GLORY MAIN

Books written under the name Vincent H. O'Neil

Interlands: A Tale of the Supernatural
Death Troupe

The Frank Cole / Exile Mystery Series
Murder in Exile
Reduced Circumstances
Exile Trust
Contest of Wills

www.vincenthoneil.com

GLORY MAIN

The Sim War: Book One

HENRY V. O'NEIL

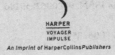

HARPER
VOYAGER
IMPULSE

An Imprint of HarperCollins Publishers

This is a work of fiction. Names, characters, places, and incidents are drawn from the author's imagination or are used fictitiously and are not to be construed as real. Any resemblance to actual events, locales, organizations, or persons, living or dead, is entirely coincidental.

EPub Edition July 2014 ISBN: 9780062359186

Print Edition ISBN: 9780062359193

10 9 8 7 6 5 4 3

This book is dedicated to the memory of
Lieutenant Colonel Charles Henry Buehring
Killed in action in Baghdad, Iraq in 2003
The Citadel Class of 1985
U.S. Army Special Forces
U.S. Army Infantry
Loving Husband
Devoted Father
Our Chad

ACKNOWLEDGMENTS

As always, I would like to express my deep gratitude to those friends and relatives who took the time to read the various drafts of *Glory Main* as it progressed. Special thanks to my West Point classmates Michael McGurk, Meg Roosma, Andrew Kerber, Keith Landry, and Ginni Guiton, who provided invaluable insights that made this a better book.

Who has placed me here? By whose
order, by whose arrangement,
have this spot and this period
been assigned to my existence?

—BLAISE PASCAL

GLORY MAIN

CHAPTER 1

The lieutenant awoke to darkness, but was too much of a newbie to know that was wrong. Instead of feeling concern, he lay there in his transit tube congratulating himself for knowing where he was after being asleep for so long. He'd traveled in this fashion once before, during a family vacation, but that had been a short Step between two systems and nothing like the multi-Threshold voyage now completed.

Unlike that earlier ship—a luxury craft befitting his father's exalted station—this was a massive military transport ferrying him to his first war zone. Although humankind had been fighting the Sims for four decades and he'd grown up in the conflict's lengthening shadow, he still felt a rush of excitement at finally having arrived. A lifetime of physical fitness and competitive sport, officer candidate instruction at university, and specialized infantry training after graduation had all combined to bring him to this moment.

He was to be assigned a combat platoon in the Twelfth Corps, the "All-Victorious and Ever-Glorious Twelfth" of the Human Defense Force. On Earth the Twelfth was referred to as The Senate's Own, but out here on the cutting edge they were simply known as the Glory Corps. The lieutenant already understood that the level of respect or mockery when uttering either nickname depended a lot on who was speaking. And where.

But that was all bullshit now. Soon a group of technicians would open his coffin-like transit tube, and shortly after that he would be delivered to his new unit. His platoon would consist of roughly forty soldiers, mostly combat veterans and many of them older than his twenty-two years. Three platoons to a company, all led by a company commander overseen in turn by a battalion commander directing three companies. As a team they would be facing an implacable enemy contesting humankind's claim to the habitable planets of distant star systems. A brutal opponent known for extreme cruelty and fiendish treachery. An enemy that spent the lives of its own troops with such abandon that it was believed to outnumber mankind drastically.

The Sims.

In the classified briefings he'd secretly received from his father's personal staff, he'd been surprised to learn that even the Emergency Senate knew next to nothing about their opponents. Nothing, that is, except that the

Sims resembled mankind so closely that some experts quietly asserted that they had once been human. Even their name suggested the link: Sim. Facsimile. Similar. The war had been in progress for so long that no one was sure how or where the name had first originated.

But none of that mattered either. Not now. He'd been warned that there was no way to completely prepare oneself for combat, and in the vanity of youth he only half believed that. He could now make out the gray silhouette of his long legs inside the tube, using the dull light from the observation window just inches over his face, and he was pleased by the sight. Exactly six feet tall, well muscled and athletic, he felt he was as ready as he was ever going to get.

Let it come. I might not be ready, but I am prepared.

The face that appeared in the observation window was so unexpected, so close, and so white against the dark background that he gave out a brief scream.

"**E**asy. Easy. Take it easy." Gentle hands helped him into a sitting position on the transit tube's lid. The face that had startled him so badly belonged to a woman not many years his senior, clad in an olive flight suit. Her hair was dark and cut short, but it was hard to tell much more in the low light.

Her companion looked like a teenager, and so far he'd said nothing. Tall and lean, he wore a tan flight suit and waited a few steps behind the woman.

The cabin was a wreck, with cables looping from

the ceiling like vines and an overturned transit tube lying next to his own. The lieutenant's mind was still groggy from the long sleep and the compartment was cloaked in shadow, but he could just make out substantial cracks running across the white ceiling.

"There. Just sit still for a moment and let yourself come to." The woman turned to the teenager. "See if anything's working in here."

Her companion nodded minutely and moved off, squeezing past the fractured transit tube toward a console set into the wall. The lieutenant watched him for a moment before turning back to the woman.

"What did you say your name was?"

"Amelia. Captain Amelia Trent. I'm a psychoanalyst." She gave a slight smile. "I'm a counselor for Force personnel who are having difficulties."

She motioned toward the printed label next to his thigh. "And you would be Jander Mortas. Lieutenant, Infantry. Well thank heavens for that."

"Huh?"

"Oh, don't worry. I'll help you all I can. But I really haven't got any survival training, and Force regulations are quite clear that in a circumstance like this the ranking individual with combat specialties training is in command."

"Circumstances like this?" Mortas surveyed the ceiling cracks again. Obviously they'd been involved in some kind of a crash, but the true extent of their current situation wasn't clear. "What circumstances?"

"I'm sorry, I should have told you this before we

pulled you out." Trent's face adopted a look of true sympathy. "Apparently our Insert was ejected from the transport and Emergency Stepped to the nearest habitable planet. It's the standard response to a catastrophic event on ship. I don't know what happened—I was out cold same as you—so they might have been attacked, they might have hit something, or . . . I don't know. So many things can go wrong out here."

Mortas extended a hand and gripped her shoulder.

"You mean we're alone?"

"So far, yes. We've checked the rest of the Insert, and apart from Chartist Gorman there—" she pumped a thumb over her shoulder "—and one other survivor who I don't think is going to be any help at all, we seem to be the only ones left."

Mortas looked about him, remembering the walk through the connected cabins of the Insert before he'd climbed into his transit tube. There were twenty tubes to an Insert, which was then slid into the side of the transport which would carry them. While individual passengers were sometimes revived and disembarked separately, the standard usage was to transfer the Insert with its contents all at once. Inserts sometimes passed from ship to ship traveling under their own power. This meant they could also act as escape pods or life boats, carrying their sleeping contents alive for an indefinite period or delivering them safely to the ground of a habitable planet.

That prompted a question, one which he was hesitant to ask. Trent seemed to sense it.

"There were fifteen other passengers with us." She looked down. "Seems we landed pretty hard."

The teenager now spoke, turning from the wall console that hadn't so much as beeped no matter what he did to it.

"Hard is right. This one doesn't work any better than the others." He shrugged evenly, as if pronouncing a meal slightly overcooked. "I'm a chartist first class, but without a set of functioning gear I can't tell you what planet we're on, or even what system we're in. I have no idea where we are."

Mortas looked back at Trent, confused. "But you said this is a Hab planet, right? If nothing's working, how did you know that?"

The captain smiled tolerantly. "Our Insert cracked in half when we hit the ground. You're breathing planet air right now. If it wasn't habitable . . . we wouldn't be talking."

"Most of my stuff is missing." Mortas had recovered sufficiently to retrieve his uniform from under the transit tube, but the bag containing his personal effects was nowhere in sight.

"Not surprising." Captain Trent had just finished searching the cabinet beneath the overturned tube. Mortas had been careful not to look after seeing that a rust-colored liquid had seeped out from the tube's cover and dried on its side. "Some of the loading crews have sticky fingers."

"The emergency gear all seems to be gone too." The teenager, now identified as Chartist First Class Gorman, spoke in a soft voice. "No rations, no communications equipment, no medical kits. No weapons."

Something in the way he'd said the last word caught Mortas's attention. He'd just buckled his gray fatigue pants, and now reached for the long shirt that went with them.

"Given the circumstances, I would have mentioned the weapons first."

"Oh I understand that, Lieutenant. Don't mind me; I'm Holy Whisper."

The captain's face appeared above the broken transit tube, surprised. "Really? And they sent you out here anyway?"

"Being an objector doesn't necessarily get you out of combat duty, Captain. There are all sorts of assignments we can handle that don't involve the taking of life."

Mortas began fastening his multi-pocketed fatigue shirt down the front while still regarding the chartist. Trent stood up slowly, brushing off her flight suit as if preparing for inspection. The lieutenant's eyes had finally adjusted to the darkness, but it didn't mean he liked what he was seeing.

Some platoon I've got myself here. A lady headshrinker and a pacifist mapmaker.

As if conjured by his thoughts, a figure appeared in one of the cabin's connecting hatches. He was short, but his long-sleeved shirt hugged a tightly muscled chest. A black skull cap covered most of his close-cropped hair and much of his forehead, and he wore gray-and-black camouflaged fatigue pants over a set of black boots. He stopped long enough to look each of them directly in the eye, and then started to move toward the cabin's opposite hatch.

"He's the only other survivor, Lieutenant. The one I told you about. Says he's a Spartacan Scout." Trent's voice was cold, and she directed a scowl at the short man as he passed from sight. Just before he vanished, Mortas noticed the handle of a black fighting knife in the back of his trousers.

"A Spartacan?" Mortas allowed the interest to jump into his voice even as his face lit up. He regretted it instantly, concerned that he might have hurt the others' feelings, but then he dismissed the silly notion. If they were going to survive long enough to be rescued, they were going to need better guidance than a green lieutenant could provide.

Once again the captain seemed to sense his thoughts.

"Don't get your hopes up. He told me not to mess with him. Not in those words. Said he's a Spartacan Scout on a mission, and that it's a death penalty offense to even question him about it." Trent's voice rasped bitterly. "Of course, out here just about everything carries the death penalty."

Mortas was already aware of the harsh discipline exercised in the war zones, but he also knew that the Spartacans were considered the cream of the cream. A strict selection process followed by training that bordered on the inhuman had forged them into an elite reconnaissance element feared across the cosmos. The war had spawned many such units, frequently at odds with one another for resources and accolades according to his father, but the Spartacans were at the very top of that pile. They reported only to Command itself, and even a green-as-grass lieutenant knew that any Spartacan encountered by his platoon was to be aided in any way requested.

"Said he was on a mission?"

"Yeah." Trent's eyes roved over the wreckage with intent. "If you want to believe that."

"No." Mortas hopped down from the tube, the unmarked soles of his boots ringing on the deck. "No I don't."

"You know, the same regulation that puts you in charge of us puts him under your command too. This *is* an emergency survival situation."

Tired of the goading, Mortas gave her a long, searching look and was pleased to see her shrink from it. "And how would a psychoanalyst know something like that?"

She recovered quickly. "I've been counseling combat cases out here for three years, Lieutenant. You'd be surprised what I know."

There was better light in the next chamber, due to a wide crack in its ceiling. It meandered over his head like a bolt of lightning, and through several feet of pipes, insulation, and wires, Mortas could make out a sky that was tinged slightly purple. Trent had tried to accompany him, but he'd made her stay with Gorman. If she'd managed to get on his nerves in such a short span of time, she was unlikely to be of help in convincing the Spartacan to cooperate.

The adjoining space was at one end of the Insert and twice the size of the transit-tube cabins. Though it showed similar damage, at least one part of that disarray might have occurred since the landing. An access panel lay on the floor near a pair of legs in camouflage trousers and well-worn boots. The Spartacan Scout had burrowed underneath a console sporting numerous gauges that Mortas couldn't have identified if given a year, and from the movements of his legs was struggling with something.

Mortas decided to try and establish some kind of rapport with the stranger.

"Need any help there?"

The legs didn't stop moving, but the Spartacan did lean out just far enough to see him. The skull cap was slightly askew, and the blackened dagger was now in his hand.

"Sure." The short man disappeared under the console, and reemerged clutching what appeared to be a handful of long, shiny snakes. He held these out in a clump, and Mortas bent over to accept them without a word. Standing back up, he decided that they were some kind of insulated tubing that the scout was harvesting for a purpose known only to him.

"What are these for?"

The other man began smashing at something, presumably with the butt of the knife, and Mortas was on the verge of repeating himself when the Spartacan emerged once again. This time he slid out fully, coming to a seated position on the floor while holding a rectangular metallic box festooned with a number of small dials. He levered one of these off with the knife, and then held out an empty palm for one of the lengths of tubing.

Mortas handed it over with mounting annoyance, but this subsided slightly when the Spartacan jammed the dial into one end of the tube. It fit snugly, and curiosity got the better of him.

"What's that for?"

"No food, you die in weeks. No water, you die in days."

"So it's a canteen of some kind?"

"Yep." The short man drew his weathered boots up close to his buttocks and stood with surprising suddenness. The knife was still in his hand, long and thin and lethal, and Mortas took a step backward. The Spartacan noticed the movement, and glanced at the blade before reaching back to slide it into its scabbard. "Don't worry about that."

The voice was distant, bled of emotion, but Mortas decided this was a good moment to introduce himself. "I'm Lieutenant Mortas. New to the zone and . . . wherever this is."

By then the short man was sorting through his harvest, measuring the tubes against his outspread arms and discarding the ones he found wanting. Studying him, Mortas was dismayed to notice that he seemed to be a teenager like Gorman. The scout stopped working at that moment, and fixed him with a quizzical expression. "Death?"

"Excuse me?"

"Lieutenant Death. Your last name means death. *Mortis*. You know—*rigor mortis*."

"Oh, I see. Actually it's Mor-*tas*, with an *a*. What's your name?"

"Cranther. Spartacan Scout."

"What's your first name?"

"Corporal."

Cranther finished sorting the tubing and began tying off one end of each of the hoses he'd kept. "Listen, Lieutenant. Can't interfere with me. Command will have your ass if you do. Stay out of my way, don't ask me questions, and don't follow me."

There was no heat in the words, and for the briefest moment Mortas felt stymied. Bucking Command was unwise, and he knew so little of the Spartacans that he wondered if this busy little scout actually knew what he was talking about.

But that did it, of course; the Spartacan obviously knew a lot about survival and there was no way Mortas could just let him walk off. The group needed him, and the notion that their crash-landing on this place was part of some secret mission was so absurd as to be almost laughable.

"Yeah, I'm going to have to go ahead and disagree with you there." Mortas spoke slowly, letting his voice take on the slightest timber of command. He'd heard this tone before, by officers and noncoms sure of their authority who were trying not to go directly to the yelling stage. He hoped it would be enough.

The short man's head came up slowly, and he seemed to be taking Mortas's measure for the first time. His hands were full of tubing and dials, but it wouldn't take him long to get to the knife if he decided to go that route. Instead, he locked eyes with the lieutenant and scowled.

"Any interference with a Spartacan Scout is a death-penalty offense. You're new, so—"

"Brand new, actually. Which means I don't know much and you know a lot. Right now I've got a psycho-analyst and a chartist, no food and no weapons, and no idea where we are." He gestured toward the scout's makeshift canteens. "But you look like you might know what to do here, so you're not leaving us."

That sounded a bit too direct, and he decided to take it down a notch. "Heck, where would you go, anyway?"

"Never mind where I go."

"You got eyes in the back of your head? Never sleep? Who knows what could be out there? Might be nice to have someone watching your back."

Cranther gave him a slight, ghostly smile. "Don't know much about how Spartacans operate, do you, Lieutenant?"

"No. Which is another reason why you have to stay with us." He remembered Trent's words. "I'm declaring this an emergency survival situation."

The Spartacan cocked his head to one side, still looking into his eyes. He pushed his lower lip up as if giving the whole thing serious thought, and then let it go slack. "It is that. So I'll help you out. Why not?"

He turned easily, corkscrewing downward to scoop up the discarded tubes and starting to drape them over his arm. Mortas headed for the hatch, pleased with his success and unwilling to push it, but still hearing what the scout muttered under his breath.

"We're all dead anyway."

Trent and Gorman were no longer in the adjoining compartment when he came back, but he could hear them in the cabin next door. They were obviously continuing the search for anything useful, and Mortas wondered bleakly if there was any chance that they might find some food. The scout's estimate of how long it took for a human being to die without nourishment seemed wildly optimistic to him, as he hadn't eaten since the moment they'd sealed him in his tube. Mortas knew that people emerged from the tubes in a state akin to low-level shock, but that once it wore off they quickly became ravenous.

He let himself ponder just what that meant in terms of the "weeks" it would take for them to starve to death, and decided that the clock on that deadline had been running for quite some time. As if to confirm his finding, his intestines rubbed against each other and gave off a low growl. He reached out for the transit tube's lid to steady himself just as Trent and Gorman returned.

"Any luck?" he asked, straightening slowly as if he'd only been stretching.

"No." Trent shook her head, and then lifted her chin toward the hatch behind him. "How about you?"

"He's on board." Mortas took a step closer, inclining his head and speaking in a whisper. "I think he's waiting for a reason to ditch us, so go easy with the comments. It won't take much, and we need him."

"Not sure about that." The reply was also given in a whisper. "I've seen his type before, usually when casualties are coming in. Their buddies are all beat up, half of 'em FUAD, and all they want to know is where the hot food is."

"FUAD?"

Trent's face took on a pained expression. "Oh, I didn't mean to say that. I promised myself I wouldn't pick up that kind of thing . . . it's an acronym the triage techs like to use. It stands for 'Fucked Up and Dying' and I swore I'd never use it."

"Captain, you don't know anything about my type." Cranther stood in the hatch behind Mortas, a dozen hoses draped over his brown shirt. Again the words lacked heat, spoken as if proclaiming an unassailable truth. "If we don't locate something to eat right away, you'll find out why my 'type' asks about the hot chow."

Mortas was about to suggest that the scout busy himself with more important things, but Cranther had already moved on. He walked up to Gorman and held out the bundle of hoses. The chartist took them without protest, but seemed confused.

"What are these for?"

"You and I are gonna go fill them from the water heater's reservoir."

Gorman selected one of the tubes and flipped it back and forth in one hand. "This is the best we can do? How are we going to carry them?"

"Nothing but water has flowed through these. If you wanna drink hydraulic residue, small holding tanks make great canteens."

Gorman nodded. "I guess you know more about this than I do. Let's go."

The scout turned to Mortas. "Don't know how long we've been here, but judging from the burn marks on the hull it's been at least a day. We need to get the water together, make one last sweep for anything worth taking, and get out of here."

The sinister implication struck Mortas in a mix of both fear and embarrassment. This was his first trip to a war zone, and he'd completely forgotten the enemy. For all he knew, they'd landed on a Hab planet colonized by the Sims.

"You've been outside?"

"Of course. First thing I did. The place is mostly rock. We got lucky, the Insert's hidden pretty well. Between two hills, one a lot bigger than the other. Went up on the low one, didn't see much."

Trent's face had switched from anger to concern as Cranther spoke. "Did you see *anything?*"

"Yeah. I told you. Lots of rocks."

CHAPTER 2

Though winded from the climb, Mortas still took one last look at the Insert far below. Its reactive pigmentation had colored the fuselage to match the orange-and-brown environment, but the break midway along the giant cylinder still showed up clearly. He marveled at his own desire to return to it, and couldn't decide if that impulse came from a wish to maintain his only link with civilization or simple fear of the unknown.

Turning away, he looked across the rough plateau at the top of the ridge they'd just climbed and decided it was fear of the unknown. There was plenty of that.

Cranther had been right in that the entire planet seemed made of rock. Their ridge, and the smaller one next to it, represented the only high ground for many miles and gave them an excellent view of an appalling nothing. A flat plain stretched away on every side, ending on an empty horizon except for two dark elevations so distant that they could have been mountains or clouds. Or maybe a mountain chain with clouds. The rock beneath their boots was alternately red and orange, although it was covered in places by thin topsoil that was either brown or tan. Tiny vegetation in the form of yellow grass or sickly star-shaped creepers clung to it, but in the ravine there had at least been some scrub.

"Water. Gotta be water somewhere." Cranther had whispered, pointing at the bushes before they began the climb. He'd schooled the group in the need for silence before they'd left the Insert, after giving each of them three of the black water tubes. The material of the hoses hadn't distended after being filled, and Cranther had tied the two ends of each tube together with wire so that they could be slung, stopper-end up, over a shoulder.

In addition to the hoses, Cranther had given Gorman a thin piece of pipe as tall as a man and handed Trent a plastic holding tank the size of a human head. When asked about the two items, he'd grunted something about being able to collect water from a stream without getting eaten by whatever lived in it, and Mortas had let the subject drop.

The sun had moved close to the horizon while they'd been walking, and Mortas mentally berated himself for not recording how long that had taken. Although he'd trained and traveled on worlds other than his native Earth, it was maddening to think he'd have to learn an entirely new planet without mechanical aid or prior briefing. Cranther appeared beside him as if reading his thoughts, his voice an airy murmur.

"Sun was about there"—he pointed into the darkened sky at roughly a 45 degree angle— "when I first went out. Been about three hours since then."

Mortas opened his mouth to ask how he'd estimated the time, but the scout pulled back the sleeve of his shirt to show the chronometer strapped there. "You gotta hide your important stuff from the loading crews."

"What else do you have that the rest of us don't?"

The short man gave him a wintry smile and then moved off toward the spot where Trent and Gorman were standing. His voice was too low to hear, and Mortas was too overcome with weariness to follow. Not that he was physically tired; the climb up had been merely a good stretch of the legs and the planet's atmosphere had so far proved similar to Earth's in pressure and temperature. No, the fatigue was mental . . . and emotional, even if he didn't want to admit it.

The onslaught of such extreme revelations, one on top of another and each seeming to be worse than the ones before, was proving more than he could process. The shock of awakening to their dire circumstances had been abruptly displaced by fear of an enemy that might be approaching the Insert even as they tarried inside. That fear had abated quickly once they'd emerged to find nothing threatening them, but that was its own problem in itself: There didn't appear to be a single moving, living thing on the planet at all. Nothing flying in the air, nothing crawling on the dry ground, not so much as a breeze to carry a scent.

Starting the walk up the steep ridge, Mortas had felt

his concern changing to a feeling of unreality. His companions were so unfamiliar, and their environment so hopeless, that it was easier to believe it wasn't actually happening. In short, it didn't fit his idea of war and so he rejected it. The training cadre had played their share of mind games on him and his fellow lieutenants in the pre-deployment exercises completed not long before, and more than once he looked around in the hope of seeing hidden referees adjudicating his performance.

But now, having reached the deserted plateau in the gathering darkness, able to see just enough to know that they were truly marooned and that there might not be another living soul on the planet, Mortas could finally admit the crushing disappointment of it all. He'd come out here to serve humankind, to lead others like himself in combat, and to die if necessary in that effort.

Instead, it was beginning to look like he was going to die very slowly on a planet whose name he didn't even know. A planet that was so worthless that neither side had even bothered to claim it.

Cranther produced yet another unexpected item, this one from one of the cargo pockets of his camouflage pants, and handed it to Gorman. He pointed over the edge of the ridge in the direction from which they'd come, and the mapmaker obediently walked away with his eyes fixed on whatever Cranther had provided.

For his part, the scout moved off toward a rock formation in the dead center of the plateau. It was twice the height of a man and many times that in width, and he vanished into the shadows while Mortas watched. Trent came over to stand next to him, her eyes on spot where the short man had disappeared.

"He's going to run off on us."

"Not much we can do to stop him, is there?"

"I guess not." She shifted her feet on the gravel. "Maybe talk to him? If he gets to know us, finds something about us that he likes, maybe he'll stick around."

"Back at the Insert it sounded like you wanted him to leave."

"I did. Like I told you, I've seen his kind before. Only out for their own skins. I've always avoided them because of that." She cleared her throat. "Except now *my* skin's on the line."

"That never happened before?"

"Of course not. My job's been aboard ship the entire three years I've been out here. We got attacked a couple of times, sure, but I've never been—"

"What did he tell Gorman to do?"

"Gave him some paper and a marker. He's got him making a sketch of where we are in relation to the Insert and that high ground over there, so we don't get completely lost."

"Sounds like he plans to stick around."

"Or maybe he wants a clear conscience when he sneaks off. Wants to think he's not leaving us completely helpless."

"Maybe." He was finding the whole conversation

depressing, and decided that if he did survive this and was ever feeling a little down he would never visit a Force counselor. "I think I'll go and see how Gorman's doing."

The loose scree underfoot crunched as he walked, and night had fallen to the extent that Mortas had difficulty making out the edge of the plateau. He stopped in place, to let his eyes adjust further, but Gorman's voice came at him from close by.

"Over here, Lieutenant." The mapmaker was kneeling with his hands pressed together in prayer.

"How's the sketch coming along?"

The light color of Gorman's flight suit allowed Mortas to see his hands part and swing to his sides as the other man gracefully rose to a standing position.

"Done. Not much to it, really, but the Corporal's right; with so few reference points we need to be sure of where they are in relation to each other."

Mortas shook his head, glad no one could see his frustration. Here he had a man trained in stellar mapmaking, and the only equipment he could give him was a pen and paper.

"Too bad they can't tell you what planet we're on."

The objector turned toward him and, even though he couldn't make out his features, Mortas could have sworn Gorman was smiling. The tan arm came up to point at the overhead sky.

"Have a little faith, Lieutenant. Sometimes you have to seek guidance from above."

He tried to keep the discouraging words from

coming out, but it proved impossible. "Somehow I don't think that's going to be quite enough, Gorman."

Mortas walked away quickly, annoyed at himself, but still certain that the other man was smiling at him.

Mortas found his way to the rock formation and sat down with his back against it. Too dark to move around, and no food. Cranther and Trent were nowhere to be seen, even if his eyes could penetrate the darkness, and Gorman had no doubt returned to his prayers. A sensation of guilt swept across him as he realized he hadn't posted a guard, but his eyes were heavy and he allowed them to shut.

Guard? Against what?

"Though physiologically almost identical to humans, the Sims are different in several key aspects." The instructor at the front of the class spoke in a clipped, rapid manner that suggested he'd given this block of instruction many times before. His uniform showed none of the service badges or medals associated with the war, but he was an intelligence officer assigned to the training of new lieutenants and presumably knew his stuff. On the screen behind him, a succession of color photos depicted the enemy in various stages of battle, surrender, and decay. Sitting in the audience, Mortas admitted to himself that the photos could have easily been pictures of humans.

"First, the Sims are biologically incapable of reproduction. Though the enemy population separates by gender into males and females, and they do possess the same genitalia as humans, none of the reproductive functions of these organs actually work. No one has ever encountered a Sim, male or female, who was not at least in late adolescence, and just how the Sims reproduce is currently unknown. With that said, the status of females in Sim culture is presumed to be quite high. The enemy has not utilized females in combat roles to date, and very few of them have been available for capture when enemy settlements have been overrun.

"Which leads us to another difference between Sims and humans: They can't derive nourishment from the food we consume. Their nutritional requirements are still a mystery to us, even though we have captured large quantities of preserved food which serve as their field rations. Analysis of Sim foodstuffs has been inconclusive, as whatever makes up those nutrients is of an origin that is completely alien to us. Sims are seldom captured alive, but even when they are, they don't stay alive for long. Even fed with their own rations, Sim prisoners expire within days in captivity. Command suspects that either the rations require special handling in order to remain potent, or that the Sims require something more than those rations to live.

"And of course they can't tell us about that, as the Sims are physically incapable of forming the syllables of any known human speech. Their language, such as it is, consists of a collection of chirps, peeps, and squeaks—" the assembled lieutenants tittered at this, reinforcing Mortas's suspicion that many of his fellow young officers considered the Sims a bit of a joke "—and so far it has resisted the efforts of any of our translation technology."

The instructor punched a button on the podium, switching off the projected images on the screen behind him. "Are there any questions regarding the material I've just covered?"

Mortas knew better than to raise any of the obvious issues presented by this shallow dive into the nature of their opponents, so he sat still. As was always the case, somebody just couldn't keep his hand down. Luckily it was one of his more intelligent classmates, a lieutenant named McVries who was popular with both the students and their training cadre.

"So if they can't make little Sims themselves, where did they come from, sir?"

"You know the answer already. Which came first, the chicken or the egg?"

"Excuse me, sir, but that's not an answer. That's a question." The students laughed at this, partly in mirth and partly in support of the young man's point.

"The truth is we don't know where they came from, but it hardly matters." The intelligence officer gave a nervous glance toward the back of the auditorium, where a long row of mirrored windows hid whoever might be sitting in the monitoring rooms. "They're taking planets we need, they fight us whenever we encounter them, and there's one heck of a lot of them."

"I understand that, sir. In fact, I think I've heard those exact words somewhere before." More laughter ensued, as the briefer's response was a verbatim recitation of the government line. "It's just that it strikes me as odd that they can't eat our food, can't talk to us, and die off after they've been with us for any time at all. They can't make little Sims, and even though they haven't yet mastered the Step, they've traveled across an awful lot of space to snap up those planets you mentioned."

"What's your point, Lieutenant?"

"My point is that they're identical to us with the exception of those traits that keep them from spending any time with us." An earnest expression replaced the humorous one that he'd worn through much of the exchange. "They're tailor-made to fight us without any possible way of joining us. So the real question is, who's making them?"

Mortas awoke with a start much later, to see the plateau bathed in a dull blue light. The stars had come out while he'd slept, showing through the blackness arched over his head. Having so recently come from that void, he stared up at it for a long time as if looking at a picture of home.

Nature called after a short while, though, and he stood up and walked across the hard ground to where he could clearly make out the edge of the ridge. The floor below was too far away to be seen, but he took himself out and pissed on it anyway. The lack of sound, which he'd earlier considered so disturbing, now seemed to comfort him personally. The stillness created a similar sensation within him, and the slightest hint of a breeze finally played across his face as if a hand were gently ruffling his hair.

Finishing, he turned and saw that Gorman was also awake. The mapmaker stood many yards away, eyes and arms skyward, as if beseeching the heavens for a reprieve.

The sun was above the horizon when Mortas awoke. He'd slumped over on his side at some point, and came to with a sore neck and a raging belly. He slowly shifted to a sitting position, happy at least that he was still warm. This led to the thought of how much worse things could have been if they'd been deposited on a Hab planet in wintertime. From the look of things this planet didn't have a winter, but even if it did they weren't likely to see it.

Mortas came to his feet slowly, stretching his muscles and looking out over the plain. They'd arrived on the plateau too late the previous evening to see much, and he'd been mistaken in his belief that the region was barren. The sky still showed a purplish tinge, but there were no clouds to impede the sunlight and he could see for miles.

The ridge sloped away from him with a covering of yellowed grass that he'd missed earlier. Rocks of all sizes broke the topsoil in various spots, and not a mile away there was a minor hill that glinted with surface minerals. The dark outlines he'd seen the night before were indeed distant mountains of some kind, and even though the general hue was still orange and brown the whole region seemed somehow friendlier.

Studying the small hill, Mortas noted the way that the ground rose and fell as it approached the top. It reminded him of a game he'd played with the family cat as a child, where he'd moved his legs around under his bedcovers and the feline had jumped all over them as if they were prey seeking escape. That game had created myriad terrain shapes in the blankets, some of them similar to what he was seeing now. The contours of the hill suggested paths to the summit, and he allowed his mind to imagine the platoon he would now never lead, separating into squads and occupying the escarpment as they set up a defensive position.

A sound behind him interrupted these thoughts, and Mortas turned just in time to see Cranther emerge from a dark crevice in the rock near where he'd slept. He marveled at the way the short, wiry man had folded himself into the crack and decided a second later that all the Spartacans must have been taught to do things like that. Reconnaissance outfits relied on stealth and concealment to make up for what they lacked in firepower, and so hiding like that had probably become second nature.

Cranther squatted down, limbering up while his eyes roved all around. He adjusted the skull cap to make it sit more squarely on his head, and then approached.

"See any other Inserts?"

"No." Once again Mortas felt like he was a step behind, as it hadn't occurred to him to look.

"Their camouflage would have kicked in when they landed, so they might not be easy to see." Cranther walked a little closer to the edge, his gaze slowly sweeping over the terrain. "Look for smaller wreckage, and disturbed ground. Our Insert left quite a gash before it ran into the rocks."

He joined the scout and diligently searched the open plain for a full minute before speaking. "There should be others, right?"

"Depends. With a sudden shipboard crisis, factor in the time it takes to work up an emergency Threshold, and in the end maybe they don't manage to get a lot of the Inserts launched. And if they were attacked . . ."

"Think they might have sent a distress call?"

"Of course they did. Before they even *thought* of launching the Inserts, you bet they sent the message trying to save their own hides. Problem is, an emergency Step isn't like a normal one. It's supposed to throw us at the nearest Hab, but sometimes that's not how it works out." Cranther looked up at him, actually smiling. "Did you know the original name for the Step was *Transgression*? It means 'to step across' but somebody decided that sounded too negative, like we didn't have a right to go anywhere we damn well please, so they came up with nice words like *Step* and *Threshold*. Bet Command had something to do with that."

Mortas tried to get back to the original topic. "Even

with an emergency Step, a search party wouldn't have too many places to cover, would it? I mean, starting from where the transport sent the distress call."

"Search party? You kidding me? No such thing, El-tee." As disturbing as the words might be, Mortas did find some small comfort in the less formal address.

"Really?"

"At least not for a bunch of nobodies like us. Have a general go missing, or a colonel with the right friends, maybe they'd send somebody. But the big boys don't travel in the Coffin Ships. Nah, they're always in fancy shuttles with big-tittied technicians and booze and lots of good food. I caught a ride on one of those, once. That's probably where all our emergency gear went, to give the important people a double chance at survival."

"Good morning." The light female voice, coupled with the outlandish greeting, caused both their heads to turn. The dark green of Trent's flight suit was tracked with orange where she'd slept on the ground. In the full light, Mortas now saw that her hair was a reddish-brown and that her eyes were a striking blue. "I haven't heard any birds, or seen anything moving . . . at all."

"Big surprise, huh?" Cranther's friendly tone had changed to mockery. "With us being so familiar with this place."

Mortas fired a disapproving look in Cranther's direction and was pleased when the scout pursed his lips and resumed surveying the plain. Trent seemed not to have noticed.

"I just thought it would be helpful if we had some

kind of indigenous life to observe. A flock of birds, maybe they'd show us where the water is."

"Gotta be careful, though." Cranther tilted his head skyward. "On Platinus the Sims had these incredible reconnaissance robots that flew just like the birds. Took Command forever to figure that one out.

"But there is something alive here other than the plants."

"What? Did you see something?"

"No." The scout pointed at the seat of his trousers, where a darkened area had bled across the camouflage pattern. "I slept in a pile of guano last night and didn't notice it until this morning. Little bead-like things, no idea what made them."

As hard as he tried not to, Mortas couldn't keep from snorting in laughter. Trent joined in uneasily, but Cranther didn't seem to care. Taking a step back from the edge, he canted his head toward a spot on the other side of the plateau. "Let's see how the Wisp is coming along. He was making some kind of a rock garden last time I saw him."

Mortas recognized the pejorative term for members of the Holy Whisper cult, but decided not to say anything. The modest connection he'd made with Cranther could be broken at any time, and he'd already laughed at him for no good reason at all. He was still dwelling on that when the trio arrived at the spot where Gorman had been praying the night before.

At first he thought that the objector had gone insane. Gorman stood in the middle of a broad arrangement of fist-sized rocks that were connected by shallow gouges dug in the dirt. The mapmaker was busily writing in the notebook Cranther had given him, and only detected their presence when he stopped to review a segment of his arcane artwork.

"Oh, hello." Gorman tucked the notebook under one arm and pulled back the sleeve of his flight suit to reveal the timepiece Cranther had been sporting the day before. He unbuckled it while speaking to the scout. "I started the timer when the first rays came over the horizon, Corporal. Just as you asked."

Cranther accepted the chronometer and replaced it on his wrist. He glanced at Mortas, who was once again kicking himself for having forgotten to track the movement of the strange planet's sun. "I had to pee a few hours ago and the Wisp here was awake so I asked him to help out."

Gorman didn't indicate he'd taken any offense at the insulting term, instead returning his eyes to the rock pattern at his feet. "I was up anyway. Thought I heard thunder at one point, but it was somewhere on the other side of those mountains."

Mortas looked at Cranther, and the scout shrugged in reply. Not knowing what to make of the thunder comment, he pointed at the chartist's confusing handiwork. "What's all this?"

"Well, it's like I told you, Lieutenant. Sometimes you have to seek guidance from above. I studied the star formations last night, and tracked the movements." Gorman grinned as he swept a hand across his primitive chart. "I know where we are."

"This is the Tarlo system. Based on my estimate, I think we're on the very edge of Twelfth Corps space."

"That's the Glory Corps. I was headed there for assignment." Mortas looked at Cranther. "Know anything about this place?"

The scout was studying the makeshift star map. He walked back and forth slowly, as if orienting himself. "Makes sense. One of the Tarlo planets is listed as a Hab. And you say your orders were taking you to this sector. What about you two? Where were you going?"

"They almost never tell me. Psychoanalysts get rotated pretty frequently."

"Must keep you from going nuts. How about you?"

"I'm assigned to the *Jonas*. It's a cruiser with Twelfth Corps. I was granted leave to make a mandatory pilgrimage to Pacifica."

"Wisp Central. Got it. So our transport was passing through the area, something happened, and they Emergency Stepped us to a known Hab."

Mortas tried to keep his eagerness from showing. "But you're familiar with this place, right?"

"Spartacans are required to memorize the locations and characteristics of all Hab planets in our sector of operations, Lieutenant. That's so we can get to the nearest base when we've got priority intelligence."

"The nearest base? Wouldn't you head for Glory

Main if you had key information?" Mortas asked, secretly proud that he knew the war zone nickname for the Twelfth Corps main headquarters.

"Spartacans don't call it that. We get shifted around so often that half the time we don't know who we're working for. So for us it's just Main or Forward. The forward headquarters is usually on a ship looking for trouble and nobody, not even us, ever knows where Main is. Nah, we just head for the closest base and then get passed up the chain."

"Don't they come get you?"

"Most of the time, yeah. Other times a ship gets diverted to scoop us up or we hitch a ride with a friendly unit, but sometimes they lose track of us and we have to make our own arrangements." He waved a hand at Gorman's model, his voice dropping and the words coming out more slowly. "It's a funny thing, war in space. Fleets Stepping every which way, one minute they're here and the next they're not, but Command makes damn sure we know how to find the things that are more or less permanent. First the military bases, next the human colonies, after that the Sim colonies, and as a last resort the Hab planets that haven't got anybody living on them yet, human or Sim.

"And we've landed on the last kind." He looked up at Mortas. "There's nobody here but us."

Gorman seemed to have missed Cranther's diagnosis. "Corporal, why would Command want you to head for a Sim planet if you carried important intelligence?"

"Like I said, we make our own arrangements when we have to. The Sims might not be completely human, but they're human enough for us to use some of their ships. Wren shuttles work the best. You'd be surprised how easy it is to steal one of those on a busy base. But there's nothing like that here, so it's not like I'm gonna get a chance to show you how."

"How can you be sure of that?" Trent's voice was high, strained. "Just because they told you this wasn't inhabited, why couldn't that change? That's what this war is all about, right? Grabbing up all the good locations? Maybe somebody *is* here, maybe somebody human, and we just have to find them."

Cranther raised an open palm toward the sky. "Sure. Why not? Which way you want to go, Captain?"

"That's enough." Mortas was startled by the hard edge in his own voice. "That goes for both of you. We need to think here, not fight. Gorman's given us the most important information we could get right now, and we need to use it."

"Use it for what? An entry on a pile of stones?" Cranther's voice maintained its irritating calm, even when he saw that they didn't understand. "I've come across them on other planets, you know. Markers of all kinds, left by the maroons. Like it was important to convince future colonists that the heap of human bones they'd found knew what planet they were on when they starved to death."

"I don't accept that at all. There has got to be a way for us to survive. And to get out of here."

"Really? No distress beacon on the Insert, and nobody's coming to look for us even if there was. There's no one else on this entire planet." Cranther pointed at Trent and Gorman. "These two are gonna drop within a day's walk—"

"You saying that because I'm a woman?"

"No. It's because you're a ship jockey and the most walking you do is to the galley."

"This ship jockey runs ten miles on a treadmill three times a week."

"Great. If running in place will save us, you're in charge."

"Enough!" Mortas stepped between the two, glaring down at Cranther. "Where, exactly, would we be doing all this walking, Corporal? Where does your experience say we should go from here?"

The scout smiled up at him, his face an animated skull. "My experience? My experience tells me to head for those mountains."

Mortas looked into the distance, doubtful once again. So far. Too far.

"Why? Get up high? Maybe see something?"

"Nah. There's nothing to see here. What we need is a nice tall cliff, several hundred feet at least."

Mortas's mind struggled with the riddle. "What would that do for us?"

"It'll make sure we're good and dead when we finally get so hungry that we jump off of the thing."

CHAPTER 3

Walking. Walking. Starving.

Mortas had managed to stay in charge for a full five minutes after deciding that they would move off the ridge. Cranther had walked away from the group momentarily, and Mortas had used that time to direct the others to get their meager gear together. He'd warned Trent and Gorman that the pace would be quick and that they would have to work hard to keep up, but that hadn't turned out to be the case.

Cranther had rejoined them with his three water hoses draped across his chest and the sullen question of which direction Mortas felt was best. Despite the scout's dark suggestion regarding the mountains, Mortas chose to head for the escarpment for the simple reason that he couldn't see anything in any other direction. He also hoped that the mountains might be a source of runoff water, which he doubted they'd find on the empty plain.

The day before, just before the sun went down, the mountains had looked like they might have clouds on top of them. And Gorman had thought he heard thunder from that direction sometime that night.

Hoped. Might. Looked like. Thought.

The sun was climbing high in the sky when Mortas asked Gorman to take the lead, intending to point him at the highest peak of the distant chain, but Cranther had stopped him.

"Just because nobody's here doesn't mean we can just go walking across the flat in broad daylight. There are some good ravines down there that we can use to hide our movements. I'll take the first turn on point."

The scout had addressed Trent and Gorman next. "Okay, the key here is if we do meet somebody or something, to meet them on our own terms. That means we walk at a nice steady clip, but not fast. Keep your eyes and your ears open, no talking while we're moving, and only whisper when we're stopped. Don't go kicking any loose rocks no matter how bored you get. And we're gonna be walking all day, so you will get bored."

Cranther couldn't have been more right. Mortas had been on many long marches during his training, but the terrain involved in those exercises had at least been interesting. Once they'd moved off the ridge and into the ravines, their world had basically folded in on itself. The canyons resembled huge cracks in the rock-hard orange ground, and they quickly swallowed the small group. The ravines were deeper than Mortas had first thought, and even though they provided excellent cover, the walls dramatically reduced his field of vision.

Vertical furrows ran down the sides of the gully walls in places, and he initially found hope in the idea that they might represent the runoff he expected to see in the mountains. The sky overhead showed no signs of clouds, however, and the longer they walked the more Mortas began to doubt his earlier idea. The width of the chasm's floor varied, with the walls sometimes pinching in so that the walkers had to press their hands against the sides to keep from tripping.

Cranther stopped them from time to time, usually near a spot where an outcrop allowed him a foothold to check over the rim. At first Mortas would move up from his place at the rear of the group to have a look too, but Cranther had finally admonished him that he was simply taking a bearing. Returning to the end of the tiny column, Mortas soon found himself fighting a malaise that threatened to rob him of any awareness at all. The sameness of the tight surroundings, the dull plodding of their movement, and the soundless, windless nature of the ravines might have caused him to lose his concentration entirely if he hadn't been so hungry.

And he was hungry. The gentle swigs from the rapidly emptying water hoses did nothing to ease the pangs, and Mortas's insides rumbled in rebellion at not being fed. He'd played tough, demanding sports all his young life and was no stranger to fatigue, but this was a level of debilitation with which he was completely unfamiliar. It seemed to sap his energy and consume his attention all at the same time, dulling his mind but heightening his awareness that he hadn't eaten since before being loaded into his transit tube. Mortas tried not to speculate on how long that might have been.

To take his mind off the ugly sensations, he tried to focus on their current predicament. He had to admire Cranther's choice of a route; anyone watching the plain would miss them entirely as they moved along below its surface. Mortas now remembered tales of the battles at the very start of the Sim War, where positional defenses interconnected with trenches very much like these gullies had been overwhelmed by the wave attacks of massed Sims even though they'd been cut down in the thousands. Looking about him, Mortas decided that he would have been able to move his entire platoon this way, and perhaps the entire company of which it was a part, had he only made it to his destination.

Thoughts of the platoon he would never see prodded his mind toward what he'd been taught in training, and Mortas wondered if he should be trying to exert more control over the situation. In a platoon-level movement he would have been close to the front of the formation while his platoon sergeant managed the other half. That would have put Mortas in a position to direct events if the point of the spearhead encountered the enemy, and leave his platoon sergeant free to direct the remainder of the platoon to flank the enemy or pin them down with fire.

What was the phrase they'd used for that? Ah, yes.

Develop the situation. A platoon leader was supposed to be just far enough up front to see what was happening and direct the response, but not so far forward that he'd get nailed in the first volley from a hidden enemy. *Develop the situation.* Mortas smiled at the utter absurdity of the phrase in his current circumstances. Here he was, walking in the rear of the group for the simple reason that he was concerned that Gorman or Trent might not be able to keep up. Cranther was leading them, and for the life of him Mortas couldn't say there was any real point to this movement at all. Except that it was movement. And that movement was better than standing still waiting to die.

Cranther halted them again, slithering up the gully to peek over the edge as he'd done so many times before. Gorman leaned back against the wall, adjusting the plastic box slung with his water and looking tired. For her part, Trent planted the metal pipe on the ground in front of her like a walking stick and stood motionless, scarcely breathing.

Guess she wasn't lying about the treadmill.

Cranther slid back down from his perch and walked back toward Mortas. He stepped up on a large stone so that he was almost at ear level, and whispered. "We're veering off course, so we're going to have to crawl out and get into a different ravine. I think we should take a break here for a few. Okay?"

Mortas's stomach growled with authority before he could speak, so he nodded instead. The scout's hand left his shoulder and Cranther stepped off the rock to tell the others. Gorman gratefully slid to the gully floor, and when Cranther sat across from him the two officers joined them. They were close enough to converse quietly, and Mortas decided to ask a question that had formed in his mind as they'd walked.

"Corporal, I couldn't help noticing how much your speech has improved since the first time we spoke."

Mortas had hoped to get some kind of acknowledgment that he hadn't let his mind go completely to sleep, but it wasn't forthcoming. Cranther gave him a bland look before replying. "Oh, I can speak well when I need to, Lieutenant. Just one of the many little improvements they made on us in the Spartacans. You see, Command doesn't trust anybody below a certain rank to accurately transmit what some smelly scout said about a hill or a spaceport or an enemy column. They like to hear it straight from the guy who was actually there. That's why you're supposed to pass us along to the next higher echelon as soon as possible.

"So while they were beating us into reconnaissance troops in Scout Basic, they were also pounding the right grammar and pronunciation into us so the bigs could hear our reports without an interpreter."

Cranther let that sink in before continuing. "Didn't know Command had such a low opinion of you, did you, sir?"

A flashback, brief as the flare on a match. His father warning him that there was no way Senator Olech Mortas's son could go to combat without every major commander knowing who he was—for both good and ill. That the Twelfth Corps, The Senate's Own, was the best place for him despite his objections because all of its senior officers owed their appointments to the Emergency Senate. Darkly suggesting that there were people out in the war zone who held deep, personal grudges against him and his supporters.

Be careful out there, son. Some of those people might hurt you to get revenge on me.

"I'm new. Why would they have an opinion of me at all?"

They'd moved into a different ravine after that, Cranther crawling across the open and the others following once he signaled that it was safe. The scout had hung his water tubes around his neck instead of across his chest, and they'd all done the same thing once they'd seen him inch across the open with the black hoses resting on his back. As last man Mortas had forced himself to move slowly, not from fear of being spotted but because he wanted to get a better feel for the terrain. It had been much too easy to become focused on the constricting walls of the passage they were following, and Mortas was surprised by the amount of vegetation he now found.

It wasn't like moving across a field of grass, but the dirt was home to acres of small, spindly bushes that were the same color as the rest of the plain. That was why he hadn't been able to make them out from up on the ridge. The brush was connected by surface roots that split as Mortas slid over them, and he took a moment to feel the broken ends for moisture. If it was there, he couldn't detect it.

At the edge of the next gully Mortas lifted his head to gauge how far they'd come, and was encouraged by the distance they'd put between them and the ridge. The sun was already past its zenith, and when he turned his head to look at the mountains he was dismayed to see that they appeared no closer than before they'd set out. Mortas lifted his head still further, trying to see more, but a hand then reached up from the chasm and lightly swatted his arm. Cranther's face appeared right next to his.

"Fallin' asleep there, Lieutenant?"

His mouth formed to give a response, but the short man was already gone. Annoyed by the comment and not sure why, Mortas swung his leg into the ravine and found the ledge where Cranther had been waiting. Rearranging his water tubes so that they hung across him again, he noticed that the orange dirt of the plain had ground into the fibers of his uniform. Its gray coloring had stood out against the gully walls all morning, but now his front was almost perfectly camouflaged.

Cranther had put Gorman in the lead by then and signaled him to move out, but Mortas gave out an insistent hiss that stopped the other three. He moved up to them and pointed at the now-orange fronts of Trent and Gorman's flight suits. Removing his water tubes, Mortas dropped to a sitting position and then lay back before squirming away from them, grinding new dirt into the unstained fibers. Trent and Gorman under-stood immediately and began imitating him while Cranther watched.

"Who are you camouflaging us from, Lieutenant? I told you; there's nobody here."

Mortas draped the tubes across him again before standing. "You don't know that for sure. Besides, you're halfway there already. Your front's camouflaged, so why not do the rest?"

"Maybe because I don't want to have to walk with sand in the crack of my ass?"

Mortas took a step forward, towering over the other man. If it bothered him, Cranther didn't show it. "Well don't do it then. But from here on out, consider every-thing I suggest to be an order. As in, no matter who's walking point, the last man in this column should be either you or me. We're also going to start designating rally points as we go, so if we get separated we know where to link up. Now you take the rear, and I'll take the lead."

Mortas stepped out smartly after that, making sure he got around the next bend with enough time to shake the sand out of his trousers. It trickled down the sides of his legs, and much of it went into his boots.

They were only halfway to the mountain when the sun went down. Cranther was insistent that they push on through the night, but Mortas had been watch-ing Gorman and Trent carefully and overruled him.

Gorman was clearly limping, and Trent seemed to have withdrawn inside herself. Cranther's hostility had shut her up early on, but Mortas could have sworn he'd watched the psychoanalyst actually shrink in size. A tense, worried expression was now permanently stamped on her face, and she kept looking skyward in the tunnel-like canyons as if hoping to see a rescue ship hovering overhead.

"Let me see your feet." Mortas stood over Gorman, who had slid down the canyon wall to a sitting position when they'd halted. Cranther was on the surface looking for a hole large enough for them to spend the night in, and Trent was staring at the sky.

"I'm all right, sir." Gorman whispered, his voice dry. They were down to one tube of water apiece, and hadn't consumed any for several hours.

"I'll tell you if you're all right. Take 'em off."

The mapmaker bent one leg over the other and pulled off the smooth-soled shipboard boot. His sock almost went with it, a sodden rag that had obviously slid down and bunched up around his heel. Mortas recoiled slightly at the sight of the raw flesh, surprised that the man's foot could be that blistered after only a day's march.

"Shit, Gorman. Didn't you feel that happening?"

"With every step, sir." The voice was peaceful and accepting, and Mortas wondered if the objector had viewed his suffering as some sort of holy purification.

Mortas pulled the damp sock all the way off, seeing wrinkled white flesh and more blisters on Gorman's toes. His hands folded the sock and then wrung it out, a reflex action from the hard training he'd received as an infantry officer. Rusty blotches smudged the fabric, reminding Mortas that they had no medical supplies. In training he'd learned to cut and place bandages around blisters so that the aggravated flesh could heal without further friction, but here he had nothing.

Mortas handed the sock back. "When we're in the hole where we're going to spend the night, take your boots and your socks off. Let some air get at your feet, and let the socks and the insides of your boots dry."

"Wrong." Cranther slid over the edge of the ravine. "Only one boot off at a time, never two. And be ready to put that one on in a hurry. If we have to run suddenly, you'll end up barefoot."

The scout picked up Gorman's boot and shook his head. "Shipboard piece of shit. Doesn't breathe, doesn't lace up; no matter how many times he pulls up his socks they're gonna slide down." A finger pointed at the blood-stained garment. "Better off throwing those away."

Mortas felt his anger rising. "You find us a spot?"

"Yes. About fifty yards that way. It's a hole big enough for the four of us, nobody's gonna find it who isn't actually looking for us."

"You crawled fifty yards?"

"No. There's more brush here than where we started. If you move in a crouch you should be all right."

"More brush? You think that means we're close to water?"

"Gotta be. But we won't find it sitting in a hole."

"I already told you we're stopping for the night."

"We should be *moving* at night. Less chance of being seen, sweat less."

"Yeah, well, we've been going all day." Mortas reconsidered, suspecting the scout was right but concerned about the other two. "We'll lay up until the stars are out and then maybe move on."

"I'm okay, Lieutenant." Gorman stood up, hiding the pain.

"And don't worry about me." Trent had joined the group while they'd been talking.

"How are your feet?"

"They're fine. I told you: I can run for miles."

"Let me see."

"Shouldn't we be getting to this super-nice hole I've been hearing about?"

"It'll be too dark to see then. Let me see your feet."

Irritated, Trent jammed the pipe section against the wall and dropped to the ground. She yanked off the same kind of boot Gorman was wearing, but there was no sock underneath. The foot was suddenly thrust in Mortas's face, and even in the failing light he could see it was unblemished. It didn't even smell.

He took hold of her ankle before Trent could pull away, gently pressing a thumb against the flesh. It was soft and dry.

"That's incredible. You've got some magic feet. No calluses, no blisters. They're not even sweating."

"It's why I don't wear socks."

He was just about to hand her boot back when Cranther's voice sounded in a rasp from the surface. "When you're done with the foot massage, can we get going?"

Without the clouds from the previous evening, the stars came out almost immediately after nightfall. Cranther had timed the day's length at twenty hours and reset the timer to measure the hours of darkness. The hole he'd found for them was just deep enough for Mortas to see out of if he stood up, and the scrub around it provided even more concealment. It wasn't lush, but it was taller than anything they'd yet seen and actually had some kind of trunk area.

Water's got to be around here somewhere.

His stomach had quieted down as they walked, like a sullen child sent to bed without supper, but now it started protesting again. Coupled with his thirst, it was a constant reminder of their situation and he was truly beginning to resent it. His feet were sore, the backs of his knees were strained, and Mortas was beginning to understand something his training hadn't taught him: It's easy to rise above one or two minor inconveniences or even injuries, but pile a few of them on top of one another and the obstacle can become very high indeed.

He was suddenly feeling very tired, and decided they would spend the rest of the night right where they were. "Assuming ten hours of darkness, that's two and a half hours of guard apiece."

"So we're staying here after all?" Cranther spoke from a sitting position, his back against the dirt.

"Yeah." Mortas let the fatigue enter his voice. "I don't know about anybody else, but I could use the break."

"The Sims don't take many breaks on a march. Did you know that?" For once the scout's words weren't hostile. "One time I was hunkered down in the brush, a place a lot like this, when a Sim column came trotting by. Close enough to smell, hundreds of 'em, all combat loaded. Not a sound other than their feet, none of that chirping that passes for words with them. Four abreast, really moving out, going somewhere in a hurry.

"I stopped counting at two hundred and just put my face in the dirt. Didn't even try to send a report, too scared they'd hear me. I called it in after they were gone, got chewed out like you wouldn't believe, but I did have a direction for them.

"An aerobot found the column hours later, so far away that they must have been moving the entire time. No breaks at all. Hustling along that whole distance, under those loads, knowing that if they got spotted we'd drop everything we had right on 'em. Which is what happened. Heard later the entire column was annihilated. That they were rushing up to reinforce an outfit that was under heavy attack. Only reason they tried to pull a stunt like that in daylight."

The stars allowed Mortas to see the scout's head shake. "They're tougher than we are, you know. Command laughs at them for being so far behind us technology-wise, but from what I've seen they don't need it. They understand how important it is to be able to do without. Even the stuff they have, they train for the times when they don't have it. They practice hard on things like bayonet fighting, for the times when they run out of ammo. They have these amazing signals that they all understand, hand signals, smoke signals, lights, heck, even music. They can trot for hours under a full combat load. No breaks at all. And look what happens to us when we don't have all our toys. We crap out and hide in a hole."

"You sound like you think we're not going to win." Gorman was on his back, his boots elevated against the wall to reduce the swelling.

"We're not gonna win, Wisp. Weren't you listening just now?"

"Stop calling him that." Trent rasped from his left.

"What? Wisp? If he's Holy Whisper, he shouldn't mind. They don't mind anything. Right, Gorman?"

"Actually we mind a lot of things. Killing, for one. That's why we're all objectors. But you're right, in that we don't get excited about silly name-calling. But as insults go, that one's not that bad at all and it reminds us of our origin. God's call isn't a shout, it's a whisper." He raised himself up on an elbow. "And a wisp can be a very important thing, if you think about it. A wisp of smoke, for example. You ever had to fight a shipboard fire, Corporal?"

"Not yet."

"I only fought one. Pulling mid-deck watch, smelled smoke. Sensors went off right after that, and of course the hatches all sealed automatically, so it was just a few of us against this wall of flame." His voice trailed off.

"So tell me. Did you get down and pray, or did you fight that thing alongside the others?"

"You can pray and fight at the same time, Corporal. Especially if you learn how before things get rough. It's important to have a philosophy of life . . . and of death."

"Well I'm an orphan, so nobody ever bothered to give me one of those. Guess I was robbed, huh?"

"You can't be robbed of something you never had. Even less of something you gave away."

Trent's voice rose from the shadows. "You're an orphan?"

"Yes. I was born on Celestia. Escaped from the orphanage just before they would have sent me to the mines. Did you know that on Celestia the word for orphan is the same as the word for slave? It's true. So I ran off when I was probably ten."

"Probably?"

"Your guess is as good as mine. They don't keep very accurate records on the slaves."

Mortas turned away from watching the surface. "How old are you now?"

"At Scout Basic they ran a whole bunch of tests on us and one doctor said I was fifteen. That was five years ago."

"Amazing. How long were you in the service before you went to the Spartacans?"

"I wasn't. Like I said, I was fifteen when they caught me and handed me off to the Force. Cleaned out this entire slum of every runaway, piled us into these massive corrugated boxes, and next stop was Scout Basic."

"I thought the Spartacans were all volunteers."

"Don't know who Spartacus was, Lieutenant? Don't worry, nobody seems to. He was a slave of the Romans, led a revolt and ended up getting executed for it. That's one of the first stories they tell you at Scout Basic. Not that they needed to."

"Needed to what?"

"Tell us a scary story to keep us in line." Cranther's voice became thin, bled of emotion. "They left us in that box for hours, no food, no water, no toilets. I swear they waited until the fights started before they opened this one hatch. Five or six guys in those massive armored suits came walking in, all of 'em holding these big shock-sticks. Man, did those things have a jolt.

"They started at one end of the box and just worked their way through, shocking the heck out of every one of us. We attacked them, of course, but that was a waste of time because of the armor. How they knew who hadn't been jolted I will never figure out. I pushed this one kid in front of me, got around behind them while they were letting him have it, and the next thing I knew I was on the floor screaming, all my muscles going berserk and my insides feeling like they were being ground up.

"And then they just walked out. Left us there in this pile of shit and piss and vomit and bodies, half my muscles didn't work for I don't know how long."

"Why'd they do that?"

"Every Spartacan's got a different opinion, but I go with how I felt right at that moment. Completely helpless. I think that's why they did it. To let us know we were totally in their power, that they could do whatever they wanted. I swear, lying there thinking of what they might decide to do next was worse than anything they did later.

"So finally we'd recovered enough to stand up, and that's when the loudspeaker said that they were going to drop one wall of the box and that we were supposed to get our toes on these white lines that were painted on the pavement just outside. We were all happy to do that, but then the loudspeaker said that the last guy out of the box was going to wish he'd moved a little faster."

The stars allowed Mortas to see the little man shudder before he continued.

"So the wall comes down with a crash, this mass of bodies goes tumbling over it, it's daylight outside so nobody can see, everybody's running into everybody else, 'Where are the lines? Where are the lines?' and then somehow we found 'em and we were all standing like statues in three long rows. Still wearing our civilian clothes, covered in filth, but we were really dedicated at that moment to standing in that formation.

"And the armored suits came back, just took this one guy, just grabbed him at random, no *way* they could have known who was last out of that box, and they dragged him out in front of the others. They pinned that poor bastard to the ground, *stood on him* with those massive suits, and shocked him until he passed out screaming his head off.

"And nobody in that formation made a move to help him." He gave a short laugh. "It was a thing of genius."

They all waited for him to say more, but after a time it was clear that he was finished. Gorman lifted his boots off the rock where they'd been propped and curled himself up into a sitting position.

"I'm not doubting you, Corporal, but how do you know they just picked that one guy? How do you know he *wasn't* the last one out of the box?"

"Because I wasn't last."

Mortas had the final guard shift of the night, and he leaned his chest against the hole's dirt wall as the sky slowly began to lighten. A breeze had sprung up over time, causing the brush in front of him to sway back and forth. In the predawn darkness it reminded him of undersea grass he'd once seen while snorkeling at home, gently rocking to invisible currents.

One of the others moved at his feet, and Mortas looked down to see Trent stretching and yawning. Cranther and Gorman were still asleep, the mapmaker with his feet elevated once again and the scout curled up into a ball. Trent stood up without disturbing the other two and joined him at the wall.

"Sun's coming up."

"Yeah. Seen anything out there? Animals? Birds?"

"No, but it was pitch dark during most of my shift. And the wind's kept the brush moving, scraping against itself, making noise. Might have been something out there but I missed it."

"I could have sworn something flew over us during

my shift." She stretched again, raising her arms over her head and arching her back. "Ya know, as hungry as we all are, I can honestly say that what bugs me right now is that I haven't had my coffee."

Mortas gave her a friendly smile, relieved that she'd found something to say that didn't irritate him.

"We'd pull these long shifts when the wounded came in, and when the last ones had been sorted and handed off to the doctors I'd sit with the triage techs and drink this awful coffee and shoot the breeze. You wouldn't believe the jokes they told, just to stay sane."

"Sounds like a tough job."

"For them it was. Not a lot of latitude. The scanners told them how bad off the patient was, and they sorted them according to Force guidance." Trent shook her head. "They used all these codes and phrases so that anyone who was being set aside wouldn't know what was happening."

"Like FUAD?"

"Yeah. I guess making an acronym out of it made it less ugly. The doctors would try to get involved with triage every now and then, so Command posted guards between the receiving bay and the surgery. Some of the techs wondered if that meant the triage guidance was wrong, but speaking up got you a tour in the brig, so they pretty much kept it to themselves."

"They talked to you, though."

"Hey, you move enough gurneys for them and they forget you're a headshrinker. Besides, I think they felt sorry for me. All that training and no job."

"Huh?"

She gave off a short, helpless laugh. "The only cases I ever got to handle were mandatory referrals or the ones who'd actually cracked up. Oh, I did get to listen to a couple of higher-highers complain about how lonely they were and that their subordinates didn't like them, but all that did was piss me off. Every one of them spent years chasing that rank, some of them did really shitty things to get ahead, and now that they finally had what they'd been after so long, they had the nerve to say they didn't like it. Boo fuckin' hoo."

They exchanged fraternal smiles, Mortas wondering if his own father might sometimes feel the way Trent was describing.

"Anyway, most people know that everything they tell me gets reported. So there's not a lot of walk-in traffic. Heck, I was originally assigned to triage so I could comfort the dying, but then they changed the regs because the psychoanalysts were supposedly upsetting the wounded. But that was a lie; they just didn't want anyone getting into the Waiting Room who didn't absolutely have to be there."

"Waiting Room?"

"Another one of those phrases. More like the Waiting To Die Room, but it's not as bad as it sounds. They've got attendants and plenty of painkillers, but once you go in you're not coming out."

A dark rumor from Officer Basic tiptoed into his head. A former enlisted man, veteran of numerous fights, promising them that if they made it back to a ship their chances of living were better than fifty-fifty no matter how badly banged up they were. And that even if they couldn't be saved they'd never know it.

Mortas was so engrossed in the memory that he didn't realize Cranther had moved until the scout was standing next to him. The skull cap was in his hand, and he was scratching the stubble on his head. Yawning, he murmured, "Now you know why my 'type' always wants to know where the hot chow is. You gotta be crazy to hang around the sick bay."

CHAPTER 4

They were approaching the mountain when the ration bag blew by. The dark edifice had grown massive with all the hours of walking, even when seen from inside the chasms. They got lucky with the timing, as Cranther had climbed up to check the surface when the bag appeared. One moment he'd been crouched on a small ledge near the top of the ravine and the next he was gone, as abruptly as if a giant bird had plucked him from their midst.

Mortas, robbed of energy by the constant ache in his stomach, had been sitting with the others when the scout scrambled away. He'd looked up in a daze, telling himself that he really should climb up there to see what was going on, when Trent beat him to it. She hopped up onto the spot vacated by Cranther, squatting while in the air so that only her head was visible when she landed. Mortas shook his head, not sure that he'd actually seen the display of acrobatics, but he didn't get any more time to consider it. Cranther rolled over the side and dropped into the gully with a thud, his arms wrapped around his torso.

Mortas and Gorman both pulled him to his feet, confused by the theatrics until they saw that he was clutching the dull yellow rectangle of a combat ration. The rubberized pouch had been torn open at the top, and the scout upended it to show it was empty. Even so, its effect was explosive.

"Is it real?"

"Is that what I think it is?"

"Are there any more? Did you see any more?"

The words spewed from their mouths while the four of them passed the object from hand to hand like a priceless artifact. Mortas simply stood there, one hand on Cranther's shoulder and the other on Gorman's, swaying with fatigue and hunger and staring at the empty bag. He finally found the words.

"How old is it? Can you tell?"

Cranther spit a few flecks of dirt from his lips before smiling up at him. "We may not have to find that cliff after all, El-tee. That bag hasn't been blowing around here more than a few days."

"**W**e need to get up on that mountain, Lieutenant."

"How?" Mortas's patience had finally worn thin. It had taken a remarkably short time for the elation caused by the ration bag to erode. They'd walked for two more hours, finally reaching the base of the new ridge and also discovering that it ended only a short distance from where they now huddled. His head throbbed from dehydration, and his hands were shaking from hunger. Gorman's feet were obviously torturing him even though he hadn't said a word in complaint, and even Trent was showing signs of exhaustion.

"We won't have to climb it. If we just skirt around the end there I'm sure we'll have a nice, easy walk up."

"Why? We need water, and I guarantee there's none up there."

"What we need is to find whoever left that ration bag. If the Force put a survey team down here, they'll be cruising around in some kind of vehicle. And the only way to see where they are, or where they went, is to get up high."

"What if they're not a survey team?" Gorman was holding the metal pole now, his hands gripping it tightly as he shifted his weight from one foot to the other. "What if they're a recon outfit? What if they're Spartacans?"

"They're not Spartacans. If they were, we'd never have seen that ration bag. But if they're some other kind of recon, they'll be up on the high ground."

"The water's not up on that mountain. Look around you; the vegetation's actually got some color to it, there are roots right here"—Mortas reached out and gave a tug at the tiny brown shoots protruding from the wall—"and we're out of water. You said it yourself, we die if we don't find more."

"We die anyway if we don't find whoever dropped that bag."

"What if we're wrong?" Gorman's voice was a thin rasp. "Wrong about who dropped that thing? What if it's the Sims?"

"The Sims. Come on, Gorman, even a shipboard type has to know they can't eat our food and we can't eat theirs."

"I do. But that doesn't mean it couldn't have been dropped by them instead of us. You never picked up something the enemy left behind, Corporal? Just out of curiosity?"

"Looking for intelligence is more like it. But this planet was listed as uninhabited when we went into the tubes, and now we found a human ration bag on it. What are you saying? Both sides landed here while we were being shit out the back end of that transport?"

"Actually, the Inserts are launched from the sides."

"You know what I mean." Cranther turned away in disgust. "Listen, Lieutenant, let me go up there alone. I can be up and back in no time."

Mortas's brain bucked against him weakly. So tired. So sick of walking. So hungry. Perhaps it wouldn't hurt to let Cranther go and check it out . . .

"We shouldn't split up." Trent spoke with her eyes on the ground.

"What's wrong, Captain? Afraid I'm gonna run off?"

"Right now nothing would please me more."

"Okay, enough of that." Mortas struggled to his

feet. For an instant he envisioned himself running off instead of Cranther, finally free of the advice and the complaints and the bickering. "Cranther and I will go up on the ridge while you two—"

"Lieutenant." Gorman's voice was a hiss, and for a moment Mortas expected him to protest that he was fit enough to make the climb. He looked over sharply, but the mapmaker was pointing at something in the distance, his arm fully extended. Standing there leaning on the pipe, he looked like some ancient sage guiding his people through the wilderness.

They all looked, and a moment later got to see what was so important. A large bird had flown between the two ridges, less than a mile from where they stood. It descended gracefully, as if coming in to land, and just before it disappeared below the level of the underbrush it unfurled an appendage from its beak.

"What was that? Its tongue?"

"Wait." Cranther had stepped among them, his finger pointed as if imitating Gorman. His arm kept moving, though, tracing the bird's flight behind the bushes. Judging the location of the ground, he gently brought the same arm up in a low trajectory, as if predicting where the bird would reemerge. He was only off by a second or two, as the creature rose into view again with a loud flap of its huge wings. Mortas didn't want to say it, fearing it was in his mind, but he could have sworn he saw drops of water trailing from the bird's tail feathers.

"It wasn't a tongue. It was some kind of a straw. There's standing water right over there."

"**H**ow much longer are we going to wait?" Gorman's voice was barely audible, but from lack of water more than caution. The group was huddled back-to-back in a bed of tall yellow grass on the edge of the most beautiful creek Mortas had ever seen.

"It's like I told you. The predators always stake out the water source." Cranther's eyes were in constant motion, roving along the opposite bank. He'd guided them to a spot where the stream took a sharp turn and then had them hunker down in the grass near its edge. The plastic bucket was now tied to the end of the pipe they'd carried for so long, but the scout still insisted they wait.

The stream was probably only fifty yards wide, but the current was fast and the sound of the running water was driving Mortas mad. All twelve of the empty hoses were stacked in the center of their tiny perimeter, waiting to be filled. The dust of the long journey had turned them a dull red, and when he spared a glance at the others he saw the same color on faces, clothes, and hands.

"Okay." Cranther slowly shifted from a squatting position to his stomach in the weeds. He gently spread the brush directly in front of him and then, instead of extending the pole, began handing back some of the stones that obviously formed the stream's bed.

He whispered without turning, his eyes fixed on the water. "Be ready to start heaving these things if something tries to grab me."

"Just get the water, will you?" Mortas hissed.

The scout turned his head long enough to give that ghostly smile again, just before taking the pole and sliding the plastic container toward the water. He extended it to almost its entire length before gently easing it into the flow. It filled quickly, and he had difficulty lifting the weight as he retracted it. The laden bucket scraped against the stones and then it was in his hands. The short man rolled over into a sitting position, holding the precious container like a baby.

All four of them were now staring at it, gummed tongues playing across pasty lips. Cranther looked up, and for the first time Mortas saw indecision in his eyes.

"Remember: Just because this place is a Hab doesn't mean all the water's drinkable. With no colonies here, maybe none of it is."

"It has to be." Croaked Gorman. "The bird drank it."

"Bird comes from here. We don't."

"So what do we do? Stare at it?" Mortas could feel his throat constricting, begging for the liquid.

"Somebody has to try it."

Shuffling forward, Gorman took the container by the sides and raised it to his lips, the pole still attached. One small sip. He stopped, licking his lips and blinking quickly as if trying to identify the taste. Then another one, longer. He slowly sat back, still clutching the bucket and looking thoughtful.

"It's definitely water. Not sure if anything else is in it." He drank again, long, slow swallows.

"So now what?" Mortas was finding it hard not to reach for the receptacle.

"By the book, we should wait a full day and see how he's doing once it's gone all the way through his system." Trent spoke as if in a trance, not accepting her own words. "But even then if there's a bug in this stuff we might not know it."

"And we've got to get moving again." Cranther. "We've got to get back up on the high ground if there's any chance of finding whoever left that ration bag."

Mortas could feel the three pairs of eyes boring into him even though he was still fixated on the bucket. So many decisions. Couldn't *one* of them be easy?

"Everybody drink some. After that we fill up the hoses and get moving."

Cranther nodded and took the bucket from Gorman, raising it to his mouth. His eyes shut as he drank, ecstatic, but he left enough for both Mortas and Trent. When Trent had emptied the vessel she fed the pole over Cranther's shoulder where he once again lay in the brush. He started extending it again, and was about to ease it into the water, when he whispered, "Everybody keep your eyes open."

It was as if he'd recited a summoning spell. One moment Mortas was greedily watching the container dipping toward the surface, and then everything was motion and terror and noise. The rippling water bursting upward like a geyser, its center a black-green tube the width of a man's thigh. Open jaws and teeth, snapping madly. Hurtling toward the group even as Mortas dived backward, panic-stricken, a choked cry of insane prehistoric fear springing from within.

Seeing, even in his panic, the jaws smashing down on the plastic bucket. The pole bending as Cranther tried to ward off the beast, hollering, "Hit it! Hit it! Hit it!" before desperately scuttling backward. Gorman grabbing the short man by the collar, yanking him away, into the brush.

Trent kneeling, snatching up the forgotten stones and heaving them at the beast with incredible speed. Gorman bouncing off of her when his hand slipped from Cranther's shirt and he fell over. Cranther flipping onto his stomach and crashing through the brush in a frenzied crawl. Trent throwing one of the rocks perfectly, smacking the awful maw with a wet, meaty thud. Mortas grabbing her arm as he scrambled past, his eyes darting back over his shoulder. The nightmare thing dropping onto the mashed grass where Cranther had been, already wriggling in retreat toward its element. In a moment it was gone, but that didn't stop him from pushing Trent in front of him, running hard after the other two.

They might have fled for quite a distance had Cranther not managed to get his feet tangled up in the pipe that he miraculously still carried. It sent him sprawling in the grass, and Gorman was so close behind that he went down too. Trent almost managed to stop before running them over, but Mortas barreled into her so hard that they both ended up in the pile.

All tangled arms, legs, and weeds, Mortas found himself face to face with Cranther. The scout's eyes were huge and his mouth opened and shut more than once before he finally got the words out.

"What . . . was . . . that?"

"They're coming, Corporal."

Gorman gave the warning in a flat, low voice. Cranther was prone on a narrow rock that jutted out over the stream, the pole down in the water. They'd lost the bucket in the first attack, but the current was strong enough to fill the water tubes if they were dangled in just the right way. Filling, they swished back and forth and took on an eerie resemblance to the serpents that had tried to kill them.

And that was what they were: Serpents. The riverine monsters varied in size, the largest ones twenty feet long and as big around as a man's waist. After composing themselves from their earlier flight, the group had traveled upstream in search of a safer spot to try and get more water. They'd been left alone briefly, but disturbing the current with the hoses had alerted the serpents to their presence no matter how many times they'd moved. Although these predators weren't amphibian, they hadn't hesitated to launch themselves up onto the bank a short distance once they'd noticed that a possible meal was near.

Perhaps the worst part was seeing just how many of them had gathered over time. The presence of food and the thrashing of the earliest arrivals had drawn quite a crowd. The humans had been driven from two different spots before finding the overhanging rock, and even though they knew it wasn't out of range for the leaping predators, it at least provided some protection.

The dark water began to ripple unnaturally, lines crossing the current and revealing the approach of the underwater hunters. Mortas was holding Cranther's boots in both hands, primed to pull him back, and Trent stood ready with more rocks. She'd proved a dead shot with the projectiles and seemed to derive great pleasure from striking the monsters even after Cranther had moved to safety.

The scout pulled the pole back up, water draining off the teardrop-shaped water tube at its end. He was just about to start sliding backward when he stopped as if stuck. Mortas shifted his hands to the man's ankles, getting ready to pull, when Cranther spoke.

"I don't believe this."

He quickly crawled backward, dragging the pipe and the tube with him while Mortas moved out of the way. As if on cue, the approaching runnels in the water either veered off or disappeared entirely as the serpents dispersed. Mortas watched with revulsion, eager to be away from the stream now that most of the water carriers were filled. Even so, he remembered Cranther's odd statement and turned to where the scout sat in the grass. The Spartacan wore an expression mixing chagrin, exhaustion, and wonder.

"What is it? What did you see?"

Cranther pointed with his thumb toward a spot upstream, blocked by the tall weeds.

"There's a bridge not five hundred yards that way."

"A bridge?" Mortas's voice cracked, but he hardly noticed. He stood up eagerly, trying to see over the brush. "You mean, a man-made bridge?"

"Sort of." Cranther looked up, a critical expression appearing on his face. "And get down, sir. I've seen this kind before. It's temporary. New colony stuff, until the permanent bridge can get built." He blew out a long exhalation, his eyes on the ground.

"And it belongs to the Sims."

They circled around, using the brush for cover as they worked their way up to the bridge. A knob of high ground overlooked the structure from a hundred yards away, and they crawled forward on their stomachs to view it.

It didn't look temporary. Concrete supports had been built into the bank on either side, squared-off rock over which the metal span was laid. Honeycombed plates made up the bridge floor, and a railing stood up on either side at what was probably waist height. It wasn't long, and looked only wide enough for one-way traffic, but it was impossible to know about that because it was absolutely empty.

They were losing the light by then, but Cranther insisted that they remain motionless, observing the bridge and the far bank. The ground on the opposite side rose into yet another ridge, and it was covered in the same yellowish grass as the knob where they lay.

"See that?" Cranther spoke so softly that Mortas could barely hear him even though the scout's lips were almost in his ear. "They graded the other side. It's not exactly a road, but it means the settlement is on that side of the water."

Mortas found the whole scene simply incredible. First the ration bag, then finding the stream, then being menaced by enormous water snakes, and now finding proof positive of an alien presence was almost too much for him. He'd had his fill of water and was feeling more composed as a result, but the onslaught of unexpected developments still left him baffled.

"If there is a colony here, how come we haven't seen any shuttles in the air? Or even ground vehicles?"

"No idea. None of this is making any sense. This planet was uninhabited as of my last briefing. And I'm still trying to figure out how a human ration bag connects to a Sim emplacement." He raised a finger. "Look. Another bird. It's like they're coming back after running away from something."

"But what?" Mortas pondered his own question. The absence of enemy aircraft, vehicles, and even personnel seemed to offer an answer. "You think maybe they had an accident? Blew up the whole colony? Chemicals, maybe?"

"Could be. Thought I smelled smoke the first night, but just figured it was natural. Brush fire, something like that. But it still doesn't explain how this place suddenly has a Sim colony."

"Why does this mean it's a colony?" Gorman pointed at the bridge below. "Maybe it's just a survey party, like you thought when we were looking for whoever owned that bag."

"That kind of bridge means a settlement, or at the very least a battalion-sized force. No survey team would be cruising around plunking those down. But hey, look on the bright side: That big a bunch of Sims, they gotta have a ship we could steal." He looked up at the darkening sky. "We need to find them. So let's wait until full dark and then use their bridge to cross without getting eaten."

"He sure seems confident that we can steal a ship from the Sims." Gorman looked over his shoulder at Cranther, who was asleep behind them. The scout had worked his way into a Z-shaped crack in the ground and pulled weeds over him so that he was practically invisible.

Mortas lay on his stomach next to the mapmaker, watching the empty bridge as the stars slowly brightened overhead. Trent had slid back from the edge a short time earlier, and Mortas had assumed she was going to catch some shut-eye in imitation of Cranther. He silently congratulated himself on having decided to make them pull guard shifts the night before, now that an enemy presence had revealed itself.

"Remember we haven't seen a live human or a live Sim yet. It sure would make things easier if they were all dead." A disturbing thought: the Sim colony that Cranther believed was somewhere on the other side of the creek might have suffered an accident so severe that they'd packed up everything and gone home. It would be a disappointing explanation for why they hadn't seen any of the aerial traffic normally associated with a Sim emplacement, and he pushed it away. "Right about now I'm up for anything that brings us closer to a meal."

"Me too. Trying not to think about it, but it's hard not to."

"Hey Lieutenant." Trent's voice came from just behind them, low. "Take a look at my foot."

He raised himself on an elbow to see that Trent was sitting in a small depression with one boot off. The bare foot was crossed over the opposite leg, and so Mortas crawled over. The stars were bright enough for him to make out a lump on Trent's heel, and when he poked it she gave off a hiss of pain.

"Looks like I get blisters just like everybody else."

"Yeah. Sorry about that. Nothing we can do for it."

"Keep walking on it and it'll toughen up." Cranther's voice rose from the crack in the dirt. The corporal slowly sat up, adjusting the skull cap. "Human bodies can adapt to a lot of things. Walk far enough and your foot will build callus like a boot heel. Go without food long enough and your stomach will shrink. You can get used to just about anything that doesn't kill you outright."

Mortas briefly considered arguing that last point, but decided against it. They needed to get moving. Movement meant getting closer to the chance of food. And a ship. Or maybe a radio of some kind that they could use to call for help.

"Lieutenant!" Gorman's voice shot at him in an urgent whisper. "Something's coming on the other side of the river."

The three of them lunged toward the mapmaker, landing in a tight pile facing the bridge. On the opposite bank, with a low rumble that became only slightly louder as it approached, a pair of muted lights bumped along the track. The vehicle was almost at the bridge when Mortas was finally able to make out its general shape. Some kind of mover, a cargo hauler perhaps, with two seats in front and a covered back.

It stopped with a sigh, and one door at its front opened. The starlight was sufficient to identify him as a tall individual, two arms and two legs and carrying some sort of weapon. He appeared human in every aspect as he walked to the rear of the mover and opened a large hatch. Mortas had seen plenty of footage of captured Sims, and had heard their gibbering language on tape, but even so he was unprepared when the thing spoke.

Sim language had so far evaded the efforts of mankind's finest linguists and supercomputers, and he now knew why. The tall Sim uttered a stream of chirps and peeps loud enough for the group on the hill to hear clearly. The syllables seemed to bounce off of each other, and even though he understood not one of them, Mortas was almost certain the speaker was annoyed.

The chirping brought two more Sims out of the vehicle, both of them dropping to the dirt carrying weapons. Mortas didn't recognize the devices, having expected to see the long, skeletal rifle common to Sim infantry. These were stubby, short-barreled things that didn't look like they had much range to them, and the two Sims who'd emerged from the mover both hugged them to their chests as if for warmth.

All three of them were clad in some sort of uniform that appeared gray in the darkness. The speaker was bareheaded, but the other two wore helmets and combat harnesses. The helmets were also foreign to Mortas, flimsy-looking headgear that hugged the skull and covered the ears. The speaker gestured with an arm as he turned and walked onto the bridge, and the other two followed.

"Son of a bitch, he's posting a guard." Cranther whispered right into Mortas's ear. For the first time the lieutenant was aware that the four of them were so close together that they were basically a pile.

He turned, cupping a hand over the scout's ear and bringing his mouth close. "What are they? Never seen outfits or guns like those."

"Probably colony militia. Those guns are a generation behind what the mainline troops are slinging these days. They're called Maulers."

A remembered slideshow from training, enemy weapons they might see on the battlefield. A trainer referring to one picture of a squat, ugly thing that fired a burst of low-velocity pellets that shattered internal organs so badly that human troops referred to it as the Mauler.

Mortas looked back down just in time to see the first Sim start back toward the vehicle. The two helmeted enemy were left standing in the center of the bridge, looking abandoned. That soon turned out to be the case, as the mover hummed into life and turned around laboriously on the narrow track before heading back the way it came.

"Good." Cranther brought a finger up in front of Mortas's eyes, pointing downstream after the vehicle. "Colony's got to be that way."

The lieutenant looked at the two guards, who still stood there uncertainly. It was madness to have posted them in the center of the span, or on it at all, if they were expecting trouble. There was plenty of cover and good vantage points on both sides of the stream from which they could have covered the bridge with fire. One more item on a growing list of things that didn't make sense.

"So what do we do?"

"Gotta get across the water, which means we use the bridge. We got lucky; these two haven't got a clue about what they're doing. Shouldn't be a problem for us."

"You mean kill them?"

"No choice. We need to be across and up on that high ground before daylight if we want to see where this colony is."

"Won't that bring the rest down on us?"

"They must know about the serpents same as we do. We leave one of those helmets on the bridge, toss the bodies over, let their bosses decide it was an accident. One of the guards sat on the rail, tipped over, the other reached for him and they both went in the drink."

"But how do we approach them? They're right in the middle of the bridge."

It was as if the guards had heard his question. A burst of angry chirping carried to them through the darkness, and he looked down to see one of the Sims pointing a finger at the other. Standing close up, accusatorial. So very human-like. The other one looked away, but not in fear; Mortas tried hard to make sense of it.

"They're arguing." Trent's breath was hot against his neck. "One of them is hardcore and the other one doesn't care at all."

"She's right." Cranther raised up on his elbows just a bit, slowly. The angry guard poked the quiet one in the chest before turning and stomping off toward the opposite end of the bridge. The quiet one watched him go for several steps before tossing a hand gesture at his back. "I think I know what that meant."

"Are they splitting up?" Gorman had to lean in to be heard.

"Maybe." Cranther's face was lit by a malicious grin. "But I doubt it. I think they got told to walk around and one of them doesn't want to."

He lowered himself back onto his stomach, the

smile still there. "Let's watch for a while and see if they develop a pattern."

"Okay, here's what we're going to do." Cranther's voice broke the stillness. "One of us is going to crawl up under the bridge and cross to the other side. Shouldn't be too dangerous. When these two aren't arguing, the hardcore one walks up and down the bridge. Every time he heads for the opposite side, the other one sits down.

"When Hardcore comes back and starts chirping and whining at Lazyboy, that should leave plenty of time to slide out on the other side and get ready." Mortas couldn't help noticing that Cranther was looking at him now. "The next time Hardcore walks off the bridge, turns around, decides what he's gonna say next to Lazyboy, when his back's turned it'll be easy to stab him."

A movement. Mortas looked down and was surprised to see the butt end of Cranther's knife held out in his direction.

"Me? I've never done anything like that. Besides, you'd fit under the bridge a lot easier than I would."

The knife disappeared. "Fine. I'd rather take the one on the other side. He'll never know what hit him. But the guy in the middle there, whoever gets him is gonna have to run across all those metal plates, making all sorts of racket, and then kill him with a rock or his bare hands.

"Figured I'd do that part, but if you want it, it's yours."

"Why do we have to kill either of them?" Gorman. "Why can't we all just crawl under the bridge?"

"Because one man can cross under that bridge without getting spotted. Four people? No way."

"We'll go one at a time, then."

"Sure. And end up with two of us on the other side, one under the bridge, and one left over here when that mover comes back." Cranther shook his head minutely. "Lieutenant? It's your call. Take the knife and do the guard on the other side, or take the one in the middle with a rock. Oh, and remember that if the one on the other side gets off a shot, whoever's doing the one in the middle is gonna have to move like lightning."

The knife came up again, and Mortas grabbed the handle angrily. He hefted the thin dagger, surprised by its weight. "Give me the scabbard too. I'm not cutting myself on this thing while going across."

A prolonged outburst of Sim talk jerked his attention back to the span. The guard who'd been walking the post swatted the other one on the helmet, hard, before walking toward their side of the stream. Cranther nudged Mortas, and the two of them slithered back from the edge of the hill on their stomachs.

"Now listen." Cranther unbuckled his belt and began feeding it through the loops toward the scabbard. "Take your time. The water sounds are gonna cover your movement, and whenever that one guy's in motion his boots hitting those plates are all he's gonna hear even if he's right over you. If he stops, you stop. And don't start moving again until he does. We've got all night to do this."

"I thought we were worried about the mover coming back." Mortas slid the dagger into its sheath and began buckling his belt again.

"We are. So keep your eyes open for them too. Once you're on the other side, cross the road and get in the weeds so if they do come back you're not exposed. When the guard reaches your end, wait until he turns away from you and come up behind him quick." He raised his left hand with the fingers pressed together. "You're tall, so this will work for you. Cup your hand over his mouth, hard, and drive the knife in from the side of his neck."

"You mean stab him? I thought it was better to cut his throat."

"No." Cranther's left hand clamped down over an unseen mouth and his right hand came up in a fist, as if he was trying to stab his left arm. "Do it all at once, punch in with a lot of force because the meat's tough, and then rip straight out.

"Don't believe what you've been told, Lieutenant. The Sims are human. Any luck, you'll tear out his arteries and his windpipe. It'll be an ungodly mess, but make sure you hang on to him. Take him to the ground, and hold him until he stops moving. Then get his gun—you do know how to use one of theirs, right?"

"The newer ones, they let us shoot them in training one time. Not these."

"Same basic idea, just lousy range. Don't shoot unless you absolutely have to. Drag his body into the grass on the other side of the road and wait until the three of us come across."

Mortas could feel his heart thudding in his chest, and he wondered if the sensation of lightheadedness was because of hunger or fear. His mind fogged up on him, unwilling to accept what was happening. Could he do it? Could he *not* do it? What if he messed it up?

"Lieutenant." The voice was stern. "Relax. You'll be fine. He won't be expecting a thing. Take your time getting across, get hidden on the other side, and kill him when he comes to you. Once I see he hasn't come back I'll make my move."

The short man craned his neck over the grass. "He's heading away now. Time to go."

Mortas looked at him expectantly, hoping the scout would at least accompany him to the bridge. It was a foolish thought, but real nonetheless.

Cranther stuck his hand out, and Mortas took it firmly. "Be careful getting under the bridge, and don't let your legs swing down while you're crossing. Those serpents are under there somewhere."

And then he was gone.

CHAPTER 5

The rocks shifted dangerously underfoot as Mortas moved. It had taken him some time to screw up the courage to actually approach the water, but the idea that he might end up trapped under the bridge or waiting on the opposite bank when more Sims arrived spurred him to action.

The ground between the hill and the bridge was relatively open, probably cleared when the structure was put in place. Still, there was enough shrubbery to shield him if he hustled from clump to clump, bent over as if crushed under a tremendous load. The knife felt strange in the small of his back, yet another goad pushing him along.

An odd thought came to mind as the dark expanse got larger and more distinct. It was from a training exercise during his early lieutenancy, and he'd been sent out on a night reconnaissance to observe the mission's target. A live opposing force was supposed to have been defending the location, a signal-bounce station on a small ridge, but they were nowhere to be seen. He and another lieutenant had spent an hour crawling and crouching their way to the top, only to find the place deserted. A mock-up of an enemy antenna had proved they were in the right spot, and to leave their mark they'd pulled up its anchoring stakes and tipped it over the side.

Though only a few months earlier, the event seemed a distant memory.

The sound of the water was now louder than his footfalls, but instead of hurrying him along it caused him to draw back from the embankment. The very thought of the serpents made his legs go weak, and he now knew that it wasn't from hunger. Squatting beside a clump of tall yellow grass that was gray in the starlight, he peeped over the brush to scope out the bridge and was startled to see it was only a few yards away. That of course meant that the others, up on the hill, were watching him now. Mortas found that idea oddly comforting and, stranger still, somehow motivational. They were depending on him, and couldn't even start to come across until he'd completed his assigned tasks. The thought freed him just a little of his concern for his own well-being.

Leaving the final cover, he duckwalked to the side of the bridge. The railing hid him from the guard who was presumably still seated in the span's center, but he didn't waste time looking. The white composite material that made up the bridge support sloped down the bank like a ramp, and the shadowy stream lapped against it hungrily.

Unable to see beneath the structure, but unwilling to move closer to the water, he forced himself to scramble out onto the alien rock, his hands sliding along the cool metal overhead. His arms were now fully extended, and he could just make out the maze of struts and cables under the bridge's flooring that helped support the span. The structure's underside was much deeper than he'd first imagined, and it was with relief that he swung his legs up and into the metal framework.

His ankles found purchase on a rigid cable, so Mortas pulled himself up and forward until he'd come to a sitting position. The water gurgled below him at a distance that seemed much too close, and he pulled his boots up in a hurry when he remembered Cranther's parting words. That left him crouched on the cable, both hands gripping an overhead beam, and the position was so uncomfortable that it got him moving again.

The decking just overhead bore rows of stamped oval holes which let in enough light for him to start picking his way forward. He made good progress, thinking the whole time that the much-shorter Cranther would have been a better choice for this leg of the journey while also listening for the sound of boots on metal. It didn't come, and so he pressed on, making sure of his handholds before stepping onto the next cable or strut. The butt of the knife was starting to abrade the small of his back, but he was too frightened by the chance of falling into the water to do anything about it.

Gonna kill that Cranther when this is all over. He's probably laughing his ass off up there, waiting for me to get shot . . . or to fall.

A new vibration in his hands made those thoughts vanish, and he stopped moving. It was rhythmic, a steady beat, and it could only be the footfalls of the returning guard. He looked ahead, trying to determine where he was in relation to the sitting guard, and that was when he saw something that almost made him lose his grip.

Just a few yards ahead, probably in the center of the span, the underside of the bridge was completely taken up by a thick metal beam that completely blocked his path.

Mortas felt the backs of his legs cramping up first. He was still squatting there in the murky darkness, fixated on the obstacle, when the walking guard reached the sitting guard. They seemed to converse for a bit, the chirping sounds hard to distinguish against the rush of the water. It hardly mattered that they seemed on the verge of a rapprochement, as he wouldn't have been able to keep moving even if they'd separated as expected.

The beam blocking his path was directly beneath the sitting guard, so he wouldn't be able to slide around it by grasping the railing above. There appeared to be a cable looped around the obstacle, but using that would require him to swing underneath, dangling over the stream like a worm on a hook. He shuddered just thinking about it.

The cramps began asserting themselves more forcefully then, and he looked around in panic for a means of stretching his legs out. The chirping overhead grew louder, and he was able to locate the standing guard by the way the light changed in one row of holes up ahead. The back of one of his thighs began to scream just after that, and he was forced to sit back onto the cable and reach out with his boots, pressing them against the next stanchion while the two Sims argued.

What if they shoot each other?

His heart leapt at the very thought, and he imagined climbing up onto the bridge next to two dead bodies, freed of the confines and the water and the serpents and the looming task of killing one of them himself. With a knife. In cold blood.

The utter impossibility of his predicament came home at that instant, and it took a conscious effort not to actually start crying in frustration. His strength was quickly ebbing, and he looked about wildly, as if willing some kind of egress to appear. It did not, of course, but just then the light through the holes changed yet again, quickly, and he heard the meaty thud of a boot on flesh. The plates began to vibrate as the walking guard came toward him, stomping hard, clearly furious as he walked away from his lazy partner.

Thanks a lot, Fuckface. Now I gotta sneak up on a guy who's really pissed off.

Anger welled up in him, and he pulled his boots back onto the cable to resume a squatting position. The barely loosened muscles immediately wanted to constrict again, so he started grimly moving forward. The beam seemed to bounce in front of him, taunting, and the cable wrapped around it took on the consistency of a thread.

He finally reached it, and rested a palm against the metal while searching the shadows for any kind of a handhold. The water rushing by below got louder, and he could have sworn he heard a different, living kind of swishing sound down there. Mortas raised one foot and reached out for the cable, nudging it to see if it was actually attached. It didn't move, but that didn't mean it would support his weight. His head began jerking around madly, his eyes almost round as they tried to penetrate the gloom and find some other way, any other way to do this.

There was none.

His breath came in short, shallow gasps as he reached down with one hand and took hold of the thick rolled wire. The rush of the water turned into a roar as he steeled himself, and he knew, he just knew, that the cable wasn't really attached to anything. It was probably just a discarded piece of support wire tucked out of the way by a Sim workman as lazy as the bastard sitting above him, and it would come loose the instant he swung under the beam. He watched in disbelief as his other hand released the firm safety of the bridge and wrapped around the cable as if directed by someone else. He inched his buttocks forward slowly, reluctantly, feeling the weight shifting off of the last contact while his mouth filled with the brassy taste of adrenaline and his boots swung against empty air and then he was falling.

The handhold came loose almost immediately, dropping him toward the water and the waiting, snapping jaws. He was in free fall, the air rushing around but not supporting him, his mouth and eyes widening in absolute terror. He was just about to scream when the slack went out of the line with a jerk. The cable had slid along the beam, an abbreviated rasp, loosening but not letting go at either end, and now it caught on something and shot him under the obstacle like a trapeze artist. Incredibly, the extra play in the wire was exactly what he needed, and his momentum sailed him straight up and into the supports on the other side.

His boot hooked on one of the diagonal support bars, his opposite shin barked against unyielding metal, and for an instant he was hanging almost upside down. The image of one of the serpents launching itself for his head sent him shimmying upward into the safety under the bridge's flooring, and he grabbed his shin as the pain soared into his brain. Tightened into a ball, hugging the frame with his upper arms while squeezing his leg with his hands, he practically shouted when something thumped on the plates directly above him.

He looked up to see the holes in the flooring change from light to black, and then back to light.

The walking guard passed over him, so close that he could have poked a finger up into the sole of his boot, and he froze until the rhythmic footfalls went silent. He clung there for what seemed like a long time, letting his heart and his breathing slow down. Stress perspiration covered his entire body, and a slight breeze brought a cooling release. The water below kept gurgling at him, but he could now see all the way to the end of the bridge.

The far bank was much steeper, almost sheer, and so he had to worm his way through the remaining metal latticework and over the rock-like support until there was simply no more room. The walking guard had already headed for the other side, and so he wriggled out on his back, the girders just over his chest and gravel working its way down his neck. The stars overhead were shining, he was safely across the abode of the ravenous water snakes, and he simply lay there for a long moment. Finally rolling onto his stomach, he pushed himself up into a kneeling position and looked around.

It was as if he'd discovered the planet all over again, and he felt like an explorer. Of the group, he was the only one who'd seen this side of the river up close, and he looked down the hard pack of the road until it melted into the darkness. Remembering the enemy mover as well as his grim purpose, he got to his feet and dashed across into the weeds. It was intoxicating to move freely, to run over solid dirt and then collapse in a bed of grass. The ground sloped upward sharply from there, into what he already knew was a high ridge. Cranther had suggested it as their next destination, and Mortas tried to focus on that instead of the approaching brutality.

The trip across had left him both dazed and elated, but he knew that the Sim guard would be returning soon and that the hardest part of the night had not yet arrived. He reached back and slowly drew the knife from its sheath, awkward in his hand. He hefted it a few times to get the feel, like lacrosse warm-ups back at university, hoping to gain some kind of familiarity with the strange tool. His lacrosse stick had become just another part of him after enough games, but he truly doubted he'd ever get that comfortable with this evil blade.

The thought of school days brought unwanted images of his father, his sister, even the dim memories of his dead mother. Prone in the weeds on a foreign planet, stomach empty, waiting for an unsuspecting entity to cross his path. What would his people say if they could see him right now?

His father, always ready with an answer, would probably say something about doing things that had to be done no matter how distasteful or difficult. But then again, he and his cronies of the Emergency Senate had murdered the Interplanetary President and his entire cabinet, so they'd had lots of practice portraying their actions in terms of necessity.

His sister Ayliss would have a different opinion. She always did. She'd tried so many times to dissuade him from signing up for the Force. Accurately warning him that their father was using him yet again, either to learn the truth about what was actually happening in the war or to hold him up as an example of the family's dedication to that very conflict.

He doesn't care if you live or die out there, Jan. Either way he'll make you a hero.

Beautiful, golden-haired Ayliss, just one year his senior but a lifetime more mature. From his earliest memory she'd been able to predict their father's every move. Her one flaw was that she didn't see that this mystic understanding of the dreaded Senator Mortas came from the fact that she was almost exactly like him. In looks, brains, and temperament.

And she'd been wrong about the reason Mortas had signed up. She thought it was his way of finally gaining the parental attention that no number of nannies or coaches or mentors could replace, but that hadn't been it. It was something else, far more personal, far more primitive. It was something he'd found on the lacrosse fields and in dormitory fights at boarding school: he liked competition, enjoyed testing himself, and simply wanted to know how it felt to go to war.

Mortas managed a weak smile of self-mockery at the notion of having actually wanted this. Lying there in the grass like an animal, it was crystal clear that he should have been able to figure this out without actually doing it. After all, now he knew. Now he knew what it felt like. He was ravenous, exhausted, and dirty. He was dreading the very sight of the enemy he was supposed to conquer. The only thing he knew for sure was that he'd mess his trousers at some point in the next few minutes if the guard showed up, if he didn't show up, if he took too long showing up, or even if he showed up and presented the perfect, unsuspecting target that Cranther had described.

The only chance that he wouldn't void himself rested with the high likelihood that there was nothing left in his system to soil his uniform.

The thought evaporated with the hollow metallic ringing of the Sim's boots on the bridge plates. It had an electrical effect on him, like the throwing of a switch, but unfortunately this switch turned to the off position.

I can't do this. I can't do this. I can't do this.

The notion of sneaking up behind the Sim and tearing his throat out with no provocation now solidified into something so ludicrous that Mortas marveled that he'd ever thought he'd be able to do it. The helmeted figure came into view, looking broad shouldered and enormous, and Mortas hunkered down lower in the grass. Cranther had sounded so matter-of-fact in his coaching that Mortas now questioned if this was something the scout had actually done before, or merely something he'd been taught. That idea reminded him of the others, waiting up on the hill for him to act, and his face reddened with shame.

If you're not going to do it, what are you going to do? And

*what are the others supposed to do when they see the guard
keeps reappearing?*

The Sim reached the end of the bridge and stepped
out onto the road. He was making a frustrated chirping noise under his breath, and Mortas was taken
aback by the humanity of it: the Sim was so angry with
his partner that he was talking to himself. The guard
kicked a stone out of his path, still coming on, and
Mortas slowly became certain that he'd been seen.

But that was nonsense. The Sim's stubby weapon
was slung across his chest and, even though he had one
hand on it, he clearly wasn't planning to use it. He kept
moving closer, and Mortas was able to make out the
straps of his combat harness just before he turned and
started back.

Go. Go. Go. They're counting on you.

Amazed by his own motion, Mortas came to his
feet and took an uncertain step forward. The guard
was already walking away, and the sight of his retreating back aroused an animal response in the human
sneaking up on him.

*Attack reflex. Just like they warned us when they talked
about retreating. The sight of another animal's back, in flight
or not, caused predators to immediately give chase. Sign of
weakness. Vulnerability. Bloodlust. Hunger. Rage.*

Eyes. Eyes. EYES. No no no no EYES!

He couldn't believe that the Sim had turned around.
Looking absurdly human, the guard's mouth opened
wide in consternation. There were barely two strides
between them, but to Mortas he seemed impossibly

distant. They both looked down at the weapon in the Sim's hands, and then they both moved.

The Sim reached across, dragging some kind of lever back, maybe loading the weapon, maybe taking the safety off. Mortas, fueled by that most primal terror, the fear of death, lunged forward with the knife held straight out.

It felt like he'd stabbed a tree. The blade stopped with a jolt, and pain shot through his elbow and into his shoulder. Mortas's mouth opened in an O shape, and his eyes followed suit just after that. The knife had gone straight through the Sim's throat, lodging in bone on the other side, and the enemy soldier merely stood there, a revolting vibration starting to pass through his entire body. His arms left the gun, sagging to his sides, but his body kept trembling. His feet began an angry stamping on the ground, and despite his horror Mortas tackled him to make it stop.

It was only after he'd taken the dead enemy to the ground, and after the ugly convulsions had finally ended, that he saw that his shirt front was covered in a warm, wet liquid that had to be blood.

He dragged the body across the road and into the grass, feeling like a child trying to hide the evidence of having broken a major rule. His hands were shaking when he went through the pouches on the guard's combat harness, residual adrenaline pounding through him. His mouth had dried completely, and so he took the dead enemy's canteen and sniffed at its contents. Sims drank water the same way humans did, but that was no guarantee that this was water. It had no odor, and so he drank from it hungrily.

After that he moved like a robot. He cleaned Cranther's knife on the Sim's uniform and returned it to its scabbard. Then he scrubbed at the already-drying blood on his blouse with handfuls of dirt, repelled by the cloying substance. With that done, he took the guard's weapon and moved away from the corpse, telling himself he needed to be able to cover the bridge even though the gun's range was far too short for that.

Mortas was disappointed not to see the others coming right away, but then reconsidered. They would wait a while to make sure the walking guard wasn't coming back, and then make their move. Ruminating on that, he now saw what a flimsy plan they'd devised. How many times had the walking guard disappeared and then returned while he'd been crossing under the bridge? What if the Sim had decided to take a break of his own, on this side of the water and out of sight, before Mortas had gotten into position? Cranther might have been running down the length of the bridge toward the seated guard at its center just as the walking guard reappeared.

To make matters worse, Mortas now saw another wrinkle that they hadn't addressed. If the mover came back in the next few minutes, what was he going to do? Fire at it with this unfamiliar weapon? Do nothing, and watch the others come hustling over the bridge right into the enemy's arms? The ramifications were made all the more frightening by what he'd just seen and done, and Mortas shuddered at the very thought.

He looked down the road in the direction the mover had gone, but the darkness closed in only a short distance out. There was no way to tell if he'd be able to see the approaching headlights far off, or if they'd be right on top of him. The mover's engine had been nearly silent from across the river, but hopefully it would make more noise at close range. He tried to listen, but only heard the rustling of the water and began to wish very strongly for the sound of three sets of boots crossing the bridge.

The adrenaline was wearing off, as was the shock of having killed for the first time, and a heavy lethargy began spreading across his limbs and his mind. He'd done what the others had needed him to do, the hard part for him was over, and if Cranther would just get a move on, they could get away from this cursed place. The image of the four of them walking up the next ridge seemed very peaceful, and he yawned as he considered it.

It would be so nice to be back out in the boondocks, away from everything. Away from here . . .

He came to rest in the room where he'd lived as an upperclassman at his prep school. A top-floor round tower, bigger than the other rooms with curved windows looking out on an ancient chestnut tree and the rolling fields of the school. A worn rug in the center of the room, beds, bookcases, and desks, and even a blocked-up fireplace where he and his roommate had liked to hide various contraband items.

It was night outside, and Mortas recognized the scene even though somewhere in his subconscious he knew he was dreaming. It was the night they'd announced that his father had been elevated to Chairman of the Emergency Senate, and he'd left the dining hall early to avoid the well-wishers. A dark-haired boy, a recent transfer named Emile Dassa, had followed him even though they didn't know each other. Mortas had feared it was yet another attempt to congratulate him, but he'd been wrong.

So far the dream was the same as the reality, or at least his sleeping brain said it was. Emile's hair hung past his ears, unusual for the school, and his dark eyes had blazed with something close to fanaticism.

"Your dad finally made the leap to the very top. Only took murdering the president, his entire cabinet, and a few dozen Force officers, too . . . unless you count everybody who's died in the war since then."

He'd felt an urge to throw the smaller boy out, perhaps even toss him down the stairs, but an old curiosity had prevented him from doing that. "What would you know about it? I was ten when that happened, so what would you have been? Eight?"

"Did Daddy tell you what he told everybody else? That the president and his crowd had to die because they wanted to radiate all the Hab planets between us and the Sims?"

The story at the time of the coup was that the president had ordered the Human Defense Force to render a large number of Hab planets unlivable, creating a kind of astral firebreak that would divert the Sims from the human-occupied planets. It was hard to know what was true and what wasn't because the plan's alleged authors were all dead, but they'd reputedly dubbed it the "Head 'em Off" plan. His father and the new Emergency Senate had ridiculed it as the "Head in the Sand Plan" just before presenting their own "Head On" strategy to the public. Head On had committed all of mankind to battling the Sims for every Hab planet, no matter where they were found, until the Sim home world could be located and destroyed.

"He didn't tell me anything. Like I said, I was ten." Mortas had given that response so many times over the years that it came out as a reflex, even in his dream. The sad truth was that he'd gotten the same explanation as the rest of humanity, right from his father's mouth, and that he distrusted the man so completely that he'd automatically dismissed the explanation. For a time, he'd believed he and his sister Ayliss were the only people outside the Emergency Senate who even suspected the story was a lie.

"And you never asked? Never wondered about those dirty rumors? You know, the ones about a whole bunch of generals and colonels dying in combat right around the time the president was getting the chop, even though half of them weren't anywhere near the war zones?"

"Did you say rumor? There's a rumor about your sister too, Dassa. Should I believe that as well?"

"I don't have a sister. And I'm not going to get one, not now anyway. My dad was an aide to one of those generals, but he was on leave when the Purge happened. Somehow they missed him, but they remembered him a year ago."

The dream shifted from reality at this point. In reality Mortas had jumped up, fearing the boy meant to attack him in some twisted act of revenge. He'd whipped Dassa soundly, beating him straight into the old rug before throwing him down the stairs. Emile Dassa had disappeared from the school infirmary that very night, and Mortas had never summoned the courage to ask what had happened to him. But here, in the dream, he stayed in his chair and kept on talking with the other boy, saying things he'd never said in real life.

"They killed those generals and colonels because they were going to carry out the president's orders and wreck a hundred habitable worlds. Which means your dad was working for a fool. Any idiot could see that plan wasn't going to hold off the Sims."

"Still don't get it, do you? There never was a 'Head 'em Off' plan. There was just a bunch of really frightened politicians who knew what we were actually up against out there, who were going to tell everyone that the Sims aren't the real enemy. That they're a front, just a great big clever smokescreen. That we don't stand a chance against whatever's backing them. And that would have ended the war."

Emile dissolved into a blonde-haired, blue-eyed woman in the uniform of the Veterans Auxiliary, the organization that handled everything from rehabilitation to retirement for the Forcemembers returned from the war. Mortas's sleeping mind wondered how his sister Ayliss could be at the prep school of his teen years when she'd only recently joined the Auxiliary, but her character picked up the thread where Emile had left off.

"Some people see the war as a struggle for survival, but some others see it as a struggle for power. And I don't mean power over the Sims. I mean power over humanity. That's why Father and his friends killed the president and his cabinet and all those senior officers. It was so they could take charge and get everyone in line behind them.

"And it all seemed to work for a time, everybody bought the cover story, and the war zones are so far away that nobody can ever really know what's going on out there. How the Sims keep developing these new tricks that should be beyond them. How no matter what we do, we can't even analyze what makes up their food. Or understand why they die in captivity, or why they can't reproduce."

"Where are you getting all this?" His voice was exasperated, and he remembered the line from an argument they'd had when he'd announced his plan to accept a commission and go to the war. Very few of his privileged classmates were doing that, even the ones who'd trained for it right beside him, and it would have been the simplest thing for him to avoid. He was, after all, the son of Olech Mortas.

"Why do you think I let them put me in the Auxiliary?" The uniform switched to a dark business suit, and the dreaming Mortas remarked to his subconscious that this was more like it because Ayliss almost never wore the Auxiliary outfit. "It's given me the run of the records database, and now I can talk to anyone I want. Even the veterans they committed to lockdown facilities because they wouldn't keep quiet."

"About what?"

"About the Purge. About the war. About the enemy. Even about Father."

"You're just like him, you know that? As much as you fight him, it's not because you hate him. It's because you want to play the game. His game. Sneak around in the shadows, find the weak spot, and squeeze. Well fuck that. When somebody's my enemy, they know it. I go straight at them and whatever happens happens. That's why I want to go."

Ayliss had laughed, quietly, that maddening way she had of telling him he was being ignorant. "You must know that some of Command's most senior officers murdered their superiors in the Purge, right? And that nobody in Command, whether they helped out in the Purge or not, trusts Father and his cronies at all? That's who you're going to be working for out there. Either the commanders who didn't know what Father and his friends were up to, or the backstabbers who helped them. Nobody knows who they can trust out there, and you know what the vets tell me? That's why we're losing."

The dream changed without explanation, shifting to a wide field of grass and sand. A mock-up of an enemy strongpoint stood in the center of the open space, with metal and wire obstacles arranged around it. Smoke was still in the air, and a disordered gang of lieutenants was seated in front of him. Their faces were streaked with sweat, and everything from their uniforms to their weapons was caked with sand. The sun was high and hot overhead, but he wasn't paying attention to it.

A taller, older man in a camouflage uniform was standing in front of him, shouting. He was one of the veterans in the training cadre, an NCO who took his job very seriously. The sergeant's face was close to his own, and he was clearly disappointed with whatever had happened in the last exercise. In the dream Mortas knew that he'd been in charge of this iteration, but he couldn't remember what he'd done wrong.

"You're why we're not winning this war, Lieutenant! You came out here with your head up your ass, unprepared and don't care, and you couldn't take out a lone enemy emplacement! What were you thinking, Lieutenant? You got half your platoon killed and the Sims are still in that bunker, eating that crap they call food and laughing at you! Are you hearing me, Lieutenant? Lieutenant? Lieutenant!"

"Lieutenant. Lieutenant." The voice was quiet, but insistent. A woman's voice. His eyes opened to Trent's face just a few inches above him, almost a replay of their first meeting, but this time he smiled at her. She was kneeling next to him, holding his arms with both hands where she'd been shaking him awake.

"How long was I out?" He muttered, sitting up as if in a daze. Gorman knelt in the weeds nearby, looking at something with terrible concentration. It took another long moment for Mortas to realize it was the dead Sim.

"No idea. Felt like forever, waiting for that one guard to stop coming back, and even after that Cranther waited and waited." The tension in the woman's voice conveyed the strain the other must have felt.

"Not right." Gorman spoke under his breath. "Not right."

Mortas pushed himself up into a sitting position, seeing that Trent and Gorman were carrying all twelve of the group's water tubes. He stood up slowly, becoming aware that the Sim's weapon was gone. Wobbling on the uneven ground, he looked down at the spot where he'd dragged the dead enemy. Gorman was staring at Cranther as the scout methodically searched the dark corpse, still murmuring that something wasn't right.

"What is it?" He asked the question simply to make Gorman say something different.

"Not right what he did. That other guard was asleep. He just walked out there and cut his throat. Not right."

With the bloody evidence of his own recent actions stretched out before them, Mortas found it difficult to sympathize with the mapmaker. He watched Cranther as if from a distance, now seeing that the dead Sim's weapon was lying on the ground next to him. Or was that the Mauler from the guard on the bridge? The one Cranther would have killed. His groggy brain finally focused on one of the things Gorman had said.

"Cut his throat? With what?"

"He's got another knife in his boot." Trent now stood next to him, her face stamped with anger. "He waited until he was good and sure the other guard was asleep before he went out there. You were exposed over here, they could have come back at any time, but he waited until he was sure."

Mortas knew that the revelation should be making him angry, but he also knew why it wasn't. The repellent memory of the killing was strong in his mind, and the only thing stronger was his recognition that the deed would have been much easier had the enemy been asleep. He was amazed by the way his mind moved off of the issue and onto the task at hand.

"What did you do with the body?"

"Tossed it into the drink." Cranther turned, still in a squatting position, pushing the skullcap back a little on his head. He held out the dead guard's combat harness and Mortas took it, noticing a similar rig on the scout's torso. "Didn't wanna give the Wisp here a chance to hold a service."

The cruel logic meshed with the new workings of his mind, and Mortas moved on. "Did those *things* get him?"

"Yeah, but not as fast as you might think." Cranther

glanced down at the corpse. "They're probably still nearby, though. Made a lot of noise when they found the first one."

He scooped up the Sim's weapon and handed it to Mortas, prompting his next question. "Where's the other one of these?"

"I left it on the bridge with his helmet. When the others come back, it'll convince 'em it was an accident. One guard takes a break, takes off his helmet, puts down his weapon, leans back too far on the rail, starts going over, and the other one reaches for him." He motioned toward the dead guard. "I'll take him out there unless you want to."

"Go ahead."

With surprising ease, the short man pulled the body up onto his shoulders and then stood up. He was gone in a moment.

"Not right, the things we've done here."

"Gorman, that's the last time I'm willing to hear that." Anger welled up in him at the thought of what he'd been through, and that one of the people he'd done it for found it unacceptable. "We had to cross the bridge, and they were in the way."

"Are you planning to kill everybody who gets in your way, Lieutenant?"

Out in the darkness there was a loud splash, followed by a sickening thrashing in the water under the bridge. For an instant Mortas was back under there, swinging through the empty air, certain that he would end up in the river with the serpents. He leaned forward, making eye contact with Gorman.

"From here on out . . . you can count on it."

The climb up the next hill was a tough one, but Mortas was happy to get away from the bridge. He hardly felt the exertion as they moved through the night, tripping over small stones in their haste. Even Cranther seemed eager to put distance between them and the river, recommending that they take a chance and move along the top of the ridge when they reached it. Gorman's feet were obviously torturing him again, but he kept up without complaint. After a while Mortas decided that might actually be worse than hearing him bitch a little, as it was clear that the mapmaker was withdrawing inside himself. Trent took Gorman in hand, whispering little words of encouragement, and he decided to leave things that way for now.

His silent position at the rear of the group gave Mortas time to think, and he found his mind focusing itself on the tactical considerations of their current predicament. It felt as if every other topic that would usually have come to mind during a march—sex, music, jokes, bad life decisions, moments of glory, hope for the future—had been rendered somehow irrelevant. His past was on a completely different planet and his future had shrunken to the next few hours. He now found himself completely and comfortably occupied with questions of how much distance they could cover before daylight, what help the one Mauler could be to them, and how to avoid any further involvement with the enemy until they'd found the colony. Something had changed for him back at the bridge, and he felt certain that it was not simply the dreadful act of having killed the guard. He was still revolted by the experience, and every now and then ran a hand down his shirtfront to scrape off a little more of the dried blood that clung there.

Just before dawn they moved off of the ridge to avoid being silhouetted, and Cranther found them a safe haven in a hollow that faced the direction from which the Sim mover had come. He'd advised Mortas that it was better to see their hideaway in daylight than to simply pick one in darkness, admitting that he'd been badly surprised more than once at how exposed a hide position could be when the sun came up.

The thick, dry grass of the lower elevation had given way yet again to thin scrub, and so they found a small depression to conceal them. Now that the enemy was definitely present they would have to hide during the day and move at night. Even that gave no guarantee of protection, as the Sims possessed infrared imagers the same as the humans. And if they got a few shuttles up in the air they'd pick off this pitiful little gang in no time.

So where are the shuttles? Where is their air?

Despite his empty stomach and the long night, Mortas was wide awake when they finally settled into their latest home. Cranther joined him as the sun broke over the ridges, hoping to see some indication that the enemy settlement was close.

"It makes no sense that they haven't got their air up. A new Sim colony usually has shuttles going out and back around the clock. Easiest way to pinpoint their location."

"What do you think was going on at that bridge? Only two guards, neither one knows what he's doing, far away from any help. Why post them at all?"

"Can't figure it. They put them out there after dark, almost as an afterthought." Cranther sighed, his eyes ranging over what the climbing sun was showing to be yet another barren plain. "Only connection I can make is that one ration bag. Maybe some of our people got landed here, like one of the special ops outfits, and they've been fucking with the colony."

"Think that's why we haven't seen any shuttles?"

"Maybe. Maybe they lost a couple flights to ground fire and stopped sending them up, or maybe somebody got onto their field and damaged them. Truth is I have no idea."

The sun was up high enough to see across the open ground to the next set of hills, probably miles away. As hard as he tried, Mortas couldn't find a single sign that anyone had ever been there before.

It was late in the day when Trent woke him. Her guard shift had been the last one, and so Mortas had been curled up in the hole with Cranther and Gorman, like three children sharing the same small bed.

The lack of food was making itself known in several ways. Though he'd slept for hours, his mind was still fogged when he sat up and tried to get his bearings. He'd laid his uniform top on the ground, hoping the sun would bleach out some of the bloodstain, and he touched his own shoulder as he shrugged the blouse back on. The usually meaty muscle felt odd to him, and he stopped to examine it with his hand. He caressed it for a few seconds before recognizing that it was actually smaller now, reduced by the lack of nourishment and the physical toil. For a moment it reminded him of a girl at university, his first, and he found the memory sad.

He took a small swig from the canteen before crawling up to the edge of the hole where Trent was on watch. The plain below hadn't changed, and she reported seeing and hearing nothing in the last several hours. They regarded the desolation in silence for some time.

"Lieutenant, there's something you really should know about Gorman."

He glanced over his shoulder at the chartist, who was on his side with his arms hugging his chest, his knees bent, and still unconscious. "Okay. Go ahead."

"He wasn't wrong to object to what happened last night."

"Really? Then he doesn't understand the straits we're in. And you don't either."

"Oh, I think he understands that just fine. Maybe more than the rest of us. Don't forget that the way he lives his life is geared toward the next life, so the concept of extinction is always on his mind."

"So you're saying he doesn't think we should fight for our lives?"

"He probably doesn't, but that's not it. The Holy Whisperers serve in the Force in noncombat roles, but they don't kid themselves about their hands being completely clean. They know they're helping out in the commission of violence by others, and the way they square that with themselves is the total refusal to tolerate unnecessary violence."

"Those two guards were watching the bridge. The bridge was the only way to cross the water. What happened was necessary."

"Maybe. But Cranther waited until he was sure that second guard was asleep before he even moved. He made certain that he was going to be killing someone who was unconscious."

"You think he should have been more sporting? Woke him up, maybe?"

"I'm afraid you're not seeing the point here. Gorman believes we could have just walked by that Sim. Maybe we could have, maybe we couldn't, but we didn't even try."

"That is absolute nonsense. Even if that would work, what were we supposed to do with the dead Sim? Leave him there? Quietly drag him down to the water and hope one of those monsters didn't get us as we pushed him in, just so we don't wake up the guy on the bridge? You know, the one with the weapon?"

"All right, maybe it was a silly idea. But Gorman believes it, and right now he's sure that Cranther did something very wrong and that you're on Cranther's side."

"As far as what happened at the bridge? You bet I am."

"Well maybe you shouldn't be. Forget the ethical questions for just a moment. Remember that I was over there too, watching everything that happened after you left. Both Gorman and I asked Cranther to get out there much sooner than he actually moved. He didn't seem the least bit concerned for you, waiting on the other side. He knew that guard would go to sleep, and that he'd be in no danger then." She looked down at the scout, her lip curling in contempt. "I heard him convince you to go across first, and all because that wasn't supposed to be the hard job. Well it was the hard job, by far. You had to climb out there, risk getting spotted and killed, and then take on the guard who was actually walking his post. Cranther convinced you to do that because killing the guard on the bridge was supposed to be so dangerous.

"Turned out it wasn't going to be dangerous at all. And he knew that when he told you it was."

"**S**ee it?"

Cranther pointed off into the gathering twilight. Mortas was trying hard to pick out the thing that had caught the scout's eye, but it was difficult with the failing light. Or so he thought.

"There." Cranther put a hand on his shoulder, pointing again. For the space of a few seconds, a dull green line appeared across the plain as if hanging in the night sky. "We couldn't see it in daylight. That's a Sim retransmission antenna. The settlement's on the other side of that ridge.

"They put those antennae up when a colony's new, before they get everything wired." Cranther stepped away, becoming a disembodied voice. "Did you know some of our generals call the enemy the Simples? Because their tech isn't as good as ours? Talk about simple. Sure, they're behind us in a lot of ways, still haven't figured out the Step, but they've got one very big advantage. Everything they have actually works. All the time.

"One mission we were orbiting a Hab planet, or what was supposed to be a Hab. They'd gotten as much information from the scanners as they were ever going to get, so it was time for some scouts to hit the dirt and check it out up close. First humans ever to set foot on the place. This was before they developed the cofferdams, so they loaded the first team of Spartacans into these one-man tubes, they're like big darts that they used to fire straight down at a planet's surface . . . half the time the chutes didn't deploy."

He stopped for a moment, and Mortas heard him wetting his lips.

"So the first team gets blasted down through the clouds, these giant wispy things that hid every inch of that planet, and there's no radio check from them. Any of them. Well, Command's got a lot of Spartacans so they loaded up the second team and shot them down there too. And the same thing happened. Nothing.

"Somebody got smart and suggested that the darts were the problem, maybe some fatal malfunction, so they put the next team onto a shuttle and sent them flying down through the atmosphere. Hab planet's gotta have atmosphere, ya know?

"I was in the ready room with the next team—you never saw such frightened faces—and we're listening over this speaker as they entered the clouds. And they're reporting like mad, calling out all the readings—there was some kind of interference with the data uplink—and then this one guy just starts *screaming* out this atmospheric pressure number that is skyrocketing and then . . . nothing."

Mortas felt his empty stomach lurch. Grisly tales of mistakes like that one were common enough, but to hear the story from someone who'd actually been there was something different.

"The funny thing was that, of all the data they'd collected from a distance, the pressure readings were actually right. The raw data was, at any rate. Turned out it wasn't a Hab at all. Its atmosphere crushed all the darts, and the shuttle too. A glitch in the analysis program kept correcting the pressure readings because they were so high. The machine didn't believe the number, so it defaulted to a livable measurement. Ho-ly shit.

"And the brass hats have the nerve to call the Sims simple."

It was dark enough to move out, but Mortas wanted to settle the issue of what had happened at the bridge.

He suspected that the scout had told him his most recent war story to keep him from doing just that.

"Corporal."

"Yes?"

"Did you set me up at the bridge?"

"How do you mean?" The voice was flat and calm.

"I mean, did you give me the hard job and keep the easy one for yourself?"

"Yes."

"Any special reason for that?"

"Of course." The dirt shifted under the scout's feet, and he'd clearly turned to face him. "I been out here five years, Lieutenant, and you've been here less than five days. I've been kidnapped, tortured, abandoned, lied to, starved, written off, threatened with the death sentence, and almost sent down to a planet wearing nothing but my uniform in an atmosphere that could crush an armored suit.

"You're a new guy, Lieutenant. Your being an officer doesn't change that. If we get out of this, and you do get that platoon you want so badly, it's gonna be loaded with veterans. They're not gonna want to take chances on your say-so until they see that you actually know what taking a chance really means."

"How do you know I want that platoon? How do you know I'm not just some guy who got scooped up into this insanity just like you?"

"It's written all over you. I'll bet you've been sucking up the lies from the Bounce all your life. The glorious cause. Humanity against the aliens. I bet you signed up just based on one of those hero profiles they're constantly running. The returning veteran, home from the zone, covered in medals and saying that it's your turn now."

Mortas could feel his face reddening and was thankful for the dark. The Bounce feed back home had influenced him greatly, particularly the tales of bravery and sacrifice of the heroes who had not come back. Even with his family background and the classified information it provided, he'd still bought into a lot of the propaganda. The other boys at the prep school and university, his privileged peers, had scoffed at the idea of serving and so he'd learned early on to hide his true feelings of excitement and belief.

It's Your Turn. He could still see the eyes of the medal-bedecked combat vet on the Bounce, repeating the slogan of the ongoing war. It's Your Turn. In the light of recent events, he now realized that the vet's face had been just a bit too perfect. An actor's face, but an actor who'd been chosen with great care. The face had been good-looking but not handsome, mature but not hardened, and he now wondered if the man had been a veteran at all.

"They don't call it the Bounce for nothing." It was the best he could manage, but he sensed Cranther was waiting for a response.

"Yeah. That was its original name way back when, because the feed ricocheted off of satellites to reach the other planets. Marketers probably thought they'd dreamed up a really cool name for a really cool technology. But look at how people talk about it now. Follow the Bouncing Story. Bounce Your Brain."

It's even slang at high levels now. When Father and his buddies put out their own version of a story, it's called bounce.

"Did you know that Spartacans are kept separate whenever we're not on an actual mission? On the planets we're kept in virtual prisons. In space we're restricted to certain decks, or just plain locked up. You know why that is? Because the truth doesn't bounce."

"Wait a minute. What happens when your hitch is up?"

A short laugh. "No such thing for us. Yeah, I know you've seen a Spartacan hero on those profiles every now and then, but that's a lie too. I knew a guy who knew one of those guys. He'd been snatched up like the rest of us, beat on like the rest of us, but never sent on a mission. He was connected to somebody big, and they finally found him. The Spartacans walking around out there as returned vets are almost complete phonies. And you can bet they got threatened with all sorts of trouble if they ever speak up.

"Follow that bouncing ball . . . but you just wait until the real story gets out. How we've been used out here. That the Sims are human. That the war can never end."

How the Emergency Senate can be an "emergency" body for over ten years.

"You sound almost like a radical there, Corporal."

"I am a radical. I'm radically in favor of my own ass. And nothing else."

CHAPTER 6

Walking. Walking. Starving.

Tiring.

Doubting.

The stars that had been providing such fine illumination had dimmed behind a veil of clouds, making it almost impossible to see where they were going. The shroud enfolded Mortas, cutting him off from the others even more than he already was. It seemed that the very ground conspired against them, as they were forced to walk along the side of the ridge for fear of encountering the enemy on its crest. The slope made walking uneven and chancy, and Gorman clearly suffered anew as the different angle of his footfalls reopened his blisters. Trent walked either directly behind him, or beside him on the downward slope, and Cranther took the lead the entire way.

We're splitting up into two groups. At least two.

Fracturing. Coming apart. Not supposed to allow that.

The scout seemed able to see in the dark, never stumbling, but still he didn't push the pace very hard. Every time loose rocks went tumbling down the slope because of the others he would simply freeze, and so would they. The frail forms would stand there on the angle, one tired leg bent and the other stretched to the limit, until Cranther was sure no enemy was nearby. Fingers of rock stretched across their path from time to time, running downward from the crest and forming excellent block positions. Every time they approached one of these the Spartacan would stop the group and go forward alone, silent, to see if anything waited on the likely ambush spot.

Each time he disappeared, Mortas feared he wouldn't come back.

The movement was simply endless. His own toughened feet began to heat up in unusual places because of the awkward positioning of his boots, and he feared he'd end up in even worse shape than Gorman. The mapmaker was moving along without complaint, and Mortas had to question whether or not he'd be able to bear up as well if injured in a similar fashion. The backs of his knees protested every step now, and he'd scraped the palm of his uphill hand more than once when the scree gave way beneath him.

The hours wore on and they continued the nonstop movement with no encouragement from the blackness that surrounded them. In the daylight they'd been able to gauge their progress, modest as it had seemed, but now there was no way to know if they were getting anywhere at all. The ridge that held the Sim retransmission antenna curved toward their own somewhere in the distance, and Cranther had recommended that they move to the spot where the two escarpments were closest. The idea was to cross the flat at that point and then gain the heights that presumably looked down on the settlement, but Mortas began to doubt the plan the longer they walked. He couldn't make out his hand in front of his face, and doubted how Cranther would know when they'd reached the right spot for the crossing. What if they'd already passed it?

Mortas had been surprised to lose sight of the antenna's intermittent glow early in the walk, and without that as a reference he couldn't tell how far they'd come. As the pain of his straining muscles and blistering feet slowly increased, he began to wistfully count off all the tools he would have had available for this march if he'd been with a regular Force platoon. He and his men would have been wearing goggles allowing them to see in the dark, and the enemy antenna would have been a bright line in the green field of vision. They would have been communicating through subdued microphones, passing everything from orders to information to encouragement. As a platoon leader he would have carried the additional aid of a navigational tablet that would not only tell him where he was, but also how to get where he was going. The wondrous thing would even tell him if he'd taken a wrong turn.

And that was only counting what his platoon would

have been carrying. Even operating alone, they would be accompanied by silent drones cruising above and around them, searching for the enemy. Command frowned on the use of flares because they interfered with the operation of the goggles and also because the Sims relied on them heavily, but under emergency conditions he could have requested enough parachute illumination to light up the ground for miles. In big operations, where his platoon would be a small cog in a massive, searching machine of destruction, spacecraft in orbit would be monitoring their movement, ready to deliver a cataclysmic bombardment if necessary.

It was almost comical; here he was, an officer in the most technologically advanced species known to man, someone who'd grown up with every kind of device and machine imaginable, and his world had devolved into mere rock and dirt. He could feel the gravel shifting every time he put a boot down, straining the outside of one ankle and the inside of the other. His concentration on not falling took up almost all of the consciousness that his exhaustion and hunger weren't consuming, and yet he could still shake his head in amusement that his life aspirations at that moment could be summed up in the burning desire to simply sit down.

Much later, after his legs were so sore that he couldn't identify a muscle that wasn't shouting, they abruptly turned and started walking downhill. Incredibly, this reprieve turned out to be even worse than the relentless inclined walk. Each step reached out into inky nothingness and then dropped until it found dirt, gravel, or rocks large enough to trip over. Mortas found his hands reaching out in front of him, grabbing air, and he slung the Mauler behind him to free up both his palms for the pointless effort. The stars had disappeared, and his only indication that the others were present was the sound of their own struggles. From those noises, he assumed they were doing a similar blind man's walk.

He finally gave up and turned sideways again, as if they were still hugging the ridgeline, and found it an enormous relief. They'd been headed in one direction for so long on the same incline that there had been no way to alternate the foot that was lowermost, but now he was able to face the opposite direction as he slide-stepped down the slope. The new blisters were finally protected from the harsh abrasion of his boots, and he almost groaned in release.

Cranther must have been angling them toward the plain for some time, because it didn't take long to reach level ground. Mortas knew this only when he bumped into the others gathered at the bottom in various postures of exhaustion. He mumbled a soft apology that was returned with a muffled chorus of surprising mildness. A variety of phosphorescent pebble was scattered across the flat expanse in front of them, reflecting what dim light was available, and he was finally able to make out the features of the other three. Cranther was leaning forward, his hands on his knees while

Trent and Gorman stood resting against each other. As much as those postures of fatigue might be expected, their sunny expressions were not. All three were smiling, and it took Mortas a few seconds to realize that he was doing the same thing, overcome with joy at leaving the brutal incline behind.

Without knowing why, Mortas stepped up between Trent and Gorman. He laid a hand on each of their shoulders, leaned in, and whispered, "Good job. Good job."

Sweaty hands came up to squeeze his arms, and they stood there grinning at each other until Cranther joined them. The short man stepped in across from Mortas, his hands on the others' shoulders as well, trying to catch his breath but doing it without making a sound. Mortas saw the other two placing their free hands on the scout, and couldn't have been more amazed until Gorman lowered his head to rest his temple against Cranther's. His dulled brain tried to sort through what he was seeing and feeling, and Mortas fought to understand. The pain and the soreness was still there, but it had now receded into a muted throb and he decided that the others must have been experiencing the same thing.

It was only much later, walking along in the darkness, that he realized he'd just gained a valuable piece of life wisdom. He spent much of the rest of the march turning the idea over in his mind, repeating it mentally as if polishing a rare gem.

Some of the things that beat the absolute shit out of you—

GLORY MAIN 123

*like that slope back there—can beat the bullshit out of you
too.*

They encountered the dead body in the ravines just as
the sun was coming up. They were getting close to the
next ridge, and Mortas had directed Cranther to pick
a spot for them to hole up through the daylight hours
when they turned a corner and saw the corpse.

He turned out to be human, marginally taller than
Cranther, dressed in an olive drab coverall and boots.
His brown hair was matted with dirt and dried sweat,
and he wore no headgear. Insulting rents had been
blasted through his uniform front and back, but it had
taken him a long time to die; a rust-colored stain ran
all the way down one of his legs and into that boot.

Cranther scrambled forward as soon as the corpse
came into view, rolling it over and grabbing at a small
shoulder bag it had been carrying. The others, mad
with hunger and mindless of the danger, clustered
around him as he upended the sack. Mortas recognized a plastic medical kit when it hit the dirt, and then
his entire being seemed to lurch toward a handful of
energy bars that tumbled out as well.

They counted the wrappers later, and discovered
that there had been eight of the chocolate-covered life-
givers. The food was consumed with such joyous abandon that it was gone in moments. Chocolate, nuts, a
gooey substance that tasted like pure sugar, all stuffed
into their mouths and swallowed in such a rush that

only the aftertaste and the wrapping material proved they'd existed at all. Mortas could feel his stomach coming alive again, saliva and bitter juice rushing out of his throat as he consumed the first bar in less than two bites. The water at the first river had been ecstasy, but the sensation of the nutrients entering his body was simply miraculous.

Collapsed on the dirt, utterly mindless of the dead man, he looked at the faces of the others and wasn't surprised to see that Gorman and Trent were fighting back tears. He only remembered the corpse when Cranther began searching it methodically. He found nothing on the body, and further examination of the bag's contents revealed only the aid kit.

The small box gave off a slight pop when he opened it, and Cranther looked at Gorman with a broad grin. The chartist didn't understand at first, so the scout tipped the container to show stick-on bandaging and a pair of tiny scissors.

"Our lucky day. Lucky lucky lucky us." Cranther muttered. He glanced over at the dead man's feet. "And we might just be able to throw away those for-shit boots you been wearing, too. Look like they'd fit you, and believe me, he doesn't need them anymore."

Mortas was expecting Gorman to object, but Trent spoke before he got the chance. She wore a frown, and was regarding the corpse in confusion. "What's he doing here? Is he even human?"

"A Sim wouldn't be carrying our rations." Cranther gestured toward the body. "From the uniform and the boots, I'd say this was a crewman on one of our assault vehicles. No weapon, no headgear . . . probably had to bail out fast. Only time to grab the bag, and from the look of him, maybe not even time for that."

"What do you think got him?" Mortas began to look around, becoming aware that they'd posted no security at all.

"Could be slugs from a Sim rifle, but from those tears I'd say it was fragments of something else. Maybe spall from the inside of his own vehicle."

"Spall?"

"Yeah, a round hits the outer hull hard enough, it fragments the inner lining and blows it through the personnel compartment. The Sims have gotten real creative with munitions like that."

Mortas was already climbing up the ravine wall when Trent spoke, her voice trembling. "So where's this vehicle? Why is he here? And why's he alone?"

The plain stretched out in front of him when he peeked up over the edge of the gully, and he saw nothing unexpected. The brush was thin here, and he could see a great distance even though the sun had not yet risen. The next ridge loomed in front of them, but the high ground spread away on both sides and he was certain he could see thicker vegetation where the river they'd crossed was located. He heard Cranther's voice behind him.

"Who knows what went on while we were in the transit tubes? No one's supposed to be here, but there's a brand-new Sim colony and at least one of our guys in a tanker suit. Probably explains that ration bag we saw."

"You mean there was an attack?" Trent, growing even more upset.

"Had to be. What else would explain him being here? Bailed out when his vehicle got hit, ran off, probably covered a lot of ground from the looks of that bloodstain."

Movement caught Mortas's eye, and he hissed down to the others. "Hey! Birds!"

Cranther was beside him almost immediately, looking at the brightening horizon. Three or four birds of indeterminate size were slowly circling in the distance, perhaps all the way back at the bridge. Their behavior reminded Mortas of vultures on Earth, and he shuddered at the thought that they were closing in on the remains of the guards they had killed.

"Don't seem to be 'bots," Cranther mused. "Hey El-tee. You think maybe we didn't see any of these things for the first couple of days because there was a battle here? Scared them off?"

"I thought fights attracted birds." Remembering a history lesson about how medieval armies marching toward each other were sometimes accompanied by huge hungry flocks, eager for the coming feast. "You know, scavengers."

"Sure, when they're used to it. But on a new planet the life forms usually run off for a while, just from the settlers. Add in the bang and the boom of an actual battle, something they've never seen before, and they clear out for a long time."

"Makes as much sense as anything else." Mortas looked over his shoulder and saw Trent pulling off one of Gorman's boots, the aid kit open at her feet. He leaned closer to the scout. "That body couldn't have been there for long. And chewed up like he is, he couldn't have walked all that far from wherever he got hit."

"I know. So you're thinking there might be friendlies in the area and we could link up?"

"Aren't you?"

"Sure. That would be great. Except for one thing. We haven't heard any shooting or any explosions the entire time we've been here. Those guards we nailed were colony militia at best, but they didn't act like they were in any danger."

"What are you saying?"

"If there was a fight here, I think we've missed it." Cranther raised his head a little further, straining to see. "And it looks like our side lost."

Mortas stayed on guard when Cranther slipped back down into the ravine to fix Gorman's feet. It was warm up there in the sun, and he could feel strength returning as his body rapidly processed the nutrients he'd just consumed. His stomach still wanted more, but he found it comforting that the rest of him seemed to know it had been fed. He listened to Cranther's gentle criticism of Trent's attempt to bandage Gorman's blisters.

"For a distance runner you don't know much about this." The scout whispered evenly. "See what I'm doing? You cut a piece that will cover the blister and a small area around it, then you cut out the center of that piece so that it leaves the blister exposed to the air. The bandage keeps the boot from rubbing against it, but the air will help it heal faster."

Mortas glanced down in time to see Cranther peel off the backing and stick the first bandage onto Gorman's outstretched foot. The blistering didn't look too bad from that distance, but the pale, wrinkled flesh spoke volumes. The synthetic material of Gorman's shipboard boots had trapped the moisture from his feet, and so he'd developed his own little case of immersion foot in the middle of what amounted to a desert.

Trent had already removed the dead man's boots and socks, and Cranther took them before turning to Gorman. "You're not gonna refuse these, are you?"

"No." The chartist's thinning face showed the relief he'd already gleaned from the small amount of food and the medical attention. "If the roles were reversed, I'd want him to take mine."

"Imagine that—something about the Holy Whisper that I can understand."

"It's not possible to understand all of it, Corporal. That's why they call it faith." Gorman looked at the corpse. "Can we bury him?"

"We'll be holing up nearby for the rest of the day, so I can't see why not."

"I can." Mortas called in a startled grunt. "Get up here."

Cranther hopped up onto the ledge next to him and followed his pointed finger out onto the plain. At the base of the next ridge, in the direction from which they'd come, four massive machines had rumbled into view. Brown or black, belching exhaust from stacks, they moved in a lurching motion side by side. Though it was impossible to gauge the distance, they were clearly enormous and still far away.

"What are they?" the lieutenant asked.

"Sim mobile excavators. See that diagonal bar sticking off the back? It's a conveyor belt. They can shift it in a bunch of different directions, depending on the job. Taking down a hillside, digging a ditch, whatever."

"So what are they doing?" Mortas could now make out the shapes of movers like the one they'd seen at the bridge, tiny against the mechanical mammoths, bumping across the plain. More birds appeared, fluttering up from the brush as the machines approached and flying off in haste.

"They're working in pairs. See?" Cranther pointed again. "Two of 'em just diverged from the others. They're . . ."

"They're filling in the ravines."

The scout's face twisted in thought, his mouth open. "I think you're right. All that weight, rolling along so close on either side, would collapse the walls."

"Why would they be doing that? Gotta be thousands of miles of these things."

"Maybe they're not worried about every mile, just the ones closest to where they live." Cranther's words came faster. "The colony's gotta be on the other side of this ridge . . . and if they're filling in the ravines, it means somebody's been using them to cause trouble."

"They after us? Because of what we did at the bridge?"

"Nah. Even if they figured out that wasn't an accident, it's just two guards. For them to put in this kind of effort means somebody's been scooting down these ravines to hit them and then using them to run away."

"Survivors from that fight."

"Gotta be. And for them to be working this hard on a low-speed avenue of approach means something's happened to their air."

"Maybe it got taken out in the attack."

"Maybe." Cranther looked in the opposite direction and then up at the ridge that held the antenna. "But that colony has to have real troops with it, a battalion at least. All we've seen is that squad of militia."

"The regulars are probably out looking for whoever's been hurting them."

"Could be. But they also might be waiting to see who runs away from these guys here." He looked up at the ridge again. "We need to move."

They found a crack in the base of the canyon wall and forced the dead man's body into it, more to hide it than bury it. Not knowing if the oncoming machines were acting as beaters to drive any remaining humans toward a waiting Sim force, they'd briefly argued the merits of leaving the corpse where it might be found versus concealing it. Cranther felt it would be unwise to give the excavators an indication that enemy troops had even reached this area, and that decision gave Gorman a chance to say a few words.

Standing with his eyes shut, his head tilted skyward, and his palms up, the chartist intoned a prayer Mortas had never heard before.

"Father. Mother. Sister. Brother. Son. Daughter. All are one, from the beginning of time until its end." He opened his eyes and looked at the hasty grave. "Thank you for helping us, dear brother. Find rest."

And then they were moving. The gully walls were still tall enough to completely conceal them, so they moved at a fast trot behind Cranther. The scout stopped every so often, usually at a sharp bend, but he also periodically climbed the wall to scan the ridgeline that was now looming large. The ground was trembling slightly by then, an indication that the earth movers were closing the distance, and Mortas joined Cranther during one of his brief stops on the wall.

"Think somebody might be up there?"

"So far, I don't think so. If there is, they're well camouflaged and very patient." He flashed the lieutenant a brief grin. "I don't think anybody's up there."

Then they were moving again, sloshing water tubes bouncing on shoulders and the Sim weapon growing heavy in Mortas's hands. Soon the ravine began to shrink, the walls growing shorter and shorter until they were all hustling along in a crouch. Low brush provided some cover at ground level, but if anyone was indeed waiting up on the ridge Mortas had to believe that they would have been spotted by then.

The machine noises had steadily grown from a dull rumble to a mechanical roar, and the ground around them was visibly shaking. Runnels of dirt cascaded down the sides of the gully, and they felt the full vibration when Cranther finally threw himself flat and the others followed suit. They were only a few yards from a wide finger of rock which sloped down from the ridgeline, and the scout popped his head up over the nearest bush to determine the excavators' location.

"Okay, there's nothing else we can do here. We gotta move in the open. We'll go straight up this finger, on the side away from the Sims, and hope for the best. Don't stop until we get to the top; even if there's nobody up there, anybody on the other ridges is going to be able to see us as we move.

"We take fire, get back into the ravines. Run as fast as you can, and don't wait for the others. We'll meet up at . . ." He poked his head up again. "See that ridge over there? See that column of rock out just past it? That's our rally point."

Mortas tried to keep the skepticism off his face. If they were spotted by Sim troops going up the slope, there was no way they'd live to reach that distant spire. His mind was racing along with his pulse, but the thoughts flashed by in perfect clarity. The enemy earthmovers were busily crushing the ravine walls, and the only explanation was that human troops were using them as movement channels. The farther the chasms went out into the flat, the more chaotic their patterns became. It was highly unlikely that the Sims had enough troops to ambush all of those canyons if they didn't even have enough to secure the approaches to the settlement. With no air support, even the tightest blocking cordon hidden in the ravines would leak like a sieve.

Something more: If they had enough troops for that human wall, they'd certainly have enough to provide flank security on the high ground as the excavators passed. Even without air support, it would be simple enough to get a patrol up there, and it would serve as an excellent set of eyes.

Air support. Where were their flying machines?

"Corporal!" He almost didn't get the word out in time. Cranther was rising from the ground with the intent of rushing up the ridge, but he dropped back down instantly. Mortas quickly crawled to him on his elbows, both Trent and Gorman doing the same. The excavators were still distant, but their engines were so loud that for the first time in days they were able to speak in normal voices. In fact, they had to shout.

"Listen: They got no air and not enough soldiers to secure the ravines closest to the settlement! They might have enough bodies to put someone up on this ridge, but there's no way they've got enough to cover all that!" He waved a hand at the flat. "That's where we gotta go!"

Cranther's face tensed as he turned it over in his head. He pushed himself up to get a look at the approaching enemy, and then came back down. A hand went up to the skull cap, swirled it around as if rubbing his scalp, and then stopped. Mortas saw the flesh whiten over the man's knuckles, and noticed for the first time just how dirty and scuffed Cranther's hands had become. He absently looked down and was shocked to see the same level of grime and the same number of tiny cuts and bruises on his own.

"Okay, Lieutenant!" Cranther turned to the others. His words vibrated with the ground, and he had to shout to be heard. "Stay right on my ass! We're gonna follow this gully away from here! They'll see us if we climb out, so we stay in this ravine unless it turns us all the way around! Remember the rally point if we get separated, and don't stop for anything!"

He began crawling back down the ravine, and Mortas waited until the others were gone before popping his head up once more. The excavators were still several hundred yards away, but their enormous size made them seem closer. The much smaller movers were sticking close to them, and he could make out individual Sim soldiers on foot. Many of them were carrying Maulers, but he did see some of the longer, skeletal rifles more commonly found with Sim infantry. Militia or regulars, they didn't seem eager to fan out.

They've taken a beating. They might have won the fight, but it cost them. They've learned to be careful.

More convinced than ever that his choice of the flat would now lead to their salvation, he began worming his way across the dirt after the others. This time, when the sand started working its way between his shirt and his belly, he didn't mind at all.

They covered the ground quickly once the ravine got deep enough for them to stand, but even so it wasn't a pell-mell run. At first Cranther took the lead while the others hung back a distance, but once the ground stopped shaking Mortas called a halt. A covert glimpse over the rim gave them a good reason to slow down, as the enemy machines had actually turned and gone in the opposite direction.

"Filled in one set of gullies. Now they're going back to start a new set." Mortas was impressed by how easily he'd slipped back into whisper mode after all the shouting they'd just done, but Cranther merely nodded at him in answer. "I'll take over on point. Just in case they are out here waiting, make sure the others don't close up on me."

The movement was fast, and the sun was only slightly past the midpoint when they approached a broad hump of dirt. Panting with exertion, Mortas stopped the movement so that they could rest a bit and take advantage of the comparatively high ground.

Cranther passed him without being told to check it out. He wore an expression that Mortas normally would have associated with a bad smell, and so the lieutenant wasn't terribly surprised when the short man crawled up onto the hump and sniffed the air. The three of them joined him, hunkered down on their stomachs amid the bushes, waiting for an explanation. The vista was what they'd expected: More brush and rolling plain with the next ridge rising ahead of them and the excavators receding behind them.

"What is it?" Mortas kept his eyes moving as he spoke.

"It's faint, but it's there." Cranther tilted his head backward and sniffed again, dog-like. "Cofferdams. Had to be a lot of them, for that smell to still be here. A battalion at least."

The term took Mortas back to the end of his predeployment training. The final war game had been a full-on dress rehearsal, launched from transports orbiting a conquered Hab planet. Each transport had created a transit tunnel hundreds of yards in diameter by generating energy beams that formed a cylinder running from the ship's hull through the planet's atmosphere all the way down to the surface. The tube was nearly invisible and reduced the effects of atmospheric friction, but it did have its drawbacks. The planet's gravity was lessened but not negated, and the pressure inside the cofferdam was extremely high to keep it from being crushed by the forces it was holding at bay.

Mortas had ridden in the back of a pressurized personnel carrier that had been dropped right into the cofferdam through one of many hatches in the belly of the ship. They'd glided down the miles to the surface, stabilized and decelerated by thrusters attached to the carrier for the journey, but still landing with a surprising amount of force. The cofferdam's walls had equalized with the planet's pressure at ground level by then, and they'd simply driven out of it. The initial assault element was always composed of armored carriers like that one, and so he'd been able to watch from a nearby hill as the second wave, composed of individual foot soldiers, was delivered.

Those personnel coasted down the cofferdam in giant wheel-shaped carriers whose outermost rings hugged the transparent walls of the transit tube. It had been astounding to see these giant metallic snowflakes expand from mere dots in the sky to enormous rings of connected personnel compartments. Powerful deceleration rockets had fired when they approached the ground, kicking up a cloud of dust that had erupted from inside the cofferdam, but most of the snowflakes were so badly damaged on impact that Mortas had suspected they'd never be repaired. Hundreds of unsteady foot soldiers had emerged from the damaged rings and the war game had continued from there. Even with that experience, Mortas was still confused by Cranther's comment about the odor.

"I didn't know they had a smell."

"The beam is always a little off when they hit a new planet. As they adjust—" He stopped suddenly, focusing on something in the distance. Cranther raised himself up on his elbows, shading his eyes with both hands as if holding a set of binoculars. "Oh no."

"What is it?"

The scout lowered himself back to the dirt, his eyes on the ground. Without a word, he put an elbow on Mortas's shoulder and pointed with his fingers in a knife edge.

Trent and Gorman saw it before he did, and Mortas heard them both uttering subdued words of alarm. He squinted in the sun, expecting to see the fractured snowflakes of an assault landing that had come to grief, but what they were viewing was farther out. Several hundred yards away, presumably in the direction of the enemy settlement, he could just make out the gun barrel of a heavy fighting vehicle. It was raised as if to fire at the sky, and a moment later he saw that the tank itself was stuck in the ground as if it had plummeted from a great height.

Once he recognized the wreckage, the rest came into focus. He knew he was probably looking at the near edge of an entire debris field, but even so the tank was surrounded by personnel carriers and scout cars that were likewise jammed into the dirt. It reminded Mortas of the queasy sensation he'd felt when the carrier he'd ridden in the war game had been released into the maw of the cofferdam. It had been a helpless, lurching fall that had gone on for several seconds before the quasi-gravity of the energy tube had slowed it down, and he'd feared the worst even though he'd been warned.

Had the cofferdams simply failed here? Had the occupants of the half-buried wrecks made the awful drop unaided, tumbling, screaming, accelerating? He shuddered at the very notion, and when he looked at the others he saw they were imagining the same thing. Gorman's lips were moving in silent prayer, Trent's eyes were fixed on something he couldn't see, and Cranther's face was still twisted in thought. The scout spoke first.

"Wait. Look there." He pointed again, this time at a spot only a hundred yards away but not in the direction of the debris field. Following the hand, Mortas was taken aback that he hadn't seen it earlier. An enormous circle of brush was flattened or missing, and the dirt inside it was furrowed as if recently plowed. A quick survey showed other sites like that one, on a rough line between the two ridges.

"That's where the cofferdams touched down."

"Right. So whatever happened to them, they landed safely and headed in to attack the settlement."

"Could it have moved? The cofferdam, I mean." Gorman's voice was strained, but his point was a good one. Perhaps the vehicles had been dropped when their transport tube had shifted.

"It's happened before, so maybe." Cranther came to his knees and shaded his eyes again. "But I don't think that's it. If that tank dropped all the way, that turret should have popped right off. And those recon cars would have flattened, hitting from that height."

"What are you saying?"

"That they didn't slam into the ground." The look of consternation was back. "I don't know how, but I think they sank."

The energy bars they'd consumed now proved to be a double-edged sword. Packed with the nutrients they so badly needed, the food gave them the strength to quickly move across the shorter expanse of flat ground and reach the next ridgeline. Mortas was amazed by the speed with which they traveled until he was able to consider that perhaps they'd been providing their own locomotion for so long, and without any nourishment at all, that of course it now seemed easier. But even as the food had given them what their bodies needed, it also served as a reminder that they hadn't filled their bellies in days. The renewed growling of their insides and the sight of the ruined fighting vehicles now combined to drive them toward a very risky decision.

The sun was setting when they scrambled up the side of the escarpment, largely concealed by a species of tall, dry grass that covered it. A hurried group consultation had given voice to what they'd all been thinking, and so they'd agreed to take a serious chance and try to raid the broken war machines for real food.

It made sense, in a way. Before the sun set they'd drawn close enough to see that most of the vehicles hadn't been hit by enemy fire. There'd been no need; whatever had caused them to sink into the now-hardened surface had stopped the assault completely.

The occupants of the tanks, scout cars, and personnel carriers had been transformed from armored aggressors to sitting ducks, and so they'd probably bailed out at the first opportunity. The dead man they'd found in the ravine, wearing the tanker suit and carrying no weapon, gave ample support to that theory. So if the crews and riders had run off in a frenzy, it was highly likely that they'd left food behind.

It was just as likely that the enemy knew this and might even have the area under surveillance, but intense hunger had helped the group to minimize that threat in their minds. The Sims had obviously sustained major damage in the attack; they had no air assets and could be expected to withdraw into a tight defensive perimeter once night came. The belching excavators seemed to verify this theory, as they hadn't ventured beyond the ridge where they'd originally been seen and now even their roaring had gone silent.

Cranther had gone so far as to suggest that the killing of the hapless guards at the bridge might have helped by spooking their opponents even further. The battle had taken place far from that crossing point, and the two militia men had probably been posted as a precautionary measure only. The bulk of the fleeing humans from the trapped assault force had most likely gone in the opposite direction, toward the series of ridges from which the group now observed the debris field. For the surviving humans to have even found the bridge, they would have had to cross an enormous amount of open ground, and for no reason. It was clear that they were harassing the Sim settlement, and the enemy's efforts to fill in the approaches suggested they were more concerned with those nightly attacks than with watching an enemy junkyard.

Having decided to take the risk of approaching the wrecks, they resolved not to easily accept any others. They moved along the ridgeline, just down from the crest on the side away from the battlefield, until they were close enough to get their final bearings. Darkness was coming fast, but the elevated position gave them a good view of the disaster. It was even worse when seen from above.

Two long, almost parallel ridges formed the boundaries of a long stretch of flat ground, a kind of a lane over which the assault had charged after it had separated from the cofferdams. Although no lights were in evidence at the end of that lane, not even a glow, the Sim settlement was presumably just beyond the open ground. Over a hundred tanks, scout cars, personnel carriers, and support vehicles were ranged over the expanse for a great distance, most of them half submerged.

"Look at that." Gorman pointed toward the center of the lane. "The ones in the middle are almost buried. Whatever caused this, it was more potent in the center."

"It's got to be something completely new. I've never heard of anything like this." Trent mused.

Mortas didn't reply. "How should we do this, Corporal?"

"Pairs. Gorman with me, the captain with you.

Only one goes inside a vehicle, and the other keeps watch. Two hard raps on the hull means come out fast, one means stay put. You're looking for bags of any kind, first to see if there's any food in it and second for carrying it away. Rucksacks are best; you want to be able to carry whatever you've found on your back. And don't stop to eat anything until you're back here. After the bags, you look for lockers; inside a tank they're in the rear and inside a personnel carrier they're toward the front."

"Done this before, Corporal?" Gorman sounded downright giddy, but Mortas understood. The prospect of real food was positively thrilling and he couldn't wait to get moving.

"I've stolen food from just about everything at one time or another. And the troops who get to ride everywhere usually stock up on the good stuff." He licked his lips. "See that tank there, the one with the gun pointed straight up? That's your bearing to get back here. Remember a walking Sim looks like a walking human, so don't say hello to just anybody you meet out there."

He stopped talking, and after a moment or two Mortas knew he was finished. It was dark enough now, and he honestly didn't think he could wait any longer. "Let's go."

The Mauler bumped against his back as he shuffled across the uneven terrain, and Mortas wondered if he should have left it behind. The stars weren't out yet, but his eyes had adjusted to the darkness enough that he was able to avoid most of the rocks sticking out of the wave-like earth. The dirt didn't feel like anything he'd stepped on during their sojourn on the planet, and its solidity reminded him of concrete. Crouched over as he was, he was able to reach a hand down without breaking stride and wasn't surprised that the surface felt like roughened stone.

Cranther and Gorman had veered to the left of the tank that was their reference point, and so he followed Trent to the right. For her part she moved as if it were broad daylight, almost jogging along toward a half-exposed troop carrier that Mortas had pointed out. She'd never ridden inside an assault vehicle, and he had, so they'd quickly decided that Mortas would be doing the searching. But that worked; he remembered the lockers Cranther had mentioned and also that the troops who'd given him the training ride in their carrier kept some wonderful treats in them.

He glanced at the shadowy mass of the tank as they passed and was reminded of an old, cracked tree on the grounds of one of his earliest prep schools. Wide at its base but topped well short of its normal height, at night it had looked like a blood-crazed ghoul waving its arms. The tank's gun tube resembled a large splinter that had jutted out of that tree, and he remembered being told frightening stories by the older students about what happened to newbies who left the dormitories at night and ventured too close to it.

And now I've found a place where those stories are true.

They scampered past the tank and headed for the carrier. Its nose was stuck in the solidified earth so that its open rear ramp didn't touch the ground, and the childhood spook stories made him think of it as the open mouth of a sleeping giant. He didn't get much time to develop that image, as Trent abruptly came to a silent halt and he almost skidded into her. His free hand landed on her shoulder, and she took that as some kind of interrogatory gesture. Raising a hand, she pointed at something right at her feet.

Mortas stepped around her, unslinging the Mauler just in case. He knew its bark would alert anyone within a mile, but it was a weapon and he'd be damned if he'd carry the thing this far and not have it ready. He needn't have bothered.

At first he thought the rectangular block in front of them was just another rock, but then he made out the arms and the combat armor that covered the dead man's shoulders. Only the very top of his chest was visible, and his head was missing. Mortas tried to think of the numerous ways in which this could have happened, but he kept coming back to a conclusion that was as likely as it was hideous. The soldier had become trapped in the same way as the vehicles, and the odds were good that the enemy had decapitated him in his helpless state.

The horrifying chain of events appeared in his mind and there was no stopping it. The machines roaring like beasts, slewing and sinking and spewing mud or whatever the ground had become. The dead man leaping from the top, feeling his body jamming straight down into the goo. Too far, too deep. Trapped. Struggling, hollering for help, drowned out by the sound of the gunfire, the explosions, the straining engines, and the cries of the others.

The others. Had his buddies left him? Or just not seen him? Had he watched them flee, knowing he was being left behind? How long had he been there, alone? And when the Sims found him, had he been frightened or relieved?

Mortas could have gone on with that for much longer, but he sensed eyes on his face and looked up to see Trent studying him, gauging his reaction.

Fuckin' headshrinker. Still doesn't understand this isn't some sterile shipboard sick bay.

He pointed a knife-edged hand at the tilted carrier just ahead, angrily directing her to get moving.

The canted hulk loomed up in front of them as they covered the final distance, and they took cover next to its mud-clotted treads. The front of the vehicle was buried, and so Mortas peered across under its armored belly and into the gloom on the other side. There was no wind and no sound, and he waited for a long while in order to make sure they hadn't been spotted. Trent turned to face in the other direction and crouched down, placing her buttocks against his own.

At least she understands three-sixty security.

When he saw no reason to wait further, he reached back and tapped her thigh. She looked at him, mouth closed, and he pointed at his chest and then at the back ramp to indicate he was going in. She nodded and turned so that her back was against the heavy wheels that had so recently moved the treads that should have propelled the behemoth. He slung the Mauler behind him before reaching up for the carrier's thick back wall, the ramp that had swung down to allow the troops to exit during the disaster. Pulling himself up over hardened clumps of dirt, he wondered how many of them had escaped.

Hatches in the roof of the carrier were also open, so a modest amount of light shone in as he slid down the plates of the sloping floor. A mounting post for a heavy weapon arrested his movement halfway, and folding troop seats on either side of him provided handholds as he moved toward the lockers at the front of the carrier. His boots made contact with something soft and for a moment he feared it was another body, but when it gave beneath his weight he recognized it as some kind of bag. When he moved his foot it landed on a discarded helmet, and he realized that the flotsam and jetsam left in the vehicle had slid to the front when it finally came to rest.

Bending his knees, he found the snaps holding the bag closed and gently began unfastening just enough of them to reach inside. As he'd expected, it was a tool kit of a kind that he'd seen on his training ride months before. He hefted a large hammer and then lost control of it when he went to move the bag off to the side. The mallet twisted in his hands and fell to the deck with a dull metallic thud that nonetheless seemed to ring for hours.

He froze for several moments, wondering if Trent had heard the noise. When her face didn't appear in the much-lighter maw of the rear opening, he decided the hammer hadn't made that big a sound after all. Right after that he began to ridicule Cranther's system of warning slaps on the outer hull—if Trent hadn't heard the hammer dropping on metal, how was he supposed to hear her bare palm pounding on armor?

Not for the first time, he pondered the notion that Cranther's knowledge of small unit tactics might be a bit deficient because the Spartacan almost always worked alone. He had no established procedure for warning fellow soldiers because he so seldom had any of them around him. Despite his extensive combat experience and survival skills, in the end he was hardly the voice that a brand-new lieutenant would seek for guidance on managing a platoon, a squad, or even three strangers.

But I bet he scrounges like nobody's business.

The thought spurred him back into action, and he shifted a large water container out of the way as quietly as possible. He was reaching for the recessed handle of the first locker when a question crossed his mind.

Where are the weapons? Why haven't I found any of those?

Mortas pressed a palm against the metal door before releasing the catch, and was rewarded with only a tiny ping when it opened. The interior of the locker was invisible in the darkness, but he recognized the feel of a ration box when he touched it and almost cried out in joy. There were twelve condensed meals in that box, and he had only to—

Where are the weapons?

It wasn't possible that every soldier riding in that carrier had carried his rifle or machine gun out with him. Mortas had already found discarded pieces of field gear, and when he reached around near his feet again he found a complete combat harness loaded with canteens and ammunition pouches.

Empty ammunition pouches.

He looked around him, his eyes now fully accustomed to the gloom, and noted that the onboard rifle racks were empty. The crewmember they'd found dead in the ravines had been unarmed, and if they'd bailed out as fast as he expected, it was reasonable to assume that at least some of their weapons would have been left behind.

They took them. The Sims took them. And the ammunition. What if they left booby traps in their place?

He reached back for the ration box, but this time in fear. He slowly worked his fingers around the carton's outline, expecting at any moment to come across the wire or the spring or whatever other device would indicate the food was a trap. He was only partially relieved when he finished the blind inspection, too aware of the enemy's fondness for rigging human equipment, and even human corpses, so that they would detonate if moved. A pressure switch either behind or below the box would be beyond his reach, and the only way to find out if it was there was to actually lift the carton from the shadows.

He might have stayed there in that position for a very long time had he not heard an insistent hiss behind him. Looking up and back, he saw Trent's head just visible over the rear ramp. Her arms came up in a gesture that was part concern and part exasperation, but it was enough. Without pausing to think, he seized the carton on both sides and pulled it out of the locker. He was still holding his breath when he slid it up the incline to Trent's waiting hands.

Mortas dropped to the ground several minutes later, holding a rucksack that he'd emptied. A more thorough search of the carrier had revealed no weapons of any kind and no food other than the rations he'd already found. Trent stepped out from the hulk's shadow, and Mortas traded her a human combat harness for the ration box. At least they wouldn't have to haul the makeshift tube-canteens anymore, now that they had real ones. He went to stuff the carton into the ruck's open top, and was mildly impressed to note that its tension bands were still intact. Trent hadn't helped herself to any of the food while she'd been waiting outside, which surprised him. It wasn't a criticism; while still inside he'd secretly hoped to come across something small that he could eat quickly and had to believe Trent was just as hungry.

Although several other vehicles with open hatches were nearby, he was already inclined to leave the area with what they had when the shooting started. It was far away, somewhere on the opposite side of the next ridge and close to where they believed the enemy settlement was located, but both he and Trent hit the ground in alarm. Despite the distance, it sounded like an entire shop full of unmuffled machinery had come to life with a startling roar of harsh pops and rippling snaps.

Crawling around the wreck to get a better look, Mortas watched in amazement as flares flickered into life in the night sky at least a mile away. He'd been trained to use signals like that, but these were different in color and it took him a moment to realize they were fired by the Sims. The roaring slowed for a few seconds before resuming at a lower volume, and now he heard the deeper, sharper sounds of explosives going off.

Grenades. Whoever was out there was in close quarters.

A tug on the rucksack brought his attention back to Trent, who was gesturing for them to leave the area. A glance down at the bag reminded him of its precious contents and how much he desired it, and he gave a weak nod before Trent pulled the bag from his hand and worked it up onto her shoulders.

More flares popped in the sky as the first ones fizzled out, and the firing resumed. Clearly the Sims had gained the upper hand in that contest, and were now pressing their advantage. Coming to his feet to follow the already moving Trent, Mortas experienced a thought that he would never have imagined possible even a few days earlier.

Nothing we could do for them, even if we were there.

Time to eat.

CHAPTER 7

Cranther and Gorman were already back at the rally point when they got there. The scout had scrounged a rucksack similar to the one Trent now wore, and it looked full. Without a word they formed up in a column, Cranther in the lead, and humped up the ridge while still more flares raced up into the blackness and briefly joined the stars. The far-off shooting had died down by then, and Mortas had to assume that the enemy was now pursuing whoever was left.

The climb away from the wreckage was steep and tiring, but they all knew they'd get to eat only after putting sufficient ground between them and the place where they'd gotten the food, and so they set to it with a will. Bringing up the rear, Mortas couldn't help but be impressed at the way Trent handled the climb. Granted the rations weren't all that heavy, but she carried the rucksack as if it contained nothing at all while Gorman, bearing the other one, kept overbalancing and reaching out for the ground. The flares provided intermittent illumination that improved as they neared the summit, allowing Mortas to gauge the weariness of the others. Tired and hungry as he was, he noted with secret pride that even Cranther's steps weaved from time to time in a way that his own did not. Trent was the only one who seemed more at home, and Mortas promised to add her treadmill regimen to his workouts when they finally returned to humanity.

If they returned to humanity.

His mind fought against the thought of eventual salvation, not because it was unlikely but because it was so far away. His entire existence had been reduced to the solving of simple problems such as how to move about without getting spotted and how to find water without getting killed, and now it was even more focused on finding a safe place to eat. This reminded Mortas of a veteran from his training who had warned the assembled lieutenants not to get sloppy at resupply time. Units receiving their expected rations on a normal schedule sometimes let security slip in anticipation, and the veteran had said this was doubly so with units that had missed their resupply and gone hungry.

So he knew what Cranther was looking for as they climbed: a spot near the top of the ridge from which they could observe anyone trying to sneak up on them, a hole that would hide them, and a location that would require effort for the enemy to reach them. That meant climbing high, but not so high that they'd be on a natural movement corridor for an enemy who was presumably as tired of walking as they were.

The tall grass slowly gave way to the lower, sparser brush that they'd come to know, and Mortas assumed this meant they were nearing the top. A single flare popped alight just as he looked up, and a thrill went through him when he saw they were almost at the summit. The flare washed along the ridge on the opposite side but didn't expose them, and they were so high up by then that it quickly dropped below them.

They should have stopped moving and flattened on the ground in such close proximity to a light source, but it was a sign of their exhaustion that even Cranther stayed upright. He took the opportunity to search the immediate area with his eyes, and found what he was looking for before the flare flickered and died. They were left in darkness, but Cranther began moving again and Mortas followed the others along the knife edge of the summit until they found the depression Cranther had seen. Though near the top, the ridge here was so steep that it wouldn't have allowed anyone to actually walk on it. Mortas nodded in agreement with the selection as he slid down the shallow hole's crumbling sides and joined the others at its bottom.

Both rucksacks were soon emptied, and if Mortas had ever received better gifts he certainly couldn't remember the occasion. The ration box proved to be two-thirds full, but that still meant two meals apiece. Back home such food would have been considered unfit for the family dog, and on training maneuvers two rations would have been one meal short of a daily allotment, but there in that forgotten hole it was quite simply a banquet.

Cranther had found more of the energy bars, another medical kit, and three canteens filled with the flavored water-and-additives mix that Mortas had come to love while in the field. Most of the infantrymen he knew carried the powder in packet form and added it to the water in their canteens even though Command had warned its high levels of caffeine were addictive. He snorted at the notion of fearing such a long-term danger as he took a long, grateful swallow.

They each took a ration pouch at random, unable to see its markings, and set the remaining four on the side of the dirt wall so that the next flare might reveal its contents. It was then that any pretense of control vanished, as all four of them greedily tore into the rubberized bags and began devouring the contents. Mortas would be hard pressed later on to identify the meal he'd been given, knowing only that it was covered in gravy, that it was deliciously greasy, and that it contained some kind of chunked meat. It was gone in moments, no matter how hard he tried to slow down, and he ripped the small bag apart so that he could lick its insides clean. When he was done with that he rubbed his hands hard against the stubble around his mouth and then licked them clean too.

He looked at the others then, and was intrigued to see that they'd also devoured their food but that he hadn't heard them doing it. Reflecting on this, Mortas realized that he'd suppressed more than one moan of pleasure as the nutrients had gone down his throat. The others must have done the same, and he considered it a testament to how long they'd been in a survival situation and how much they'd come to imitate Cranther.

For his part, the short man was half reclined against the hole's sloping wall across from Mortas. His knees were drawn up slightly, and the wrappings from his meal were resting on his thighs. Mortas watched as the scout began stuffing the trash back into the original pouch, and he began to do the same. The revelry of the hurried meal vanished with the memory of an enemy who was hunting humans nearby, close enough for their flares to help the tiny band find their way. It would not do to leave evidence that they had been there, and the picked-clean wrappers from one of their rations would be a dead giveaway.

"I want another." Gorman's voice was quiet and passive. He was seated across from the line of four meals awaiting the next flare, but the hostilities seemed to have ended for the night. "I don't care which one it is. I don't want to wait for a flare, or anything involving this war. I just want to eat my next meal."

"You eat it now, you can't eat it tomorrow." Mortas kept his voice level, more the tone of a parent giving advice to a child, but even he didn't find value in the words.

"Probably a good idea to wait just a bit." Trent offered. "Let our bodies adjust to what we just had. We haven't eaten in days, except for those energy bars . . . and didn't you say our stomachs would shrink, Corporal?"

"Yeah I did, but that was a lie. I just wanted to give you something to help handle the hunger pangs."

There was a long silence, but it finally ended when Gorman began to giggle. As hard as he tried not to laugh, Mortas soon joined in and ended up clamping a hand over his mouth to muffle the sound. Next to him, Trent was actually shaking with mirth and barely got the words out. "You son of a bitch."

"I know, I know." Cranther raised his hands palm upward. "But it worked, didn't it?"

They kept up the stifled laughter for some time, and Cranther took the opportunity to crawl to the top of the ridge and look over at the inky vastness below. When he came back he settled against the wall and pronounced that portion of the night's activities to be over.

"Any idea what happened to those vehicles?" Mortas asked, still mightily puzzled.

"I've seen some weird things in this war, and both sides are always developing new stuff, but that one's a cut above. No idea how they did it, but they turned dry dirt into mud so deep it bogged down treaded vehicles and swallowed men alive. And then it went back the way it was."

Mortas searched his brain for the term the instructors had used. "Temporary area denial."

"That's the name of the game out here." Trent broke in. "No point in fighting over a Hab planet if you make it an Unhab in the process."

His father's secret briefings came back to Mortas with that observation. One of the techs had used almost those exact words describing the seemingly contradictory nature of the war. Although it was a fight for survival of an entire species, it was very much a limited conflict. Both sides possessed weapons that could blow a planet's atmosphere right off or radiate the place so badly that no one could live there, but the goal of gaining a habitable planet took those weapons off the table. Instead it set the engineers from both sides working on devices that delivered their terrible effect but didn't permanently alter the ground where they were used.

The tech had become visibly disturbed when he reached the logical conclusion that the limited war calculus would no doubt be dropped the day either side found the enemy's home planets.

Cranther murmured, "Very practical boys, the Sims. It figures they'd come up with a way to turn the dirt against us."

"I heard a rumor that they found a way to defeat the Step," Gorman suggested. "Either it makes the Threshold collapse as the ship enters it, or they've got a rocket fired on the other side so it makes contact as the ship exits."

Mortas shifted uneasily. Ships had been lost in the Step since its creation, but another of his secret classes had mentioned a concern that the enemy had learned enough about the technology to turn it against the humans. There had been only a slight increase in unexplained ship losses, but Command was still greatly concerned that the enemy had indeed countered mankind's greatest advantage. It would be typical of the Sims to distill a technological achievement down to a simple question of inertia and have something waiting for the irreversible arrival of the ship making the transgression.

"I heard that one too," Trent whispered. "A pilot I know said the enemy had captured enough of our ships to figure out how it all works. Said they can't reproduce it yet, but they don't need to if they just want to stop it."

"Well, Command's gonna have their hands full countering this new thing right here," Cranther said. "Forget what the Sims might come up with later."

"Think anyone reported it? I mean, anyone got off a message or maybe even got back to the ships before they bugged out?" Trent's eyes were on Cranther.

"That's almost certain. There were no personnel rings where the cofferdams came down, so they canceled the second wave almost as soon as the first one hit the ground. First the bombers and the rockets come in, then the armor, then the individual infantry right behind them. The troops in those vehicles got written off really fast, so either somebody was watching or they sent a message." The scout made a quiet sound in his throat and then spit outside the hole. "Sometimes you're better off not letting Command know what's happening."

"You don't really believe that, right?" Mortas asked in a voice that was slowly drifting toward sleep.

"Oh you bet I do. And the troops left stranded down here believe it too. At least they do now." The short man leaned forward, his hands on his knees. "Did you know that at the beginning of the war Command used to drop huge numbers of Spartacans on Hab planets in Sim space just to get the enemy to attack? The Sims had to figure we were going to follow up those scouts with troops and colonists, so they'd send a force to wipe out the recon parties. Took 'em a while to figure out what Command was doing, buying time with Spartacan lives and getting them to waste a lot of assets on planets we couldn't hope to actually keep."

"At the start of the war? That was forty years ago. Sounds like a story to me."

"Maybe. Maybe." Cranther's voice had taken on a cautious, almost tentative tone. "But here's one that actually happened, might change your opinion of how much Command values your ass.

"I'd been operational for a year or so, finally figuring things out, when they dropped me and two others on this one planet. Had Spartacans running all over the place checking it out. We always knew when a planet was hot because it was the only time they'd send us down in groups. And that one was a special kind of hot.

"You see, there weren't any colonies there and it wasn't a standard enemy base. It was like the Sims were trying out something different. They'd hidden an entire corps on that rock, dug 'em right into the ground and inside the mountains as if it wasn't a Hab planet at all. Their camouflage was almost perfect, and man did they have discipline. They must have spotted my team and all the others, but they just sat tight and waited for the real party to arrive.

"We'd crossed this one big hill a week before the

troops came down, and of course nobody thought the enemy was there then. But some of the other scout teams started finding the signs of digging, and then the entrances to a few of the emplacements, and of course then they got taken under fire so the game was on. Our people came down in regiments and there was a lot of confusion about where the Sims were because they kept moving around underground.

"So this one platoon got told to occupy that hill I mentioned, the one I crossed with my team before we knew any enemy was on the planet. Some idiot in orbit, turned out to be a Golden Boy captain with a dad who was a general, told them to go up and dig in on this unsecured hill. When they asked if it had been scouted he said, 'Sure, the Spartacans were all over the thing,' and so they went up.

"They ended up getting torn to pieces. I was told they weren't even in tactical formation, just went for a little hike because some yo-yo who wasn't even on the planet told them everything was cool."

He stopped, and didn't seem like he was going to continue, so Gorman quietly asked the question the others were thinking. "How'd you find out about it?"

"What's that?" Cranther's voice was far away.

"I mean, how do you know the specifics if you walked over the hill a week before all that happened?"

"Oh, they tried to court-martial me for getting those guys killed. I was in the brig for an entire month. That was a bad scene; the two other guys who'd been with me had both gotten killed, so I was a sitting duck for this general and his Golden Child. You see, Command normally doesn't care about what happens to one platoon, except this one had somebody else's Golden Child in it and whoever that was, he wanted his pound of flesh."

"How'd you get off the hook?"

"Pure luck. That captain had told the dead platoon leader that he'd personally sent a recon drone over the hill just that morning and that there wasn't anything there. Lucky for me, there was a recording of that message. He was required to send that drone because my team's intel was so outdated, but he just decided not to for some reason. Wanted to get to the galley while they were still serving chow, maybe. Or maybe he was just tired. Anyway, that tape ended the whole thing. When they let me out of the brig, one of the lawyers said that captain had been executed.

"Not real sure about that, though. The Golden Children have a habit of surviving. But what happened to somebody else really isn't important; you couldn't beat the hot chow in that brig, and while I was cooling my heels there I wasn't getting shot at."

"But you could have been executed."

"Not much I could do about that, was there? And it's a lot cleaner when Command kills you on purpose . . . than when they do it by accident."

"I guess we should have waited, huh?" Gorman's voice came out of the gloom, disembodied and dull.

"What do you mean?" Mortas answered as if in a dream. His consciousness was drifting away now that they'd consumed the second ration, refusing to concentrate on even the elementary need to post a guard. The darkness was so total that it hardly seemed necessary, and even Cranther was in no hurry to broach the topic. They'd been going nonstop since the end of the day the day before, and even though their current position wasn't perfect—too easily trapped up there—it seemed impossible to think of moving.

Gorman explained his comment. "Didn't you hear that? That hissing sound? I think they're putting up more flares."

Cranther moved with great suddenness, his boots kicking Mortas's as he got his feet under him. The scout came to his full height, facing in the direction of the settlement.

Mortas stood too, a grinding sense of alarm slowly working through his lethargy. Cranther's hand gripped his arm to silence him, and that was when he heard the remotest whooshing sound, like someone brooming off a rough surface. Cranther's hand started squeezing the fabric of his sleeve, and he forced his eyes as wide as they would go in the pointless hope that it would help him see in the dark.

"No, no, no—" The scout was fairly wringing his sleeve now, and then suddenly the intense pressure relented. The voice was choked and staccato. "Back in the hole. Get back in the hole. Everybody down."

Mortas obeyed instantly, throwing himself forward and banging his chin against the dirt. He'd landed on top of Gorman's torso and Trent's legs, and they all began squirming around to make room and get lower. The hissing sound grew louder, far up in the night sky, like the malevolent warning of some giant winged predator. Mortas looked up just in time to see a faint trail of light and fire passing over the valley, sparks trailing behind whatever Cranther feared so much.

Then it burst over them. Lightning and thunder at the same time. A convulsive wind-slap on their backs blowing away the gloom like the birth of a new sun. A multitude of guttural growls, followed by a rain of spherical projectiles streaking toward the ground below, through the volcanic light. Mortas cringed in the seconds it took for the bomblets to reach the wrecked vehicles, and then the fading glow from the delivery rockets abruptly erupted into flashing fire as their deadly produce detonated.

In the instant of those explosions, Mortas was almost sure that the spheres hadn't struck the ground. Only a few yards off the deck they flashed a blinding light, which was quickly followed by a sharp cracking boom that was in turn answered by dozens of sparks and popping sounds that joined together into a rolling roar. It reminded him of strings of firecrackers he'd set off in his not-distant youth, but these were different: They were followed up by purple sparks and the pinging noise of metallic ricochets, and he recognized the weapon as a deadly Sim rocket that passed over its target area dropping dozens of anti-personnel bomblets.

He was just beginning to wonder why they hadn't heard this kind of device fired before now when a series of deeper explosions sounded from the enemy colony. His eyes were still half blinded by the light show below, but he looked up anyway, trying to see the new threat coming their way. The explosions continued, and Cranther pushed off of him to come to a kneeling position in the hole. The three others joined him slowly, uncertain, when the first artillery round landed far down the ridgeline. It struck the escarpment near the valley floor, closer to the settlement, but it was soon followed by another and another, working randomly up and down the far end of the slope.

"Let's go, let's go, let's go!" Cranther shouted above the din as the impacting rounds began to move toward them. In the momentary flash of light of each detonation Mortas saw huge plumes of dirt thrown up in the air, and imagined the particles being ripped by hundreds of chunks of jagged metal.

An insistent hand grabbed his sleeve, and then they were up and running, straight over the knife edge and down the other side, momentarily thrown back into darkness. The dirt slid under his boots as Mortas fought to stay on his feet, one hand gripping the Mauler while the other clasped hands with someone he couldn't identify. They both skidded on the loose scree, and then another set of hands was on his blouse from behind. It was impossible to take a step, but it was also unnecessary, as they were sliding down the opposite slope as if on skis.

They might have covered quite a bit of ground that way had the enemy artillery not begun to overshoot.

The explosions from the other side of the ridge now reached across for them, much closer now, and in one crack of lightning Mortas saw that all four of them had come back together, holding on to one another in an effort to stay upright. Another flash and he saw that they were already halfway down the incline, but then he saw something that almost sent him scrambling back up the slope.

The explosions reflected off a ribbon of dark fluid at the base of the ridge. Water. A stream. Serpents.

He'd just opened his mouth to shout a warning when a single round landed at the top of the ridge behind them, knocking them all over as if a giant hand had just swatted the little group. Grips lost, thrown down, rolling faster and faster, slamming into rock outcroppings and gnarled bushes, they quickly separated and crashed toward the bottom completely out of control.

Mortas hugged the Mauler to his chest, terrified that it would knock out his teeth if he tried to discard it, his eyes squeezed shut even as his mouth opened in a primal cry of terror at the very thought that they would end up in the river. His face scraped over something thorny in the darkness, he was rolling so fast that he couldn't keep his legs together, and the explosions walked closer and closer even as he started screaming, "Stop!" over and over again until he took a mouthful of sand and turned to choking instead.

His descent ended abruptly when he crashed, chest-first, into a boulder right at the water's edge. A hard protrusion on the Sim weapon smashed into his ribs, and the sudden stop knocked the wind out of him. His face was buried in a stand of grass, and he lay there simultaneously spitting out dirt and sucking for air until another body hurtled down the slope and slammed into him.

He heard a loud splash and a frantic cry, but before he could raise his head a set of hands was under his armpits, yanking him to his feet. He turned, still choking and expecting to see Gorman, but Trent's dirty face was right in front of his own. Another round landed behind them, the blast slapping their backs with an air concussion and an echoing boom that drowned out Trent's shouted words.

Cranther appeared, soaking wet, also shouting. "Come on! We gotta cross it!"

Gorman came up next, his eyes wide in the light of the latest blast. Dirt and rock rained down on them, the slap making Mortas see that Cranther was right. The enemy guns were working both sides of the ridge now, anticipating flight, and would be on them in moments. The black water of the stream appeared in the flash of a round that hit the top of the ridge, and Mortas shivered in fear at what the dark surface might be hiding.

"Go! Go! Go! I'll cover you!" He heard his voice but didn't believe the words until he was splashing, knee-deep, through the water. Rocks shifted under his feet, trying to trip him, as he aimed the Mauler into the blackness. He heard the sound of the others crossing behind him and took a quick look, relieved to see that the water was no more than waist deep. More rounds landed on their side of the ridge, making him flinch with each air-tearing explosion. The flashes of illumination allowed him to see that the stream was just that, and not a river requiring a bridge.

Maybe they don't live in water this shallow.

The thought conjured up the monsters, and in the dancing, bursting light he saw one of them rear up out of the water as if trying to get a better look. It was barely ten yards in front of him, and he shouted in fright just before the Mauler went off. His reflexive shot hit the serpent dead on with the weapon's multiple pellets, and it flipped over backward as if hooked by an unseen fisherman. The air around him came alive, buffeting him first one way and then another, as more rounds impacted near the water's edge. Dirt and rocks and dead plants slapped him, but he kept his feet because of the sight before him.

In the changing light he saw the swirling surface turn to gold and then orange and then white, easily making out the disturbances as the predators came at him under the water. He turned the Mauler on the nearest one as if in a bad dream, knowing it was pointless but doing it anyway and hoping that the end would be swift. The weapon jumped in his hands and the swirling water rippled with shot, but he might just as well have saved it because they were no longer after him.

The serpent he had shot first was thrashing about madly, and the others converged on him in a horrifying rush. They weren't as big as the ones from the river, but they were just as grotesque as they leapt from the water and pounced on their wounded fellow. The water churned in the light, and Mortas ran from it as much from revulsion as from relief at deliverance.

He rushed after the splashing sounds of the others escaping, lifting his knees high and expecting at any moment to be pulled down from behind. The far bank was only yards away now, and it was almost level with the water. Gorman appeared out of the gloom, running into the water, ducking in the flash of another explosion, grabbing his arm and pulling him forward. The next moment they were out, still running, passing between two boulders and almost colliding with Cranther and Trent. The man and the woman stood stock-still with their hands in the air as if surrendering, and as Mortas cleared the rocks a rough pair of hands yanked the Mauler from his grasp.

Something heavy clubbed him in the kidney, and he reeled forward into Trent. She caught him easily, but when Gorman was likewise propelled into her she backpedaled just a bit. It was then that Mortas saw the other figures, looming up to shove her back into position. In another burst of light he saw a Scorpion rifle, standard issue for human infantry, and the chest-and-torso armor he'd worn in training. Two human soldiers stood behind Trent and Cranther, and Mortas whooped in joy at the sight.

"Hey! *Hey!*" He stepped toward them, reaching out. "Am I glad to see you! I'm Lieutenant Jander Mortas!"

The barrel of the Scorpion gun came up into his

face and a tired voice commanded, "Step back or I will fucking shoot you."

"**F**unny thing about this war. Sims look like us, walk like us . . . but they can't talk like us." Mortas inclined his head in order to catch the words as they walked. The humans they'd literally bumped into had turned out to be a patrol led by a senior sergeant from the battalion staff of the mechanized infantry unit that had assaulted the planet days earlier. The big, beefy man wore shoulder armor over the olive drab one-piece uniform of the riding infantry and carried a stubby assault weapon known as the Flayer. The six-man patrol was a mixed bag of the survivors from the armored assault force and a company of non-mechanized infantry normally referred to as walkers. Mortas judged two of them to be the latter; their shoulder-and-torso armor and Scorpion rifles were too bulky and too long to fit comfortably inside the confines of a personnel mover.

The enemy's inability to even imitate human speech had convinced the sergeant they were friendlies, but that hadn't meant they'd reached salvation. The abandoned unit was almost out of food, so it was a lucky thing that they'd found something to eat before meeting this bunch. The armored battalion had lost well over half its strength in the attack, including most of its key leaders, and Mortas was already sensing that important positions were now filled by people with little experience in those jobs. The sergeant had already warned Mortas that the new commander, a major who'd been the assault battalion's supply officer, might not accept them as easily as he had. When asked why that might be the case, he'd refused to answer and simply looked away.

Walking along behind the man, Mortas studied the Flayer and remembered its nickname was "the Failure" because it jammed so easily and had such limited range. One of the other soldiers now carried his Mauler, and they'd walked for some distance before Mortas realized the man had been unarmed until receiving the enemy weapon. As a group the patrol's members looked pretty ragged. The two walkers still had their helmets, head-hugging protection that also housed their communications gear, but only two of the others had theirs. He imagined they'd taken them from dead walkers the same way the platoon sergeant had gotten his shoulder armor, and noted bandages on several arms and legs.

Most important, he noticed how tired they all seemed. The man in the lead appeared half asleep, trudging along a well-worn path with his eyes on the ground and his weapon hanging from his shoulder. Even the two from the walking infantry, who could be expected to be more proficient at dismounted patrolling, struck him as disturbingly careless.

"But don't be too worried about meeting Major Shalley." The sergeant spoke up suddenly, returning to the earlier topic with an abruptness that Mortas sensed was caused by a true fear of their commander-by-default.

He glanced over his shoulder at Cranther, and the scout gave him a look of concern. "He knows his stuff, he knows the enemy, and he's gonna get us off this rock."

The last man in the file, walking behind Cranther, snorted briefly before covering it with a loud clearing of his voice. After so many days of whispering to avoid detection, Mortas cringed at the sound. The stars had finally reappeared, allowing him to make out the man-sized rocks and low grass around him, but it was still dark out and noise travels farther in the dark.

"So what happened with the assault?" he whispered, hoping the sergeant would pick up on the lower volume. The man replied as if they were standing together in a crowded room.

"Damndest thing I ever saw. Our battalion and one company of walkers went in as the first wave, we were cruising straight for their settlement, and then they fired these rockets . . . sensors said it was standard stuff, nothing to worry about, we were buttoned up anyway . . . but then they burst into all these smaller rockets, like thousands of arrows, and they came down on us."

He cleared his throat. "Made a racket on the armor but no real effect . . . and then . . . we started . . . slowing down. That dirt just turned into mud. Thick, deep . . . the vehicles started to get stuck."

The sergeant's breathing became more audible, and Mortas wondered if he was the first person the man had been able to tell this story to because the others had all been there.

"The heavier ones sank fast, but the lighter ones

were slewing around so badly that they were running into each other. We were taking some anti-personnel rounds too, like the stuff they were firing tonight, but we were safe inside the vehicles . . . until somebody asked if we were actually going to sink all the way.

"I swear somebody asked that over the radio, and the next thing you knew, somebody else in another carrier was screaming that we *were* sinking all the way, and then it started." He tripped over a small rock, and took a second to kick it even though it was half buried and didn't move. "Fuckin' thing. Anyway, that's when people began bailing out. Hatches flying open, ramps dropping, guys jumping . . . of course the first ones either disappeared into the soup or got stuck up to their armpits, so the rest of us were just up there, sitting on top of our own armor while it got lower and lower . . .

"It was like we were on the deck of a sinking ship. The anti-personnel rounds started coming again— they must have had spotters somewhere—and so then there wasn't a choice. Most of the carriers had stopped sinking by then—we didn't know it but the stuff turns back into dry dirt pretty fast—but now we had to get off of them." His voice got even louder, and the words tumbled one after the other. "Some guys went back inside and you couldn't convince 'em to come out, other guys climbed down and tippy-toed off toward the rocks, people throwing away anything that made them heavier—"

"Musta been hell." Mortas cut him off, seeing that

the man was becoming disturbed. The sergeant's head snapped up at him, as if he'd been insulted, but he stopped talking. They kept moving, and his hurt expression slowly eased away. Hitching the Flayer's sling where it rested across his armor, he tried to assume a more normal tone.

"Yeah, yeah, it was rough. But we'd never seen anything like that before, that's all. And neither had Command, because they cancelled the follow-on waves. We'd regrouped up in the hills by then, and the Sims hadn't come looking for us yet, so we figured they'd drop another cofferdam and pull us out."

"That's when they stopped answering our calls." The soldier behind Cranther spoke, his words sounding like a shout. "It took us a while to figure out they ran off."

"I *told* you, they probably saw enemy ships coming!" The sergeant turned and glared at the last man. "And they'll be back for us."

He looked down at Cranther, who had stopped walking to avoid bumping into Mortas. The scout regarded the big man with a face that was completely devoid of expression, but perhaps that was why it demanded a response. "Believe it, Spartacan. Back on Primus they left us for the same reason, but they came back later. You ever heard of Primus? We were outnumbered three to one, but by the time the fleet got back we were the only living things on that planet. We killed 'em all."

"Good story, Sarge. Except the last part." Cranther

pointed past him, up the trail. Mortas turned to see that the rest of the patrol had continued walking and had almost disappeared in the night. The sergeant stepped up and poked Cranther with a finger of his own.

"What about the last part, little man?"

Mortas gently moved the scout past him, and the sergeant took a step back in recognition of Mortas's authority. Cranther spoke over his shoulder as he went to catch up with the others.

"Nobody ever kills everybody anywhere, big man. Somebody always gets away."

It didn't take long to reach the base the survivors had established in a large ravine. They passed through a thin defensive perimeter on the surface consisting of tired-looking sentries, most of them soldiers from the riding infantry with little or no body armor. It was disturbing to see how dull and unfocused they acted; Mortas had spotted them from a good distance out and decided up close that they were walking around to avoid falling asleep.

They entered the ravine by an earthen ramp that had been packed down by many boot soles, suggesting to Mortas that the survivors had been in this spot for some time. They'd followed a well-trodden trail most of the way, yet another indication that this outfit wasn't obeying the simplest rules for staying hidden. The maxims rolled through his mind: Don't stay in one place for long. Don't come back by the same route you used going out. Try to keep the natural camouflage in place as much as possible.

The ravine was deep, well over head high, and although some of the soldiers there were pulling guard on rough-hewn parapets, there seemed to be little rhyme or reason to how they were posted. Though new to the war zone, Mortas could still see gaping holes in the base security ring. Probably two dozen soldiers, a mix of riding and walking infantry, were laid out asleep in the wide ravine, and he and the others stepped over them as they followed the sergeant.

The rest of the patrol melted away, and the sergeant led the four new faces around a tight bend in the gully to meet the unit commander. The stars were fully out now, and small fluorescent stones in the walls in this part of the ravine reflected the light as if intentionally placed there. A lone man sat on a bench-like rock just a few yards away where the gully came to an end, his eyes on the dirt in front of him.

Mortas walked straight toward him, trying to remain hopeful that this senior officer knew what he was doing, but the sergeant grabbed his arm. The big man pointed at the center of the gully floor and asked, aghast, "Don't you *see* that?"

Mortas looked at his feet, and the glowing illumination revealed an odd arrangement of stones, sticks, and narrow mounds that twisted this way and that. It reminded him of a horror movie he'd once seen on the Bounce, one involving a primitive tribe that had fashioned diabolical worship markers from natural elements. Mortas stared at it, dumbfounded, until Cranther whispered, "Sand table."

That was it. He remembered creating similar terrain models in Officer Basic, although he and the other lieutenants had carried special kits for that purpose. Sand tables were a three-dimensional representation of an area where the unit operated or planned to operate, with ridges and hills created by mounding and shaping the dirt while roads and rivers were put in place using tools such as colored string or chalk shavings. Some of the sand tables he'd seen had been quite ambitious, but in a pinch natural items such as the rocks and twigs used here would suffice.

The man on the bench hadn't moved or indicated that he was aware of their presence. He only slightly raised his head when the sergeant walked over and whispered in his ear.

Amazing. The noisy prick finally decides to be quiet. I wonder why.

Mortas stepped around the ground model and approached the two, as much to break up their secret conclave as to introduce himself. The man on the bench was nodding wordlessly, and the sergeant straightened up just as the lieutenant got within earshot. He flashed a fake smile at Mortas and then headed back down the gully with a purpose. Cranther, Gorman, and Trent had followed right behind Mortas, and as they got closer the reflected light from the stars showed that the commander was somewhere in his thirties, with tight-sheared hair over a round head. He wore the one-piece coverall of the mechanized troops, and a black shoulder holster containing a small pistol.

His eyes left the sand table when Mortas got close enough to touch him, but they were active and intelligent when he looked up. He gave a bloodless smile before speaking in a serene voice. "I'm Major Shalley. Who are you?"

"Lieutenant Jander Mortas, sir. I was being transported to—"

"Mortas? Now there's a name. I'd ask if you were related to the senator, but there aren't any senator's sons out here."

There's one.

"I was being transported to a replacement center, sir. Our ship must have—"

"Where's your *platoon*, Lieutenant?" The voice was still low, but an accusatorial edge had crept into it. The mouth hung slightly open, waiting.

Didn't he hear me? Has he gone mad? My platoon?

A thought came to him then, a warm thought, and he turned and indicated the others with his hand. "This is my platoon, sir. We were marooned here a few days ago and just reached friendly lines."

A brief snort. "*Lines*, he says . . . okay, Lieutenant, introduce me to your platoon."

"This is Captain Amelia Trent, military psychoanalyst."

The man's face brightened somewhat. "Well we've got a few patients for you, Trent."

She didn't respond, so Mortas continued. "Corporal Cranther, Spartacan Scout."

"A Spartacan, huh? We could have used you before they put us down here."

"And this is Chartist Gorman."

"He seems to like my sand table."

Mortas turned to see Gorman squatting at the edge of the model, an index finger moving in the air as if tracing the course of something in the diagram.

"He should, sir. We had no idea where we'd been put down, but he built an astrochart a lot like your sand table during our first night. Tracked the stars and figured out our location."

"Well then." The man stood up, his eyes back on the model. "Maybe he can tell me how we can gain access to the enemy's spacedrome."

"Is this it?" Gorman pointed at a ring of sticks laid out on the far side of the sand table. Now able to study the depiction, Mortas quickly made out the open ground where the unit's abandoned vehicles were imprisoned. The wrecks were represented by a large number of small rocks or twigs stuffed into the sand. He imagined his little group emerging from that field after their scavenging expedition, hustling up the elongated pile of dirt that stood for the ridge they'd so recently fled. The model was extensive, showing several pieces of terrain they hadn't yet encountered, but it didn't include the bridge they'd used to get across the river. A minor depression lay between the wrecks and the enemy base, but the outlines of two landing strips suggested that was the spacedrome's location.

Mortas glanced back at Major Shalley and then tried

not to stare. The man was just standing there, his eyes fixed on the model but apparently seeing and hearing little.

"Excuse me, but we've been trying to determine where the settlement was located ourselves. Is that it?" Trent asked, pointing at the circle of sticks.

"Oh yes." The major answered as if in a dream. "You can see we had a nice straight shot at it from where they dropped us. And we were rolling along nicely when they hit us with that new ordnance. Turned the ground into mud and, well, we've been on foot ever since. Done a fair bit of scouting, though."

He smiled at Cranther, who returned it blandly.

"It's only cost us twenty men, too. That's not a bad casualty rate considering how much intelligence we've gained, and how long we've been stranded here. A lot better than our first day, getting out of that death trap. Lost roughly half the battalion."

Shalley stopped talking without looking up, and so the others simply waited for him to continue.

"Of course we didn't get *everyone* back together again, but that's been its own kind of help. Some of the other groups have been chased down by what's left of the enemy's infantry, and that's given us the opportunity to scout out that base."

"Excuse me, sir. The enemy's settlement defense units took casualties?"

The major's head snapped in Mortas's direction, an angry look jumping into place before he erased it. When Shalley answered, his voice was back under control. "Yes, Lieutenant, we actually did manage to hurt them before we got stopped. The initial bombardment from the support ships took out their air, and I estimate it killed half their defense battalion and even more of the colonists. That's why they couldn't mount up a meaningful force to come get us. They're out here, of course, but not in sufficient strength to cover all this ground. The rest of the Sims in that compound have been doing repair work on the drome and filling in the gullies closest to the settlement during the day, but they mostly pull back into their perimeter at night.

"Which means they're waiting for help to get here."

"How about us, sir?" Cranther spoke gently. "Are we waiting for help?"

The major snorted before sitting back down. "Of course not. We were only a battalion when we landed, they never sent the second wave, and then they ran off on us after that. Oh, they might be back someday, once they've figured out how to drive through armpit-deep mud, but they won't be coming for us." He paused. "But we don't need them anyway."

"What was that, sir?" Mortas hadn't known he was about to speak, but the words hung in the darkness.

"I said we don't need them, Lieutenant. The enemy will be reinforced any day now, probably a whole squadron, which will replace all their ships that we destroyed. That's why I've spent so much time scouting the arrangement of that base. Once the Sim reaction force comes down, we're going to steal one of their ships and get off this rotten planet."

He looked up, his smile widening.

"And you four are going to help us."

Help you how?

Mortas knew the question was on all their minds, but he also knew better than to put it into words. Command took a dim view of insubordination at the best of times, but in a crisis like this even a dissenting opinion could be fatal. He searched out Cranther's eyes, and the scout gave him the smallest nod.

He understood what I wanted without hearing a single word. We're more of a unit after just a few days than this grab bag will ever be.

"Major, I believe Corporal Cranther has had some experience in this sort of thing. Particularly stealing a ship from the enemy. I wonder if you might like to discuss your plan with him."

"Really?" It was the first time Shalley had appeared remotely lifelike. "That true, Corporal?"

"Yes sir. I've had to commandeer a ride from the enemy once or twice."

"Well, step up here." The major moved to the ring of sticks, producing a telescoping pointer and extending it. "As you can see, we're faced with the standard defense arrangement for a new Sim colony. Reactive wire, anti-vehicular ditch, concrete fighting positions, and active mines, all of which are a real problem. But their perimeter is elongated to incorporate their spacedrome, and their defenses weren't completed when we hit them.

In the meantime I believe they don't have sufficient troops to man all those positions anyway. The drome itself was heavily damaged in the initial bombardment, but they've repaired much of that and appear ready to accept the relief squadron when it gets here."

"Excuse me, sir, but where did they put the wrecks?"

"Damn good question, Scout." The pointer touched a wall-like heap of stones. "They pushed most of it off to this side of the main pad. It would serve as an excellent screen for our movements, but unfortunately that's not a good approach route."

"I was thinking it might hide a smaller party working its way through the obstacles."

The commander mulled this over. "Think that would work?"

"It's a good access point. Piling that junk up has disjointed their perimeter." Cranther aped the major's earlier presentation-speak, reminding Mortas that he'd been trained to brief high-level commanders in their own terminology. "Any change to a standard defensive layout is usually a good opportunity for the aggressor, and an adjustment they made in an emergency is bound to have created a hole or a blind spot or both. Not to mention it's on the far side of the settlement, and judging from what we've seen their defenses are oriented in this direction."

"They have to be. As I said, they're as short of manpower as we are . . . just a second. What have you seen of their defenses?"

"Nothing, really. That's why I think they've got the

bulk of their attention facing these hills where you are. We came from this direction here." Cranther walked around the diagram and began carving a line in the dirt with a spare stick. "We crossed a river, that was the first time we encountered the serpents—"

"Fuckin' things. Attacked us as we were retreating. They've really channelized our movement since then. Can't go near the water."

Cranther shot Mortas a look. "That's what we discovered. The enemy has a temporary bridge right about here, which was guarded by what appeared to be two colony militia members. We killed them both, dumped them in the water, and kept going. We only encountered enemy fire once we'd climbed the ridge near the battlefield. That's why I say their defense is oriented more in this direction."

"Makes sense. Our patrols never went near this bridge of yours. Our earliest efforts went down this ridge, the one closest to the settlement, and almost every time they bumped into counter-surveillance patrols. Later on I sent them around in a wider arc. Those were the ones that came back with the real intel."

"It might be helpful if I had a look up there myself, sir." Cranther made this offer as if he was thinking out loud, a subtle manipulation that Mortas recognized as the first step in getting them away from this circus. "Get an updated picture, I mean."

"Oh, I'd like nothing better, Scout." The major closed the pointer while regarding the sand table as if seeing it for the first time. "But that enemy reaction force is overdue, and I want to be ready to move when it gets here."

Shalley turned to look at Mortas and the others. "You see, there's an incredible amount of confusion when that many reinforcements land somewhere, Sim base or human. That spacedrome is going to be utter chaos for a time. And if they get attacked at one point on the settlement perimeter while that's going on, they're gonna throw a big chunk of those fresh troops directly at that spot. They'll have new guys running all over the place, no idea where they are. And if the base gets attacked just a few minutes later at a different location, whoever's left standing around is gonna get tossed at that."

The major paused, and the corners of his mouth curled up as if he'd arrived at a conclusion that pleased him mightily.

"They're gonna be jumping all over the place at that drome, and a small group using that debris pile for cover is going to have a decent shot at crossing the open and hijacking one of the ships that can handle human passengers."

The pointer came out again as the plan fell into place, and Shalley extended it to its full length. He tapped the pile of rocks that indicated the Sim ships destroyed in the initial bombardment. "Corporal, you'll be with me and the last group, coming through here. Our faithful sergeant will be leading the second attack, hitting the perimeter almost directly across from us.

"And you, Lieutenant Mortas, as the only officer

besides me, you get the prize. You get to start this show with the initial assault right here." He pointed at a spot very near the field of wrecked assault vehicles, as if Mortas would be continuing the attack that had bogged down on the first day. The very heart of the enemy defense belt.

The pointer snicked closed again, and Major Shalley looked at Mortas with a wide grin. "Right about now I bet you wish your dad really *was* a senator, huh?"

CHAPTER 8

"**A**ctually, sir, I was hoping you might let me take the others with me. They've been watching my back these past few days and it would help me recon the far side of the drome—where we'd be coming through." To Mortas, Cranther seemed to be talking from a great distance. "If you haven't had eyes-on there recently, they might have changed up on you."

"I already told you there's no time for that, Scout."

"But it's worth it, sir. Think about it: the four of us have seen the ground on the other side of the river and everything from there to here, so if you let us check out the far side of the drome, we'll be the only members of your command who've been all the way around this place."

Mortas heard the words but somehow couldn't focus on them. The strain of the last few days, the physical toll of intense hunger and sleep deprivation, their brush with extinction on the ridge, and now the discovery that salvation was going to be snatched away finally combined to overload his brain. A pair of intense thoughts did manage to fight their way through the mental murk, though.

We have to get away from this bunch.

I have to get my people *away from them.*

The major was talking. "That would be quite a valuable thing, Corporal, but I'm dead certain the Sim reaction force is going to be here in the next few hours."

"And what makes you think that?" Trent stepped up next to him, her eyes on the sand table as if memorizing it.

"Already forgotten that long, noisy bombardment a couple hours ago? The one that brought you to us? They haven't thrown anything like that since the first day. A few times they've dropped those blasted mudmakers on what was left of our vehicles, when they saw we were getting weapons and chow from them, but nothing bigger than that. So why did they just expend all that ordnance on that valley tonight?"

"Could be any number of different reasons," Trent murmured, and Mortas found his dulled mind locking on to her words. "They might have thought you were making a move on them, using the wrecks as cover. Or maybe somebody in their perimeter just got nervous. The Sims get nervous, you know, just like we do."

Her voice was soft, soothing, and Shalley turned to give her his full attention.

"That was an awful lot of ammunition if they're just nervous, Captain." The comment had no bite to it, so Trent continued. Her tone continued gentle and warm.

"Really? How would you know what's a lot for them? What if they have much, much more than that and just decided to use some of it? That's reasonable, isn't it?"

"No, if they had a lot they would have fired it by now." The major's reply carried no conviction, as if he was explaining something that was of little importance. "You see, we've been fucking with them every night since we got here, so badly that they only come out during the day. In darkness they hunker down, and if they had any extra ordnance they would have used it to defend themselves. They're so desperate that they've been filling in the ravines so we can't sneak up on them. They're shit-scared of us, and they were holding on to all that ammunition as a reserve, in case we come through the wire at them.

"But tonight they fired at least a hundred rounds at us, which can only mean one thing. They're expecting reinforcements and resupply very, very soon."

"Maybe you should let us go take a look anyway."

Mortas shook his head, not believing what he was seeing and hearing. Shalley seemed actually befuddled by the very same suggestion that he'd summarily dismissed when Cranther made it. The man's argument made sense and showed a good grasp of Sim tactics, but still he appeared to be giving strong consideration to the military advice of a psychoanalyst.

That's it—she's pulling some kind of headshrinker stuff

*on him. The low voice, the suggestions . . . the guy's probably
as zapped as we are. That's why it's working.*

"It really couldn't hurt to let us try, could it? Right?"

Major Shalley looked up with eyes that were unfocused and lost, and his mouth opened in what Mortas was sure would be assent. Unfortunately that was the moment when the sergeant came back, appearing so suddenly that Mortas almost jumped in surprise. He took a step back as if disengaging physically, and was intrigued to see that he and the major hadn't been the only ones affected by Trent's efforts. Cranther's lower lip was under his front teeth, and Gorman appeared to be almost asleep.

"Sergeant. Good, good. I've adjusted the plan to include our latest arrivals and wanted to tell you about it." Shalley drew the man with him toward the sand table, and Mortas decided he really didn't care to learn what the two were cooking up. He moved off a few steps, and the others followed.

"Nice try there." Mortas whispered to Trent. "You almost had him."

"Yeah, Captain—what was that trick? Hypnosis?"

"I wish." Trent regarded the major's back with a speculative look. "But he's practically out on his feet, so it was easier than you might think." She turned to Mortas. "You do know we have to find a way to ditch these people? Before they split us up?"

"She's right. Now's the time." Cranther cast a quick glance at the other two. "It's still dark out, and their security sucks. Let's just start moving back down the passage real quiet, and as soon as we're out of sight it's up-and-over time."

As badly as he wanted to get away, Mortas couldn't help considering just how that would look if any of the troops in the gully managed to get back to Command. Desertion was a hard charge to beat, and under the current circumstances . . .

"Okay, come with me." The sergeant was approaching, and the moment was gone anyway. There was actual buoyancy in his step, and he wasn't trying to hide the triumphant smile of having passed the worst job in Shalley's attack plan to Mortas. He ushered them down the passage, but stopped short of where the others were sleeping. The smile slipped away, but the words were almost mocking. "Lieutenant, I'll talk you through the breaching part of this operation in just a bit. We salvaged a lot of explosives, so I think you'll have enough to blow down whatever's left of their obstacles."

Blow down their obstacles. The phrase conjured up memories of a ridiculous training event he'd once been tasked to command, an infantry assault on a Sim strongpoint. It had been a complex operation, with live engineer support and numerous phases that had seemed simple when briefed. He'd ended up so focused on remembering what action took place in what sequence that he'd almost completely forgotten the robot enemy that opposed them. While he'd been busily dispatching security teams this way and support-fire teams that way, the enemy had slipped down from their bunkers and shot up the crawling engineers long before the doomed sappers got even close to the targets of their explosives.

He'd been chewed out by a crusty colonel for having flunked the exercise so badly, but right in the middle of that he'd looked over the man's shoulder at the foolishly simple arrangement of defensive wire that had thwarted him. It wasn't half as complex as the enemy obstacle belts he'd viewed on the Bounce, and the exercise of course hadn't included any of the fiendish devices the Sims could shoot and throw through the air at exposed troops like the breaching teams. His sappers had been wiped out by simple direct fire from rifles, and he'd sworn then and there that the only way he would ever try a breaching assault was inside an armored vehicle.

The sergeant turned to Trent and Gorman. "Do either of you know how to load and fire a Scorpion?"

"I do," Trent answered unhappily, and when Mortas gave her a questioning look she explained with a shrug. "I told you I don't have much to do in my job. So I ask people to teach me theirs."

"I don't." Gorman looked right into the NCO's eyes. "I'm an objector. It's against my principles to wield a weapon."

"Is staying alive against your principles?"

"It can be—and in that case I'd rather die."

The big man's face screwed up in annoyance, and he leaned in close to Gorman even though the chartist didn't move. "Oh, would you? Well that's fine when you're alone, but you're gonna be with a bunch of good men trying to fight their way onto that base, and you're going to help them."

"I can help. I just won't fight."

"So you say. But I got news for you: you're wrong. I've seen it myself. You pacifists get in the thick of it and you suddenly find out your survival instincts are as strong as anybody else's. Then you start fighting like ten mad bastards, except you're shooting like ten mad spastics because you don't know one end of a rifle from the other. So you are *going* to learn how to load and fire one of these weapons."

"No I'm not."

Cranther raised a hand, his eyes holding Mortas back. "Hey Sarge, why don't you let me teach him? And the Captain too, no matter what she says about already knowing how."

Cranther, you devious little son of a bitch. Where would we be without you?

The big man relaxed, his mind already moving on to all the things he still had to do in order to shift the hard job onto Mortas. "That would be just fine. We'll get you a rifle, but we're low on ammunition so—"

The dark stillness was broken by a sharp cry, clearly human, somewhere on the surface above. It was immediately followed by the sound of nearby gunfire, a frantic burst cut short followed by more shots. Human weapons, and Sim weapons too.

Cranther was already scrambling up the wall in the direction of the noise, and Mortas followed him in a reflex. The dirt came loose in dry handfuls as they went up, but they stopped short of exposing themselves as they'd practiced countless times in the days and nights before. A long, high-pitched scream met them at the top and the scene before them was chaos.

The few sentries still living were running toward them at a breakneck pace, terror stamped on their straining faces and some without weapons. Not many yards behind them the darkness seemed to ripple like an ocean wave, and then it cascaded into definition as a long line of armed troops charging forward. Not shooting because that would slow them down too much. Not throwing grenades because they were moving too fast.

Sims.

Cranther had his arm, yanking him back down into the gully. They landed in a pile on top of Trent and Gorman, but fear got them right back up again. All was sound and movement in the trench, the sergeant hollering "Up! Up! Up on the line!" dark figures struggling to their feet or up the incline, more screams from above, now bodies tumbling into the gully or landing full in its center, the remaining sentries reaching safety just a few steps ahead of their pursuers. A brief, roaring volley from the troops who'd made it to the top, the night illuminated by white light ripping straight out of the rifle barrels, Mortas taking in a rapid-fire succession of images as the bodies in the gully leapt about in confusion, whipping his head side to side in search of a weapon just before the wave hit them.

Dozens of bodies came jumping straight into the

ravine as if they hadn't known it was there. Sims bouncing off the opposite wall, dirt flying, humans pulled off the parapet, falling in a tangle of weapons and arms and legs and screams that rent the air. More shots now, close range, the whole world was shouts and booms and flailing arms and legs. A flare burst just overhead, swinging wildly on a parachute and casting the gully into daylight and then night as it whipped around. Light flashed off of Sim helmets, Sim combat harnesses, long Sim bayonets on the ends of Sim rifles. More humans running into the crush, more shots and screams, and a Scorpion rifle skittered down the slope a few yards from Mortas.

He jumped for the weapon, but never made it because a falling body slammed into his neck and shoulder, knocking him over. The body rolled away but then there were two more, right on top of him, fighting, wrestling, biting, kicking, high-pitched chirping and frenzied growling, he was turned the wrong way, his face stuffed against the dirt, and he couldn't reach them as he tried to push them off. Now the gunfire was all around him, the yelling so loud and desperate that vocal cords broke in the effort, more weight crushing him, helpless, dirt in his mouth and his nose and his eyes, terror and madness mixing as he realized he was going to die right there under a pile of bodies—and then the weight shifted and he fought his way out from under in a mad crawl.

Coming to his knees just in time to get kicked or clubbed in the side of the head and back down again, pushed up against one wall, knowing in the darkness that if he didn't get up now he would be pinned for good. The body against him rolled, spun; hands reached for his face and the horrible squealing turned into terrified chirps that sounded like an engine getting ready to explode. His own hands moved, found flesh—fingers gouging, wrapping around—and by some twist of luck he had the Sim by the throat, choking him. The thing thrashed, kicked, clawed at his sleeves as Mortas found he was strong enough to extend his arms to full length.

The mass of bodies lifted the Sim and he went with him, his back against the wall, pushing to his feet in shock and relief and elated surprise and not even noticing that the form opposite him had gone limp. His eyes darted all around, no longer looking for a weapon, searching for an escape route in the mad crush, and then a face was next to his; somehow he recognized it, the black skull cap. Hands were pulling him away from the fight, and then Cranther was shoving him up the wall, shouting for him to move move *move*!

The roar of the battle came back to him as he went up and over, amazed by his own speed until Cranther went by in a crouch. Shrieks and shots and the dreadful sound of gun butts striking bone, now below him but not far enough away—Cranther grabbing him again and yelling for him to run—and then they were both sprinting over the uneven ground, crushing the bushes and flinching at every shot. Driven forward by adrenaline, all thought of evasion and stealth and even thought itself gone, just the mad kick of self-preservation driving them, until Mortas felt the tearing pain in his left calf that sent him tumbling head over heels when he reached for it.

His fall took Cranther down with him, and they both crashed into the dirt. Mortas rolled up in a ball, both hands squeezing the calf muscle as if it were merely a bad cramp, fear seizing him again when he felt the blood. Cranther crawled to him on his stomach, his mouth open and sucking in great breaths of air. The scout's hands reached for the wound, stopped, and then signaled him to let go.

Slowly pulling his fingers off, Mortas was assaulted by a shower of thoughts and images that rebounded off of one another. The need for silence, and the way the distant shooting continued, but now there was less of it and it seemed muffled, like it was happening underwater. Gratitude for the little man who was now slowly tearing his trouser leg open, his face close to the wound because of the darkness. Fear that it would be bad. Fear that he wouldn't be able to get up again. Fear that the endorphins had already kicked in and that it would hurt like hell when they wore off.

The sudden, overriding fear that he had completely lost track of Gorman and Trent.

He sat bolt upright, but Cranther stopped him with a palm against his chest and an angry shake of his head. He couldn't leave it at that, though, and so he leaned forward and whispered.

"What happened to Trent and Gorman?"

"Not sure. Got 'em up and out, saw you weren't

there, so I sent them running and went back." He stifled a cough and then gave the leg two quick pats. "You got grazed by something, just a scratch. You hurt anywhere else?"

Mortas looked around, vainly seeking the image of the other two. It was the first time he registered the other pains, the scrape across his forehead and the muscles in his back that cried out for acknowledgment. That was pain too, but the athlete in him knew he could grit his teeth and keep going. Cranther's observation that his leg wound was just a scratch shamed him slightly, and he finally spoke. "No. I'm fine. We have to find the others."

The scout slowly pushed himself to a kneeling position, and the effort made him cough loudly even though he tried to stop it. He looked around, as Mortas had seen him do a thousand times, checking the area for threats, but even in the darkness something in the gesture was oddly wrong. A ghost of the previous actions, performed simply out of habit. Mortas was reaching for him when Cranther collapsed.

Somehow the stars got brighter just then, turning the ground under the scout gray. It also illuminated the spreading red oval high on his chest and off to the side. Mortas pulled up the filthy shirt and tried not to flinch when he saw the dark, ugly hole and the oozing blood. He slid a hand around, feeling Cranther's back for more blood and an exit wound as he'd been taught. There was nothing there, and the smaller man's eyes fluttered open when he pulled his hand away.

"We gotta get out of here." He croaked, and this time Mortas knew he was speaking as loud as he could.

"Easy, easy, almost there." Mortas slowly dropped to a knee and then lowered Cranther from his shoulder. At first he'd half carried him with the scout's arm stretched across his shoulders, but he'd weakened quickly and finally lapsed into unconsciousness. Only now, as they approached the bank of the river they'd crossed earlier that night, did he show any signs of life.

Mortas eased him into a sitting position against a group of man-sized rocks, and the scout seemed to fold in on himself, his hand pressed against the wound. The water gurgled somewhere beyond the tall weeds, and Mortas took the Sim canteen from his harness even though he knew it was already empty. He'd washed Cranther's wound and made him drink the rest almost an hour before, and so the decision to head for the stream had been simple. From time to time gunfire had erupted in the black void behind them, and flares had lit up the horizon more than once, but it seemed they'd eluded anyone who might be pursuing survivors.

"Lieutenant."

The word was weak, and he leaned in close to the ashen face. "Don't talk. Save your strength. I'm gonna get you some water."

"Wait."

The eyes that looked up at him from under the

skull cap were dull. "You gotta leave me here. Go find the others, and get them off this rock."

"We'll find the others, but you're coming with me. We'll rest here a bit, get you something to drink, and then push on. It'll be all right."

Cranther tried to laugh, but the attempt only made him cough again. His earlier spasms had been wet and loud, but these were desiccated and low. "Get to the drome. That crazy major was right about one thing. When that Sim react gets here it'll be total confusion. Steal a Wren and get outta here."

"I wouldn't know how. You're gonna have to do that."

"It's easy. You punch in the coordinates." His voice trailed off, and he took a long, slow breath. "Have Gorman do it."

"Coordinates? What coordinates?"

"Main. Glory Main. The planet's name is Sere. Not really a planet. Dead rock. Headquarters is inside. Not far from here. The bigs always set up near a Hab in case they have to bug out." The chuckle turned into a cough. "Generals. Trying so hard to hide, no faith in anything, contingency plan points right to them."

"That's perfect, then. Won't take long to get there. Have you in a hospital in no time." The fantastic notion that safety had always been so close was only eclipsed by the utter impossibility of actually getting there, but he had to ask anyway. "You knew that all along?"

"Woulda told you when we got the ship. No one's supposed to know. You hear things, I put it together myself. Gotta know where the safe places are." The white face turned doubtful for a moment, but then re-laxed. "You get a ship and head for Sere. You get close, you go on the distress channel, say you're carrying key intel from a Spartacan, and they'll come out to get you."

Mortas tried to laugh, humoring him. "Key intel."

"Tell 'em about the colony, about the mud muni-tions . . . *don't* tell them we met up with friendlies. All dead back there . . . no good."

"Hold still. I'll be right back."

"Wait!" Cranther's free hand grabbed his sleeve. "Told Trent and Gorman to head for that spire I pointed out. Good chance they got away. You find them and get them outta here."

"I will. We will. Let me get you some water now."

His leg wound was hurting again as he limped around the rocks toward the sound of the creek. His back ached from the fight in the ravine and the long walk with Cranther on his shoulder, and a soul-crushing weariness stole upon him while he calculated the scout's chances. The grass brushed against his mud-caked trousers and small rocks shifted under his boots, but Mortas didn't notice. He was already kneeling by the black, moving surface and filling the canteen before he remembered the serpents, and he was only mildly surprised that the memory held no fear for him.

Tears filled his eyes, and a nearly irresistible urge to just lie down right there stole over him even as he recapped the canteen and stood up. The stream had kept flowing without any sign of its terrible denizens, and he figured the fireworks might have scared them off. He and Cranther would need to cross the stream to reach the spire so many miles away, and he tried to imagine Gorman and Trent doing that at some other fording spot.

He knew he would have to carry Cranther across, and then find a ravine that would get them started toward the rally point. At least the scout had picked a landmark that was easy to see, but now it was in the wrong direction. After linking up with the others, they would have to retrace their steps, cross the stream again, and then approach the drome even as it was filling with reinforcements and enemy ships . . .

He almost didn't realize he'd returned to the spot where he'd left Cranther. He trudged up, his mind spinning with the enormity of the challenge ahead, and found himself completely stumped. Cranther wasn't there.

Mortas looked around to verify he was in the right place, but fresh blood in the dirt near the rocks said that he was. His eyes had just followed the blood trail to a tall, shadowy crack between two large stones when someone spoke behind him.

"Well well well."

He turned in a flash, prompted by a rocketing fear because he recognized the voice.

Major Shalley stood there, the front of his uniform ripped from neck to navel and an ugly bruise swelling the side of his forehead. The shoulder holster and pistol were gone, but he held a Scorpion rifle in his hands. Light reflected off of it when an enemy flare popped, and Mortas could see the rifle was pointed right at him.

"Good to see you again, Lieutenant."

Wide awake now. Amazingly wide awake. Mortas took a drink from the canteen, circling and trying not to look like it.

"Why you pointing that at me, Major?"

"Because I'm going to shoot you."

"Really?" His opponent turned in place, the gun tracking him. Just a little further and his back would be to the fissure in the rock. "What for?"

"Treason. You brought them to us, didn't you?"

"Think that's how they found you? There were so many trails leading in and out of there, it's like you put up road signs."

"Wrong. We'd been there for three days and hadn't seen a single Sim scout. And then you four came along, and minutes later they're attacking in force." Shalley's eyes lost their focus and he shook his head as if to clear it. "Just about everybody back there's dead, but I followed you to make sure you pay for what you've done."

"Are you even listening to yourself? You stayed in one place too long. Too many troops coming and going from the same spot, they probably found you days ago. I bet that bombardment was just cover so their infantry could get in close."

"That's a good story. Almost believable." The major looked around, suspicious. "The enemy teach that to you?"

"What?"

"Lemme guess. They caught you and turned you into some kind of Judas Goat. Taught you to betray your own kind."

"And how would they do that? They can't talk to us!"

Mortas watched as a hand slid out from the fissure that was now directly behind the man with the gun. The only problem was that the gun was still pointed directly at him. He flicked his eyes around, trying to decide which way to jump.

"Talking's not the only way, boy. But you already know that, right?" The major faltered, and the rifle shifted off of him. "Your headshrinker, that Trent, almost had me letting you go, back there. Those words . . . bored right into my—"

The hand turned into the rest of Cranther, detaching himself from the stone in the very moment that a string of flares lit up the sky. The blackened knife was in his right hand, and his left was out with the fingers spread. In a single blink he'd moved, one boot landing on Shalley's calf to bring him down within the shorter man's range, the left hand darting out and around, the fingers clamping down on the mouth as the other hand drove the blade straight in.

Mortas was standing there, transfixed, when the gout of blood vomited into the air and both men crashed to the dirt, the major kicking and choking and clutching and the scout rolling up in an immobile ball.

He leapt to Cranther's side, pulling him into his arms and then seeing all the new blood, knowing the damage inside had been ripped even further, that the little man had thrown away what little chance he had in order to save him. Shalley's boots were stamping out a mad tattoo that brought him close as he writhed, and Mortas kicked him away.

"Nononononononono . . ." he crooned, rocking, sure Cranther was already gone when the eyes fluttered open. Though glazed, they saw him.

"Get them out of here, Lieutenant. Sere. Remember Sere. Tell Gorman."

"I'm sorry, I'm sorry, I'm so so so so sorry. So much I was supposed to do, I should have listened—"

"Hey."

He stared into the dimming eyes.

"Yes. I'm right here."

"Tel."

"Tell who? Tell them what?"

"My first name. You asked the day we met. It's Tel."

"I thought it was Corporal."

"It was." A smile slowly crept onto the relaxing features. "Not anymore. I'm Tel again. Just Tel."

He was still smiling when he passed.

The horizon was already starting to lighten, but he simply couldn't leave Cranther lying there. He considered putting the body back in the crevice that had sheltered him this last time, knowing that the short man had habitually taken refuge in spaces just like it. Perhaps he'd picked it up on the street as an escapee from the orphanage—and the mines—or maybe the Spartacans had taught it to him. Either way it was one of the many habits he'd adopted in the name of survival, and it seemed cruelly wrong to bury him in that fashion, as if throwing him away now that he was no longer useful.

He'd seen larger rocks in the stream earlier, and decided to collect enough of them to build a small cairn. The serpents were out there somewhere, so he dragged Shalley's body many yards along the bank before positioning it, head lolling obscenely, on an outcropping near the water. Returning to Cranther, he waited until the predators began swirling in the black liquid near the fresh meat before wading out and beginning to toss the stones up onto the embankment.

The water churned far off to his left as the loathsome things lunged up on shore, over and over again, but he paid them little attention and kept working. Mortas knew when they pulled the corpse in because the thrashing reached a fever pitch and he was even able to make out the sickening splat as the scaly bodies collided. It would be helpful if they decided to turn on one another the way they had in his earlier crossing, and Mortas felt he detected the sounds of fighting as the roiled waters rippled against his thighs. He'd almost collected enough of the rocks when he sensed the approach of one of the ugly predators, and was only slightly intrigued by the inexplicable sensation, the instinctive knowing, that there was only one of them even though it was behind him.

He selected a smooth stone that was almost too large for his hand, and raised it dripping from the stream just as the thing made its leap. Completely at home in his surroundings, Mortas turned in a lazy, athletic arc and smashed the giant eel in the side of the head while it was still in the air. The blow made a revoltingly moist sound when it landed and the serpent, one of the smaller ones that had probably missed out on the latest meal, dropped into the stream. It was badly injured, and jerked spasmodically as it tried to get away.

"No you don't, you fucking coward. You start something, you finish it." He spoke under his breath, tossing the stone behind him and seizing the slimy scales near the tail. A quick twist put the thrashing tube on his shoulder, where he clutched it in both hands and dug in his fingers. Without looking back, he marched straight up onto the sand, dragging it with him as it weakly whipped and rolled and tried to break free. It was dead before he let go of it, several yards out of the water, and he dropped it with true loathing before looking out over the stream.

The dark plane eddied as if moved by a natural current, and then the others were gone.

He'd taken both of Cranther's knives and now had the long one tucked in the back of his trousers and the small one in his boot the way the scout had carried them. He reverently took the skull cap and folded it neatly before storing it in his breast pocket, believing that Gorman might want it. He arranged the small man on his back with his feet toward the water and his arms by his sides, and then slowly covered him with the stones. Most of them had dried off by then, but for some reason a few of them stayed damp.

With that done, he slung the Scorpion rifle across his back after determining that it contained only five rounds. Bowing his head, he tried to remember the words of the various funerals he'd attended as a boy and then as a teenager. They'd all been state occasions, people his father had known, and he wasn't surprised to find he remembered little about them. A more recent memory came to mind, and he tried to recall the words.

"Father. Mother. Sister. Brother. Son. Daughter. All are one, from the beginning of time until its end." He wiped his eyes and noted that the sun wasn't too far below the horizon. It was time to get moving, something he felt Cranther would understand. "Thank you, Tel. Thank you for everything. I'm glad you're finally free."

Mortas walked up the bank and took hold of the oddly deflated serpent before dragging it down to the water's edge. The spire where he hoped to meet up with Trent and Gorman was on the other side, and even though he couldn't see it yet he still knew exactly where it was. Gripping the man-sized monster with both hands, he began to turn in a gentle circle. At first it dragged across the sand, but then it slowly rose into the air. Moving faster now, feeling the coolness of the breeze he was generating, he timed his throw and heaved the thing through the air in a gracefully rotating arc that landed it far out in the stream.

The others were on it almost immediately, a riot of splashing and flailing and ripping, but still he didn't hurry. Unslinging the rifle, he held it at the ready as he waded out and plodded across.

He moved down the ravines with care, recognizing that the Sims were combing the area and that he was traveling alone. It was a strange sensation, being by himself, and with a touch of guilt Mortas remembered his fantasy about abandoning his ragtag group of survivors just a few days earlier. Cranther was now gone and he had no way of knowing if the others were alive, but the genuine desire to see them again quickened his step.

Mortas had heard one last flurry of Sim gunfire just before the sun came up, and his heart had jumped when he envisioned Trent and Gorman as its victims. He immediately pushed that away, telling himself that the headshrinker and the mapmaker had learned to move with stealth and would not have walked into an ambush. He then hoped, without remorse, that it was part of the group so ineptly commanded by Major Shalley or some other equally incautious human element. It was impossible for him to know how much of the original assault force was still left alive, but they'd had a full company of walkers with them and he hadn't seen too many of those the night before. Given his experiences with the friendlies he'd encountered so far, he had no desire to meet up with any of them—or to wish them well at the expense of his own people.

All I need right now is to find Trent and Gorman. After that, everything's going to work out.

Mortas felt forced to acknowledge the chance that the other two might not have survived the night, but he found it impossible to envision a plan that didn't include them. It was almost as if he were willing them to still be alive, and he superstitiously told himself to stop even considering the possibility that they had perished. Even so, banishing the thought didn't reduce the anxiety and he honestly didn't know what he'd do if they weren't at the rally point. The enormous task of evading the Sim forces, gaining access to one of their ships, and escaping the planet now paled to insignificance when compared with the monumentally important act of merely finding the others.

Walking along and ruminating on these morbid thoughts, Mortas realized with a start that Cranther was the first soldier he'd lost under his command. Faced with the unchangeable reality, he now felt true shame at the realization that he'd always known he would lose people but that he'd never given it much thought. It had been an abstract notion when discussed with his fellow lieutenants, and even when veteran officers had lectured them on the topic they'd made the experience sound somehow ennobling.

Feeling the sun just peeking over the edge of the ravine but still enjoying the morning's coolness,

Mortas decided that there was nothing noble about the pile of rocks he'd left behind him an hour before.

He walked faster, even though every step carrying him closer to the spire moved him that much farther from the Sim settlement that was his ultimate destination. In spite of his grief, or perhaps because of it, he allowed himself to gently mock the dead Cranther when he saw just how poor a rally point the scout had chosen. He mentally ticked off a few of the characteristics of a good emergency linkup site, and shook his head as the spire failed to meet many of those qualifications. No one in the group had ever seen it up close, so there was a chance that there was little or no cover anywhere near the towering feature. The vicinity of the tall rock might be bare ground, which made it even less attractive as a fallback position and even more difficult for him to explore if he had to look for the others. That thought brought another one to mind, even less pleasant, that such a prominent feature could have been selected as a reference point by the Sims as well.

That notion caused his eyes to start scanning the tops of the canyon walls for enemy lookouts. He moved along for some time in that fashion, alternating glances at the rock-strewn ground to keep from tripping. Now aware of his walking, he took note of the balancing act required as one foot reached out and the other followed suit, the way that his feet, though bruised and swollen, still flattened and then arched and provided the bounce that kept him going. His arms might be taken up with holding the rifle at the ready, but even so his shoulders still swung as if they hung free. His lungs expanded and contracted, blood flowed through his arteries and veins, and the engine that was his whole body provided heat that kept him warm.

Though slightly damaged and very much overused, this body, this machine, was carrying him forward in much the same way it had from the very first day on the planet. How many days had they gone without food, walking the entire time, without their bodies failing them? Only the catastrophic wounds of the battle—and the sacrificial damage when he'd killed the major—had managed to shut off Cranther's engine. Not lack of food and not crushing fatigue. Only death itself had been able to stop the little scout.

And that was why Cranther had so ardently believed they stood more than a snowball's chance of sneaking onto the Sim base and stealing one of their ships. Not his special training, though that would certainly help, but something else. Something more. Something deeper. Something much more reliable than slogans, orders, or threats. Cranther had believed they would get to that ship and get out of there simply because he'd decided that was what was going to happen. And once that decision had been made he'd started walking. One foot in front of the other, eyes on the horizon even when that horizon had been the walls of the chasms through which they'd traveled so many miles.

The scout's example flowed easily into the myriad difficult tasks Mortas now faced. First he would have to find the others, as Cranther had told him to do.

Together they would formulate some kind of a plan, something that would end with them blasting off this terrible planet and headed for a dead rock named Sere. And no matter what that plan turned out to be, its most important element would be the stubborn determination that Cranther had shown them. If they had to do it on foot, that was simply the way it had to be. If they had to do it without food, then they'd do it without food. What had he said about food and water?

"No food, you die in weeks. No water, you die in days."

With those simple words he'd prioritized the search for water, and then they'd walked until they'd found it. Cranther had been almost certain at that time that they were the only beings on the entire planet, and that they were doomed, but he'd still gone in search of the water anyway. Mortas had little doubt that the Spartacan had seriously meant to find a high cliff from which to jump if no food could be found, but that talk had disappeared the instant they discovered that they were not, in fact, alone. Even the awful revelation that the Sims were present in force hadn't changed his resolve. In fact, it had been quite the contrary. He'd greeted the Sims as a source of the ship they would need in order to escape.

So that was how they would need to act now. They needed a simple plan, made up of basic steps like using the ravines to move undetected. And when they got close enough to finally see this settlement, this promised land, this fucking mirage, they'd come up with the next step based on what they saw. Even if it meant crawling on their bellies across the ground in the dead of night, exhausted and starving. Even if it meant sneaking up on whoever might be guarding the ship they meant to steal and opening his throat with one of Cranther's knives. Even if it meant holding off the enemy firing a weapon taken from that very guard, buying the time Gorman would need to punch in the coordinates for this dead rock named Sere that supposedly held the main headquarters of the entire Glory Corps.

Glory Main.

CHAPTER 9

Mortas studied the spire from only one side before deciding where Trent and Gorman would be. The sun was well up by then, and he'd climbed a brush-covered finger on the ridge closest to the rock obelisk in order to see the ground around it. Flattened on his stomach, the Scorpion cradled in his arms, he scanned the plain beyond the spire for the ravines that had hidden them so many times before.

Strangely, this piece of dirt wasn't cracked and fissured like the expanses they'd crossed coming from the other direction. It even hosted a few short trees, gnarled things that looked dead from a distance but were probably nourished by an underground tributary of the stream not far behind him. Mortas idly envisioned the serpents swimming around in that darkness beneath the soil until realizing that there would be nothing for them to eat down there except one another. And although it hardly made sense as a steady source of nutrition, he found the image amusing.

The stone steeple itself was a wonder of nature, with no explanation for its existence. Just over five hundred yards away, it didn't appear to have once been part of the ridges that formed a semicircle around it. The striations on its shaft didn't match the lines of the nearest cliffs, and up close it didn't seem half as tall as it had appeared from a distance. Narrow and alone, it looked to Mortas as if it had stood through the years just to prove it could.

Unable to spot a hole big enough for both Trent and Gorman, he began searching the tip of the next ridge over, where it tapered down to the flat like the one where he lay. If they'd made it here and found no obvious depression to hide them, they might have opted for the high ground in order to see him coming. After all, they weren't just trying to stay out of sight. They were hoping to link up with someone who was, like them, being hunted and who would be creeping around the area with great stealth. They would want to be able to observe the ground on all sides in order to wave him in.

Him and Cranther.

A cooling breeze had come up with the sun, and it now shifted to a constant wind that moved the brush around like an unseen hand. For the first time since arriving on the planet he thought he could actually detect an odor from the bleached-out vegetation, but he soon decided that was wrong. The wind was coming from the direction of the settlement, and the scent he was picking up was the smell of battle. Smoke, fuel, the chemical components of spent explosives, and even the stench of rotting flesh. Luckily it was coming from a distance, but he had to wonder just how many humans had perished in the night just past and the days previous.

His eyes settled on an oddly shaped white stone on the spine of the opposite ridge, and it was only when he shielded his eyes with a dirty hand that he saw it wasn't a rock at all. It was the weather-stripped remains of what must have been a substantial tree before something had knocked it over. Any branches it might have once had were long gone, but judging from the width of its base it must have been supported by an extensive root structure. When it toppled over, months or perhaps years before, it probably left a considerable hole. And no matter how that hole might have filled in since then, the dead tree and the weeds that had grown up near it would probably provide enough concealment for two people.

Mortas took some time to look around before moving, alerted by the smells from the previous night's fighting. The enemy was still here, still hunting, and their sudden appearance only hours before proved it was unwise to simply assume they weren't in the vicinity. A pair of birds flew overhead, bracketing the spire as they headed out over the plain, and he took their unhurried winging as proof that the Sims weren't nearby. He slid back down the side of the finger on his stomach, only coming to a crouch once the brush was thick enough to hide him. His knees ached as he duckwalked forward, but he still forced himself to move slowly as he worked his way around the inclined ground that connected the two ridges like the webbing of a human hand.

Odd thoughts came and went as his fatigue caught up with him, and he remembered practicing a similar operation in a field maneuver months earlier. One of the most dangerous things to do in a war zone was bring two separated units together, even if they were part of the same larger unit. Unlike what he was doing now, such linkups were usually performed at night and so the danger of mistaking friendly soldiers for the enemy—or vice versa—was quite real. One group would be designated as the stationary base once the two elements were reasonably close, so that they wouldn't literally bump into each other, and radio reporting of the moving unit's progress would be almost non-stop. There was still enough hazard in the final approach that a series of signals involving lights or blips from a strobe were prearranged to avoid ugly mishaps.

None of that applied here, of course, as they had no radios and unless Trent or Gorman had scooped up a weapon Mortas was the only one who was armed. Even so, he was recalling the exact sequence of recognition signals from that far-off field problem when Trent's face appeared above the wall of dry grass in front of the dead tree's uprooted end. Time and the elements had scoured the dirt from the remaining roots, but the base was still dark and so it framed the captain's head even though she was covered with grime.

At first he thought she didn't see him, but that wasn't true at all. First her mouth dropped open in surprise, and next she simply hung there as if decapitated, a floating ghost-face that stared at him in disbelief. Then, with a yelp that made him cringe to his very soul, she leapt up from the hole and dashed the few yards to where he squatted. It was the most natural thing in the world when he simply stood, the rifle lowering to his side, and caught her when she threw her arms around his neck and buried her face against his.

In a moment Gorman was there too, joining the embrace, and he brought up the arm that held the rifle to pull them both in. Trent was whispering a flood of words he couldn't make out, but Gorman was looking over his shoulder in search of Cranther. The chartist pulled back just a little, his eyes freezing Mortas's until the lieutenant gave the slightest shake of his head. The hopeful expression sagged, and this time when Gorman leaned against him Mortas pulled him in tight.

"I'm sorry. I'm so sorry." He had no idea why he was saying that, or why it felt appropriate. Trent stopped talking then, and in the silence that followed he whispered in a voice that was hard as iron.

"No matter what happens from here, no matter what happens to me, I *promise* I will get you out of here. We are getting off this planet."

"Where are we going?" Trent's voice was low and child-like, so close it could have been his own thought.

"The one place that we know is safe. Screw looking

for any more friendlies here, or waiting for help. We're going to steal a ship from the Sims. And then we're going to Glory Main."

"So you think you can do it?"

"Yes." Gorman spoke with a hard certainty that Mortas didn't recognize. He'd adopted the tone just after being told that the location of Glory Main had come from Cranther, and so Mortas decided that was the reason. "The Sims copied our Wren shuttles so closely that the equipment is almost identical. Punching up a star chart and then selecting a destination will be child's play—don't need to be able to read Sim to do any of that. But that doesn't mean we'll just be able to fly one away if we do manage to get aboard."

"I know. But Major Shalley was right about one thing: When the Sim reinforcements arrive, that drome is going to be mass confusion. The trick for us is to be close enough to snag a Wren that's either just landed or just preparing to lift off. Which means we need to be close enough to observe the drome before they get here."

"Long way off." Trent looked back toward the ridges and the assumed location of the enemy settlement. "Shalley thought the reinforcements were going to arrive at any moment, so we'd better get moving soon."

"I thought of that." Mortas's stomach growled, angry now that it had been fed and reminded what it was like. "We're going to have to wait until dark to have any chance at all. There can't be too many more survivors of the assault force left, and there's still a bunch of Sims cruising around out here looking for the rest.

"Which also raises the issue of the route we're gonna follow. How did you two get across the river?" He hadn't told them how he'd distracted the serpents to make his own crossing.

"We got lucky and found a cut where the water flows under a partial land bridge. We had to jump across, but I think I can find it again."

"Good." Mortas's eyelids were heavy, and the quiet of their isolated nest was working on his fatigue. Time to work up a rest plan and get some shut-eye until dark . . . .

"What's that?" Trent asked, her head tilting upward and then freezing.

"What?" Mortas forced himself to come back to the moment. His hands reached for the Scorpion, and he turned on his side to face up the ridge.

"Listen."

He cocked his head to one side, noticing the expressions of silly concern the other two had adopted. It was as if they'd been asked to mime consternation or confusion, and he decided he must have put on the same expression himself. He found it quite funny, and was on the verge of saying something when he heard the sound.

It was like soft snoring, a deep inhalation that somehow never ended. It also got louder, and without being able to identify it they all flattened deeper in the hole. The noise took on a mechanical note, the snoring changing to a low growl, and then the thing streaked by almost directly overhead.

Mortas flipped over onto his back to get a better look once it was past, feeling his empty stomach squeezing even smaller. It was a two-seater Sim scout, twin exhausts trailing a thin white vapor as the triangular craft flew far out over the plain. It slowly banked when it was almost too small to see, and they watched it make a long turn before it came back miles from their position and disappeared over the ridges.

Long before that, the dwindling sound of the scout's engines had been replaced by a steady rumbling somewhere on the far side of the high ground. The roaring rose and fell, and Mortas quickly identified it. It was the sound of many spacecraft descending from orbit, throttling up or down or switching to a completely different set of thrusters now that they were flying in atmosphere.

The three of them stared at one another blankly, listening to the sound of doom and unwilling to put it into words. Another scout craft, or perhaps the same one assuming a standard patrol route, appeared far to their right and then disappeared over the ridges again.

"It's the Sim reinforcements. They're here."

"No, they're not *here*." Trent spoke glumly, her eyes in the dirt. "We're here. And they're there. The place where we needed to be. Before they got there."

They sat without speaking for a long time, but not in silence. The rumble of activity at the spacedrome continued at a lower level, but the enemy movement in the air increased significantly. The scout craft were more in evidence, passing nearby on what looked like the outside turn of a patrol arc that was bringing them closer and closer to the ground. At one point a much larger Sim gunship breasted the ridge before executing a slow turn, and moments later they heard its mini-cannon roaring at some unfortunates who'd probably been spotted by the scouts.

Or by Sim troops. The scouts and the gunships wouldn't be out there alone, not with the network of ravines that the besieged Sims had found so terrifying. Part of the relief armada would be ferrying fresh Sim troops out into the wasteland, either as blockers or beaters to help find and kill the remaining humans. Those dismounts would now be scouring the ground between them and the settlement, heavily armed and in radio contact with the aircraft and the other patrols in case they ran into trouble or their prey seemed to be getting away.

"We're fucked, aren't we?" Mortas asked in a dry voice when the noise had settled down a bit.

Gorman looked at Trent with a weak smile, the exhaustion and defeat stamped on his withered face. "Fucked up and dying, Captain?"

"FUAD for sure." Trent nodded solemnly. "But it's nice to hear you swear."

They all laughed just a little at that, and then Gorman looked at Mortas with eyes that were nonetheless hopeful. "So what now, Lieutenant?"

What now. The eternal question of leadership. And what to say when there is no answer?

"I suppose we could wait for the next scout to fly over, stand on each other's shoulders and reach way up—"

Trent's eyes stopped him when they widened in terror at something over his shoulder. She grabbed Gorman with one hand and pulled him to the bottom of the hole even as Mortas was rolling over onto his stomach and low-crawling backward to get further out of sight. He knew what it was before he saw it, but he was still amazed.

A column of Sim soldiers walked down the draw between the ridges as if asleep. Their combat smocks were dirty and ripped, and dried mud was caked on their trousers and boots. The soldier in the lead wore the flanged helmet of Sim infantry, but many of the others were bareheaded. His rifle was slung across his chest as if forgotten, and one strap of his combat harness was held in place with several wraps of dark twine. His eyes were vacant, and fixed on the spire as he walked out into the open.

The Sims who followed appeared even less aware of their surroundings, as many of them were carrying stretchers laden with their wounded. Others walked with pronounced limps or only with the aid of their buddies, and bandages were a common sight. The column trudged forward slowly until the lead soldier stopped just short of the steeple. He signaled with one hand, an untranslatable command until the first stretcher bearers reached him and gently lowered their burdens to the ground.

Mortas had been too scared to count them, but he now saw that there were roughly fifty soldiers in the group. As drained as they appeared to be, they were still well armed and even carried an assortment of human weapons in addition to their own. He was forced to worm his way further into the hole when one of them, presumably the ranking officer, posted a few guards in a loose circle around the group.

The Sims were still three hundred yards away, and quiet chirps carried across that distance as they saw to the wounded. The commander produced a handheld radio of some kind and began speaking into it while other Sims began sharing various items that appeared to be food. From a distance they could have been any human platoon, thrashed from hard service and nearing the end of their strength.

Trent's lips were on his ear, and Mortas didn't flinch as she spoke. "Must be part of the settlement's defense battalion. Out here fighting for days, they may even be the ones who attacked us last night."

Gorman slid up next to him, moving an inch at a time. The Sim guards had given up on any pretense of security, sitting down with the others, and Mortas found his shoulders aching with the tension when he finally relaxed them.

He cupped a hand between his mouth and Trent's ear. "Looks like they're being taken out of the game. Must be some kind of casualty collection point."

Gorman half-climbed onto his back so that their three heads were touching. "If more of them come here, we're going to get spotted."

"I know. But how do we get away without being seen? And wouldn't we just run into more of them?"

It was maddening. Setting up near such a prominent terrain feature had been a dreadful mistake, and Mortas mentally kicked himself for not moving them earlier. Now they were pinned down, and all it would take would be for the Sim commander to dispatch a couple of men to walk around, standard security patrol, and they'd be finished. His eyes dropped to the Scorpion, the weapon looking pitifully small and only containing five rounds.

"Just a second." Trent lifted her head a fraction, scanning, judging. "Look at them and look at us. Dirty, beat-up uniforms, a mix of human and Sim gear, and they're practically out on their feet. We're interchangeable."

A surge of adrenaline pulsed through Mortas when he saw what she was saying, but it wasn't from excitement. It was from fear. Worse than fear, mortal terror at what she was suggesting.

"You want us to walk down and join them?"

"Not right now, of course. But they're waiting for some kind of transportation, probably a flight back to the settlement with the wounded. When that arrives they're all gonna get on, and we could go with them. We'd fit right in."

"That's crazy. Think they don't know each other?"

"Right now I think they don't know their own

names. And they've been out here a long time, taking casualties, probably got some extra bodies at some point." She thought a moment. "Look there, at that group over on the left. Got those smaller helmets that the militia troops wear, the ones we saw at the bridge. One-piece uniforms like me and Gorman. They've probably mixed in plenty of new faces."

"Lots of assumptions there."

"What else are we gonna do?" The words came out in a hiss. "Try and sneak our way through a cordon of fresh troops? Walk miles through the ravines and hope we don't get nailed? And even if we do that, how do we get inside? This is the only way."

"Sure. Sure. We climb on board, the ramp comes up, and then there's some Sim medic speaking canary at us, asking if we're wounded. What then?"

Trent's face screwed up in annoyed concentration. Before she could come up with an answer, Gorman grabbed them both and pressed them down. Mortas tasted the grainy dirt of the hole, but he'd been so caught up in the argument that he had no hint of what the chartist might have seen. Whatever it was, it was close. He'd frozen as soon as Gorman had stopped pushing him down, but from that position Mortas could see nothing. For all he knew, enemy troops were walking directly at them. In a moment of fluttering unreality, Mortas was reminded of hiding under his bedspread as a small child, convinced that some horrible monster was coming toward him out of the darkness.

He learned what Gorman had seen a moment later,

when a stream of high-pitched chirping rose up from a spot only a few yards away. It was answered by more of the same, just lower and softer. Mortas didn't have to look to know another column of wounded had passed practically on top of them. Gorman's hand gave him a quick double pat as an all-clear, but Mortas took his time sliding up to peer through the weeds.

The group had more than doubled now, with almost a dozen stretchers and over one hundred troops. The new arrivals were in even worse condition, dropping to the ground as soon as they reached the others. Where the original complement had set about tending to their wounded comrades, the second bunch seemed too exhausted to care. The commander of the first element could be heard giving quiet orders to some of his troops, and these Sims, presumably medics, began examining the new stretcher cases.

"I guess our people didn't kill as many of them as Major Shalley thought," Gorman whispered, and then he looked back toward the high ground to see if more of the Sims were coming up behind them.

They didn't have to wait long to learn that Trent's idea wouldn't work after all. A pair of enemy troop carriers flew overhead and settled on the plain just beyond the steeple in a roaring cloud of dust, and when the ramps came down the stretcher cases were carried out to them. Some of the walking wounded went as well, but the rest of them didn't so much as look at the machines.

Mortas had settled in for a long wait, hoping that the airships extracting the enemy would take them all at once so he and the others could move. The strain of the last few days, combined with two sleepless nights and the warmth of the sun, now sought to rob him of reason and consciousness. He fought to stay awake, but was losing the battle when he noticed something that demanded his attention.

While most of the remaining Sim troops were stretched out asleep or seated back-to-back in tired pairs, the commander and a few of the others now gathered in the center. They were studying a rectangular device, and from the finger pointing Mortas decided they were choosing a route for their next movement. His battered mind fought back at him as he considered the various possible destinations, but he couldn't imagine this ragged bunch being fit for anything but a hospital.

The assemblage broke up, and he marveled as two or three of the Sim leaders walked off shaking their heads.

They shake their heads the same way we do. I wonder if it means the same thing.

The senior Sims now approached their troops where they'd gathered in different bunches, and individual soldiers began waking up the ones who were asleep. The chirping got louder as the officers or NCOs conveyed the new information, and there was even more head shaking after that. One soldier, seated on the ground holding a canteen, flung the water bottle away in what could only have been exasperation.

"Amelia."

Trent started, and Mortas knew he wasn't the only one who'd been almost asleep. "Yes."

"Look at 'em. Check out the body language for me."

"Never diagnosed the enemy before. Saw a few prisoners once, but they hustled 'em right by." She rubbed her eyes and looked down on the scene. "If I had to guess, I'd say they're some pretty unhappy folks."

Emphatic hand gestures from the leaders, accompanied by a sound that was more bark than chirp, soon had the soldiers gathering their equipment and getting on their feet. The leader then moved from group to group, obviously soothing raw feelings, as the back chatter quieted and then died. They began shouldering weapons and other gear, and Mortas saw the unconscious way that most of them began orienting themselves toward the high ground.

Getting ready to move. So chewed up they can't be headed anywhere but the settlement. Pissed off about something...

"They're not getting a ride back." Mortas grabbed the sleeves of the others in excitement. "They're walking. They're gonna walk all the way to the settlement. Been fighting all this time, dead on their feet, and they got screwed out of their ride."

"You sure about that?"

"Absolutely. Happened to me once in training. We'd worn this laser-tag gear for days, and at the end of one long march we stopped near a convoy of empty movers. They let us think the vehicles were for us. They had us clean up the laser-tag stuff and turn it in, and then we watched while they loaded it on the movers and they drove away. We reacted then the way the Sims are reacting now."

Trent had been studying the slowly forming column, and she began to nod. "I think you might be right."

"You bet I am." Exhilaration burned his exhaustion away as it climbed into belief. "They've got a long-ass walk in front of them and they know there's no reason for it. So if we fall in at the end, keep our mouths shut, and peel off once we're though the wire, we have a good chance of getting to the drome."

"Lieutenant." Gorman's tone was hard to identify, but Mortas feared it meant opposition. As much as his embryonic plan excited him, it also filled him with genuine terror. There were so many ways it could go wrong that Mortas knew his nerve wouldn't stand up to even the slightest argument.

"Yeah."

"We gotta cover the Captain's hair. It's short, but not short enough."

Mortas looked over at the matted tangle that was almost stuck to Trent's scalp. Gorman was right. They needed to cut it or cover it. He rolled over slightly and pulled Cranther's skull cap from his pocket. Understanding, Trent took the cap and pulled it down, but that actually made things worse: Now the longer strands stuck out, but no matter how he tried they were still too short to tuck up under the fabric. A hand nudged him, and Mortas turned to see Gorman holding out a stubby pair of scissors. Remembering them from the medical kit, he took the shears and began snipping off the excess hair. Mortas glanced over his shoulder in time to see the head of the Sim column coming toward them, and began to caution the others. Too many things to say, too many things to think of, not enough time.

"Remember: Not a word, not even a sound. We walk in the rear, we stay together, and don't make eye contact. If something unexpected happens, grab hold of each other and we'll just drift off to the side."

Snip, snip.

"Once we're through the wire, pretend you're so tired that you need to sit down and we'll all just move off together."

Snip, snip.

"They'll think we're settlement militia, and that we've got someplace to go."

"Shhhh."

He palmed the scissors and looked over the edge to see the first Sim pass not twenty yards away. It was the same troop who'd been on point with the first arrivals, and he was no more alert now than he'd been then. The others then started filing by, most with their weapons slung carelessly, and after a third of them had passed Mortas saw the leader. If he was exercising any control over this gaggle, it wasn't apparent. Perhaps he was as dead on his feet as the others. Perhaps he was annoyed that they had to walk back. Perhaps he didn't want to push his soldiers any further by insisting they assume a proper defensive posture.

Although they were barely moving, the tail end of the column came up much too soon. Mortas studied the last walkers, fearing they would be leaders posted there to encourage any stragglers. That didn't seem to be the case; if anything, these were the ones in the worst shape and the most likely to fall out. Their eyes were vacant as they moved, and most of them were unarmed. One of them sported a field dressing on his head that had seeped runnels of blood that had now dried on his cheek, and he looked ready to collapse at any moment.

With a fearful look into Trent and Gorman's equally petrified eyes, Mortas slowly came to his feet and started walking down the embankment after the Sims.

Mortas was amazed that they covered so much ground in so short a time. He wondered if the heart-racing fear of the first mile had made the distance fly by, but then he realized that couldn't be it. The Sims were walking slowly in deference to their wounded, but even so they climbed the first ridge and then left it behind in under an hour. That was when he saw both the truth and the strangeness of it: After having lived so long using cover and concealment, he was surprised by how rapidly they moved in the open because he was now unfamiliar with this careless form of travel.

And that was the correct description. Instead of seeking the higher ground in order to survey their surroundings for possible enemies, the weary Sims had climbed the ridge just far enough to find a notch that let them descend onto flatter terrain. Then they'd really begun to put the miles behind them. The brush wasn't as thick here, and the only obstacles were the crooked ravines that the humans had so recently viewed as the only safe way to move. The column, strung out in the open, twisted and turned as the lead soldiers tried to navigate around the gullies. Most of the time they found segments that were narrow enough to be jumped, but even those were too much for many of the injured. When the ravine proved too wide to leap, they were forced to slide down one side and clamber up the other.

And that was when Mortas began to believe their desperate subterfuge might actually work. Going up the opposite side of the first ravine, digging his fingers into the fresh dirt clawed by the many Sims in the front of the column, he was shocked into near-paralysis when the enemy soldier just ahead of him reached down and offered his hand. It was a common act for human infantrymen negotiating an obstacle, but Mortas was so surprised that he almost went over backward. His boots dug into the ravine wall and his legs began pushing wildly, and the Sim on the top lunged just as he was about to slide back down. The hand that gripped his was familiar, four fingers and a thumb, and the face could have been any human lieutenant from his training class.

It was all he could do not to thank him, but the Sim had already turned and moved on.

Mortas crouched down himself at that point, helping Trent and then Gorman with the last steep yards, wishing he could tell them what had just happened. Trent must have seen it, because she gave him a sympathetic look before gesturing with her chin to get him moving again.

They picked up another group of walking wounded a few hundred yards after that. These troops were sitting off to the side of an unimproved Sim road as if waiting for them, and they filled in behind Gorman once the growing column had stepped out on the new thoroughfare. It was really nothing more than a straight track of leveled dirt, and if they weren't standing on it they wouldn't have known it was there, but it was another indication that the settlement was near.

The unreality of the situation was losing its impact on Mortas, but he attributed much of that to his own exhaustion and the somnolent effect of the march. When they'd first joined the enemy formation, his mind had filled with scenes of disaster such as a Sim NCO twirping a question at them or ordering them to do something. The images had all ended in gunfire and death, but now that they'd been walking for so long without incident he came to believe this was unlikely. The Sims had stopped talking among themselves for the most part, and many of them limped along with their eyes planted on the ground.

Smelling the barn. That had been the term the instructors had used when he'd been taught basic patrolling, referring to the lapse in awareness and concentration that frequently accompanied the end of a long mission.

He and his fellow lieutenants had been warned against this time and again, and on one operation they'd been attacked by a mock enemy just short of the hilltop where they planned to spend the night. Surprised, disorganized, and lethargic, they'd been easily defeated by a force not even half their size.

Despite that experience, Mortas didn't criticize the inattentive Sim soldiers because he knew they'd been on a multiday combat operation that had frequently involved close fighting against a desperate enemy. Most of that time they'd been the only active defense of their one hope for survival on this barren planet, which was the settlement. And after they'd almost completely destroyed the humans who had come to conquer them, they were clearly being shunted aside by the Sim troops who had only just arrived. Despite the presence of large numbers of aircraft and the end of major hostilities, they'd still been left to walk in under their own steam. Given the circumstances, it was an achievement that the Sim commander had gotten this thrashed-out band into any semblance of a tactical march formation at all.

Walking along, Mortas wondered if he'd do any better with disgruntled human troops under the same conditions. He was on the verge of admitting he would not when he remembered where he was, who he was, and what he was trying to do. The laxness of this column of Sims was bringing three of their enemies closer to the settlement, and was likely to grant those three humans access to the very installation they'd fought so hard to preserve. They were inadvertently protecting three of their foes who meant to steal one of their ships and were willing to kill large numbers of their fellows in order to make their escape.

To prevent that tragedy, all the Sim leadership had to do was walk up and down the column telling the troops that humans were still on the loose and that they had to be vigilant. Reminding them that a doomed opponent has nothing to lose and that desperate enemies are capable of amazing feats. By failing to do that, they were endangering some of their comrades and maybe even the base itself.

Mortas felt his face twisting into an expression of unwilling awareness, a grave perception that now spread out and occupied his mind. A coldness grew inside him as he saw for the first time the unrelenting nature of warfare, and the ruthlessness it required because the consequences could be so mercilessly absolute. The unfeeling calculus that had called for the deaths of the two Sim guards on the bridge because they had simply been in the way. The foot-blistering, tendon-straining demands of walking down the ravines because to do otherwise was to be seen, and to be seen was to die. The necessity of fighting an unknown enemy for the habitable planets of the universe because ceding them meant the race would perish.

His thoughts were interrupted by a scout craft passing over the column, so low that he felt the warmth from its thrusters. No one in the formation acknowledged the machine's presence, and when Mortas looked down the double file he was reminded of a centipede back on Earth, its many legs working ceaselessly as the entire entity moved forward. The Sims were so covered with the planet's dirt that they blended into uniform lines on either side of the track, heads down, shoulders stooped, and the only indication that they were alive was the ceaseless tread of the hundreds of feet.

Mortas looked at his own boots then, as if seeing them for the first time. They were muddy and scuffed from all the hard days and nights, and he noted a long, deep gash across the toe which had obviously been there for quite a while. It stood testament to all the walking and crawling, the climbing and jumping, the frenzied punching and kicking in the fight the night before, and still he had no idea where he'd acquired it. The mark came into view when he took a step with that foot and disappeared when he took one more, and he became fascinated with its reappearance as if it were part of a mechanism repeating the same function over and over again while he watched from above.

He was practically asleep on his feet when a hand squeezed his upper arm from behind. His head came up with a jerk, but he quickly saw what Trent was indicating: A wheeled Sim vehicle sporting a large gun turret was parked next to the road, and several soldiers sat on top. The distinguishing feature about this tableau was its cleanliness, for even though both men and machine were lightly flecked with dirt, their dark camouflage colors stood out against the orange plain.

Reinforcements. Fresh troops. Wide awake, and looking for action.

Everything about them said they were recent arrivals. Their combat smocks were in one piece, they all wore helmets, and with the exception of the two manning the main gun they all carried individual weapons. There wasn't a bruise or field dressing among them, and their eyes swept up and down the file as it passed.

A checkpoint of some kind. They weren't just parked there; they'd been told to guard the road. And if they weren't on the lookout for humans trying to blend in with their own kind, just what purpose could they have been serving? Mortas felt his already dry mouth lose its remaining moisture, and he struggled to decide if it was better to look at them or to look away. He glanced at the troops in front of him and saw that most of them were paying no attention to the soldiers on the vehicle, and so he decided to imitate them.

It was maddening, not being able to warn Trent and Gorman to follow his example, but then again that was why he was in the lead. Unable to communicate his orders, he was relying on their ability to pick up on his signals or at least to imitate his every movement. So he now looked down at his feet in an exaggerated fashion, hoping it would serve as sufficient inducement to the others while not attracting too much attention from the watchers. He knew he was getting close to the checkpoint, and felt his heart rate climbing with each step.

A flurry of deep chirp-chatter suddenly erupted a few yards ahead, and he flipped the Scorpion's safety switch to combat mode before looking up in exhausted defeat. He was pondering the absurd notion that his puny five rounds might create enough confusion for Trent and Gorman to get away when the entire column came to a sudden halt. The troops on the gun vehicle were standing and shouting now, but not at him. A clutch of the Sims just ahead had stopped, and they were now exchanging harsh chatter with the reinforcements. Angry hand gestures were flying now, and he was struck by how human they seemed.

It took a moment, but then he recognized the source of the problem. One of the marching Sims, bareheaded and unarmed, was brandishing a ration canister at the guards. Obviously one of the troops on the vehicle had just finished eating his meal and had stupidly tossed it in the direction of the worn-out soldiers filing past. It must have hit one of them, providing the proverbial straw that broke the camel's back. As worn out as these troops were, they weren't about to tolerate an insult like that from soldiers who had come late to the fight that they had won at so great a cost.

The Sims behind Mortas now crowded forward, and he was surrounded by a chorus of hoarse chirping before being carried along toward the vehicle. In an instant he was in the middle of the argument, his head turning frantically as he looked for the others. As tall as most of the enemy, he was on the verge of panic when he felt Trent pressing up next to him and then saw Gorman in the crush only a few steps away. Trent's arm now wrapped around his waist, anchoring herself to him, but he hardly noticed because Gorman's performance simply had him spellbound.

The pacifist was right next to the armored skin of the gun vehicle, and he repeatedly smacked an open palm on the plate while staring at the guards with a look of extraordinary pugnacity. He knew better than to utter a sound, even hidden in this avian cacophony, and merely played the part of a Sim so lost in anger that he couldn't even shout an insult. His expression of righteous indignation matched the snarling faces around him, and it was difficult to distinguish him from the enemy. Mortas tried to push forward through the throng, fearful that Gorman would get carried away and attempt to mimic the Sim language, but he didn't make it before the Sim commander was on the spot.

In a bizarre mirroring of Mortas's attempt to restrain his subordinate, the enemy officer waded into the group. He wasn't shouting, though, instead relying on a calm voice spoken very close to each of the troops to convey the obvious message that he wanted this madness to cease immediately. Mortas watched in admiration as he slowly peeled the soldiers away one at a time, his insistent twirping causing others to find their composure and then start helping him regain control of their comrades.

The mob broke up slowly, and there were more than a few parting chirps exchanged, but the column eventually returned to its original shape and left the checkpoint behind. Walking away, Mortas fought to keep from muttering the words that were screaming inside his head.

That was too close. Too damned close.

CHAPTER 10

They passed into familiar terrain a short time later, skirting the base of the ridgeline where they'd first watched Sim excavators filling in the ravines. Quite a bit more of that work had gone on in their absence, but here it was patchy and obviously meant to aid the movement of the enemy vehicles. The walls of the gullies had been knocked down in several spots so that multi-wheeled movers could roll down and then climb out of those canyons that were too wide to simply run over. These cutouts were marked with metal poles and bright red flags that stood out well against the dull soil, and the column snaked first one way and then another to take advantage of them.

Still marveling at the sensation of walking freely out in the open, Mortas looked up at the sky and was alarmed to see that a lot of time remained before the sun would set. Passing through the colony's perimeter, and then separating themselves from the Sims, would be much easier if done in darkness. The encounter with the checkpoint walked with him, spooking him more with each step, because he now saw the fatal flaw in his hasty plan. They might be passing for Sim soldiers right now, but that was mostly due to the ragged condition of the enemy with whom they traveled. The cutouts on the gullies were just one more indication that large numbers of fresh troops were now operating all over the area, and there was no telling what responsibilities those reinforcements had assumed at the base. All it would take was a squad of alert troops manning the wrong gate for them to be uncovered.

He saw a brief movie in his mind, the column halted in front of miles of reactive wire and enemy fortifications. A winding passage through the obstacles, covered by fire and controlled by guards checking each soldier through individually. The obvious decision to run even though there was no way to escape, the genuine Sims throwing themselves prone on the ground as the reinforcements opened fire. The three of them crumpled on the sand, bleeding from multiple death wounds, and the film ending in blackness. Strangely, he imagined enemy soldiers discussing the event over chow later on. *Did you hear three of the humans tried to sneak into the settlement with us? Must have walked ten miles, right in the middle of our column. One of them was a female.*

They went over a small rise, allowing Mortas to see the long line of shuffling troops ahead of him. He observed that they were headed toward the plain where the stranded assault vehicles were buried, and after that it couldn't be too far to the settlement entry points. It made sense; the assault force had chosen a flat piece of ground that should have allowed them a straight run at the enemy just after touching down. And every footfall now narrowed their options just a little bit more.

Gotta get away from this bunch. But how?

He'd thought of simply falling out and taking the other two with him, as if he'd reached the end of his strength or succumbed to an injury and was being assisted by his friends. Unfortunately, legitimately tiring Sims had already dropped off to the side more than once and he'd watched the medics in the group approach them right away. There had been a conversation each of these times, so that option was out. The sun was descending, but not fast enough for him to hope that darkness would fall in time to let them slip away before they reached the settlement.

And yet even if it did, where would that leave them? The subterfuge had certainly brought them a great distance in safety, and scattered shots echoing in the distance had proved that the enemy was still out hunting for survivors, but leaving the column would leave them outside the wire. A mad, fluttering sensation rose in his stomach when he considered just toughing it out, trying to bluff their way through the gates and hoping for a lucky break. The penalty for not getting that break was certain death, but no matter how hard he tried he couldn't think of a better plan.

I wonder what Trent and Gorman would come up with. Fuck I wish I could talk to them.

He covered his mouth with his hand, as if trying to wipe away perspiration but actually to hide a smile when he remembered Gorman's antics back at the checkpoint.

Guy should have been an actor. For a pacifist he sure looked ready to kill somebody.

That thought resurrected the image of the Sim he'd killed at the bridge, the wide eyes, the surprise, the startled chirp he'd given off. He'd just been some poor slob—settlement militia assigned to watch a small bridge far from where the enemy was supposed to be. Even then he'd tried to do a good job, and what had it gotten him? A knife in the throat, and then his body devoured by those horrible reptiles.

Mortas looked up the file again, recognizing that the militia member he'd killed had been one of them and feeling guilty until the combat smocks of the Sim infantry reminded him of the fight in the gully. The sheer panic, the wave of enemy troops, the utter confusion, the weight of the bodies tumbling on top of him, the tumult that had followed, the soldier who had tried so hard to kill him. The feel of his own hands crushing the Sim's throat as if it were nothing more solid than a loaf of bread.

He shook his head, trying to rid it of the visions as well as the wadded cotton that had crept in to fill it. He was so tired . . . no wonder they were fitting in so well with this parade of corpses. They actually belonged with them. He frowned when he saw that they had more in common with this particular group of the enemy than they'd had with the humans they'd encountered. And that these stubborn, trudging forms had more in common with them than with the reinforcements who were now stalking the stragglers from a battle that was long over.

They topped the low ridge near the spot where the cofferdams had deposited the assault force, and he was able to look down on the field of wrecks again. But this was different. He almost woke up when he saw the level of activity below, and he paused as if adjusting his harness in order to take it in. Trent and Gorman moved up next to him, and the troops walking behind them passed without a chirp.

Enormous divots had sprouted on the plain where armored vehicles had once been snared. Several earthmovers were at work among the many remaining hulks, and individual Sims operating jackhammer-like devices were breaking the ground that hugged treads and wheels. At the far end of the plain, large movers were towing away the machines that had already been freed, and the answer to their dilemma almost jumped up at him. Mortas fixed the other two with a meaningful look, and their mute responses showed they'd been thinking along similar lines.

Why walk when you can ride?

They waited until the very end of the formation

passed before rejoining it and heading down toward the field of wreckage.

Up close and seen in the daylight, the disaster was even harder to contemplate. Dozens of armored vehicles were sunk into the hard terrain, and they passed close to the personnel carrier that had provided them the life-giving rations. Mortas could feel his stomach contracting again at the memory, and not for the first time did he consider leading the others out of the formation and trying to hide in one of the wrecks.

The Sims were clearly salvaging them, which was not a new development in the war, and it made sense to expect the vehicles to end up inside the settlement's perimeter. Even plunked down outside the wire, they would still be close enough to survey the layout of the enemy's defenses. Given the novel munitions the Sims had employed to trap the armored mastodons, there was a strong chance that the engines on some of them still functioned. He allowed himself to enjoy a brief fantasy of driving one of the tanks through the enemy defensive obstacles, creating sufficient havoc for them to then steal a ship, before rejecting the concept for the folly that it truly was.

Even so, it didn't completely drive the idea from his head. His feet hurt, his wounded leg hurt, his brain hurt, and the notion of finally moving by means of something other than his own boots was deliciously appealing. The thought of that comfortable ride, rocking back and forth, safely enjoying the darkened innards of a modern Trojan horse, was almost more than he could resist. There was even a chance they might get lucky and pick a vehicle with food hidden onboard.

It was a powerful lure, and Mortas shook it off with great difficulty. He still hadn't solved the problem of their approaching rendezvous with alert enemy sentries at the settlement gates, and it seemed likely they could detach themselves from the column with little trouble right there and then. Despite all that, he knew they would be betting everything on a single roll of the die if they hid themselves in one of the hulks before it was towed away. Unable to speak the enemy's language or even form its syllables, they would have no response discovered and challenged. Mortas made himself imagine that scenario all the way through to its ugly conclusion, and dismissed the idea with a shudder.

They continued straight through the center of the battlefield, studying the flatness of the soil that Sim ingenuity had turned into mud and then reconstituted. At the far end, the high-water mark of the doomed assault, they were able to see that several of the abandoned fighting vehicles had been freed already. A mix of wheeled scout cars and tracked carriers stood in a scratched-up row as if this barren spot were some kind of motor pool. Sim mechanics, unarmed and dressed in dirty coveralls, were busily attaching tow bars or climbing all over the captured equipment. A convoy of enemy movers now rolled into sight, and the infantry column reacted poorly when the large machines began backing up to the wheeled vehicles among the wrecks.

They don't like being reminded that there weren't any movers to give them a ride home, but there were plenty to haul away battlefield debris. Can't say I blame them.

The muttered chirps had an effect on the Sim commander, who signaled a halt and walked over to one of the more senior mechanics who was directing the work. He was obviously asking for a ride, and this act caused Mortas to feel genuine respect for him. He was on the verge of making a mental note to imitate the Sim leader if he was ever in a similar position with troops of his own when the enemy officer turned and gave a human-like wave to the column. He was actually smiling.

A chorus of relieved, thankful trills greeted this signal, and the Sim soldiers began limping toward the row of vehicles. The three humans held back without making a sound, following at a distance until they could identify an unclaimed wreck that they could ride by themselves. The only one that presented itself was a narrow scout vehicle with slanted armor that would make it an uncomfortable perch, but at least they'd be able to talk again. Mortas looked around as he helped Gorman and then Trent to mount the hard exterior, fighting the sensation of unreality. The feeling went beyond the simple disbelief that their ploy was working so well; what he found truly incredible was that they were finally going to stop walking. He accepted the outstretched hands that pulled him up, and just a few moments later heard the roar as the towing mover came to life.

The captured hulks rolled out of line one at a time, and as the personnel carrier next to their scout car started forward with a lurch, one of the Sims on top of it gave Mortas a grin.

As wonderful as the ride might be, the ability to talk again was a greater relief. Seated atop the scout vehicle's nose and tethered to the mover in front of them, they could yell all they wanted and no Sim in the convoy would be able to hear them. They alternately laughed and shouted, their exclamations of enjoyment mixed with astonished references to the walk just completed and their close brush with the Sim reinforcements. It was several minutes before they settled down.

The recon car's front was pointed like the bow of a ship to ease its passage through water, and its carapace was likewise canted in order to deflect enemy rounds like a boxer slipping punches. They sat side by side with their buttocks pressed against the sinister slits of the front viewports, but there was little room there, and after a few good lurches Mortas put his arms around the others to make sure they didn't slide off. Gorman wore an expression that combined astonishment with ecstasy, and Mortas chalked that up to the temporary suspension of the pacifist's long ordeal with his blisters. As for Trent, her grime-streaked face was set in a look of deep concentration while her eyes kept on the move, scanning everything in front of her.

"We've got to be ready to react if they're on their toes at the gate!" Mortas called out, unsure of just what to do if the Sims were actually checking to make sure no humans sneaked in. "We'll need to watch when the first car gets inspected. If they make the infantry dismount, we'll slide off without waiting to be told. We'll go over to the others and try to get in the middle of the group. If I start walking, no matter where I'm going, just go with me."

The valley soon turned into rolling foothills, and the captured recon vehicle rocked and bucked pleasantly with the minor crests and troughs. The vibration of the mover's engine passed into the armor on which they were perched, and Mortas had to fight the urge to laugh out loud. He was reminded of an amusement park ride from his youth, a one-man rocket ship powered through a transparent tube far above the ground by an alternating magnetic field that was supposed to provide a terrifying mix of sudden accelerations and decelerations. Something had been wrong with his tube, as he'd been quickly left behind by the children in the rockets on either side of him, and so what he most remembered was the not-unpleasant vibration as his deficient capsule had sputtered along.

All three of them took an abrupt breath when they crested the last of the foothills, because the settlement that they'd so long sought was finally laid out before them. The colony was massive, with domed structures spotted along well laid out roads inside an all-encompassing circle of defenses. From that distance it was impossible to make out the coils of reactive wire, but the low silhouettes of combat bunkers dotted the perimeter as far as the eye could see. Just before their ride dropped from the high ground, Mortas spotted the spacedrome on the far side, curved hangars and towers, fuel dumps, and flat runways. The orange dirt surrounding the drome was covered with newly arrived space vehicles, ranging from cargo transports to troop carriers and recon birds. Major Shalley had been right in his guess that the place would be a scene of chaos.

Movers and other vehicles rolled in every direction, work crews and formations of soldiers were marching to and fro, and an enemy scout screamed down to land even as they watched. Cargo carriers with lowered ramps disgorged barrels and crates in a seemingly endless supply, and mountains of both were being built on every available space. Just before losing sight of the drome, Mortas believed he spotted at least one of the Wren-style shuttles that they would need to steal.

The colony's defensive perimeter followed the layout he'd been taught in officer training, with a wide cement ditch as the first obstacle. Area denial had become such a mainstay of war on the Hab planets that both sides could lay a minefield in a matter of minutes and so the ground outside the ditch would have been sewn with man-killers shortly after the initial attack. Inside the ditch was a double wall of defensive wire, but this was no standard cattle fence.

This barbed wire was reactive, attracted by the electricity in armored vehicles, fighting suits, and even the naked human form. Some of it was stationary, some of it was loose, but its tendrils could reach out and snag anything with an electric field that came near it. Trying to blow it down with rocket fire or bombs was pretty pointless, as even severed segments were known to snake across the ground in search of electrons. Once they'd found and ensnared a vehicle or an individual, the reactive wire strands had one more trick to them. They would emit a signal calling the fire of larger Sim weapons, or glow hotly to attract the attention of spotters and infantry relying on the naked eye. It was bad enough that the fiendish stuff would trap its victim, but it was pure hell that it would then basically scream, "Over here! Shoot over here!" for every weapon in range.

Mortas felt his muscles tensing up as they crossed the open ground, his eyes taking in the irregular holes where different types of mines had either detonated outright or sprung into action. Like the reactive wire, some of these were static and others diabolically active. Detecting the same electric field as the wire, one variety would fly up in the air and explode while another actually rolled across the ground to effect maximum damage on whatever had attracted it. He didn't see any debris or body parts, and so he wondered if the Sims had detonated the devices themselves when the reinforcements arrived. Looking down at the captured recon vehicle that was now his ride, he experienced a sinking thrill at the thought that they might have over-looked one of the explosives and left it live.

Trent leaned in close to shout over the engine. "Look ahead! Maybe Shalley should have let us do a recon for him after all!"

Mortas pulled his eyes off of the ground and felt them widen in disbelief. As they neared the enemy settlement, details of the initial bombardment from space began to come into focus. Clearly the place had taken an awful beating before the attack had been called off, and the first sign of this was the absolute wreck of the ditch. Precision fire, most likely from attack craft launched from orbit, had blasted the steep sides until the waterless moat was nothing more than a gentle depression as far as the eye could see.

Likewise, the reactive wire was practically all gone. Mortas spotted several burnt-out barrels scattered on the settlement side of the moat, wrapped with scorched segments of enemy wire, and recognized them as human countermeasures. The war had been going on for a long time, and the reactive wire was not a recent development. The barrels used the wire's obsession with electric fields to its disadvantage, and a variety of delivery systems could drop these canisters right into the obstacle belt. Shorting out any strands that reached them, and spinning in place to pull down the static coils, they could denude an enemy defensive wall in only a few minutes if left to work unopposed. As they got closer, he was able to make out the holes that Sim gunners had shot into the barrels, no doubt firing directly at the glowing, thrashing tendrils engaged in the mechanical life-or-death struggle with the rolling canisters.

"These guys got caught with their pants down!" He yelled, pulling Trent and Gorman closer so they could both hear. "Our people seriously worked them over before they got their reaction going!"

"Maybe." Gorman wasn't shouting, but his words were loud enough. "Or maybe they wanted the assault force to come straight at them. They had that new ordnance to try out, and they wouldn't need anything else if it worked."

The lead vehicles were reaching the ditch now, and they all squinted into the raised dust as the movers downshifted and then crossed the depression. A small formation of Sim armored carriers was moving out to their right, and there was also some kind of vehicular traffic to their front, so it was almost impossible to see what kind of guard force was waiting for them. The grit flew up into his eyes, but Mortas kept his arms around Gorman and Trent, turning his head this way and that in a vain effort to avoid the dirt. The others used their free hands to shield themselves, and he finally couldn't take it anymore.

"What do you see? What do you see? Who's guarding the gate? How are they arranged?"

Gorman began laughing out loud at that point, and Trent soon joined in. She was still laughing when she rested her head on his shoulder and spoke as if preparing to fall into a deep sleep. "What guards? There's nobody there. The place is wide open."

The mirth was short-lived. They next rolled past a concrete bunker holding a heavy weapon of some kind, but they hardly noticed the massive barrel or the ghostly defenders seated around it. The Sim gun crew was even worse off than the infantry riding by; they sat with their backs against the chipped, sloping stone of the fighting position showing hollow eyes that barely registered life.

The humans didn't look at the exhausted enemy for too long. With their obstacle belt destroyed in the first bombardment they'd erected temporary defenses closer to the emplacement. Mortas had seen footage of these primitive devices, basically girders cut into long segments and welded together to form a metal tumbleweed. Reactive wire was strung between and among the tumbleweeds, and the ends of the girders were festooned with explosives that would detonate upon contact with a vehicle or upon command if human infantry clustered around it for cover.

Even the deadly bombs on the spokes of the tumbleweeds didn't hold their attention, however, as it was soon clear that a remnant of the walking infantry company from the initial assault had met its end right there. Different spots on the flat ground near the bunker were littered with burnt-out coils of the reactive wire, and closer inspection showed that many of them were wrapped around the remains of human troops. Some of these were so badly shot or burned that they could only be identified by their mangled body armor or ruined weapons.

Closer to the bunker, the bodies of several humans had been spread-eagled on the enemy obstacles. Their armor and weapons were gone, many of them had been dismembered, and all of them showed ugly wounds and dark smears of blood on what was left of their uniforms. Whether they were meant to serve as trophies announcing victory or scarecrows warding off further attack was unclear.

As they passed the Sim emplacement, Mortas noted the marks of a close assault on the angled rock that protected the heavy weapon. Chips had been knocked out in numerous places, and one entire corner of the bunker was gone. Fragments of stone were ranged on the ground in front of the fracture, which showed black smudges radiating from most of its edges. The human infantry had come close to taking this particular position, as the missing corner had been a rounded firing slit before someone had managed to stuff an explosive inside. To do that, the attackers would have had to maneuver right up to it, most likely under cover of darkness, and with almost no chance of retreat if they failed to capture the emplacement.

His own experience at crossing so many miles of this planet, sometimes in the canyons and other times crawling on his belly, painted the picture for him. He saw a dozen or more humans, hungry and filthy and tired, rigged out in the shoulder-and-torso armor of the walking infantry, sliding forward across the open toward the silent enemy position in the middle of the night. Guts tight with the fear of being spotted and the knowledge that their only warning would be the enemy weapons opening up on them. Different teams carrying the explosive bags, creeping all the way up to the grim walls while the others waited a short distance away, ready to provide covering fire or to charge into the breach if the bombs did their work.

Now we know why they were so bent on filling in the ravines.

Mortas turned and craned his neck to see the reaction of the Sim troops riding the next vehicle, and was only mildly surprised to see little approval for the mistreatment of the human dead. Once again he saw the shaking of a head or two, and decided that these soldiers had been locked in combat with the survivors of the assault force long enough to have gained some kind of respect for them. Either that, or they'd seen so much killing that they found excesses like these repulsive.

The settlement itself rose into life shortly after that, but the devastation simply got worse. Sim work crews were everywhere, moving piles of broken rock and smashed equipment. The domes Mortas had seen from afar had been hit by a special kind of ordnance, something that penetrated the curved roof and then detonated deep inside. All that damage would have occurred in the initial bombardment, but apparently the besieged defenders had been too busy surviving to deal with it at the time. They'd hastily pushed the wreckage off to the sides of the main thoroughfares, and now they were sifting through the detritus looking for long-dead casualties. The smell of the decaying flesh rose up over the chemical scent of the mover's engine, and as Mortas watched, a dead Sim was pulled from the rubble in two pieces.

They reached what appeared to be the town square, and Sim military police stopped the column without appearing to have much interest in it. Mortas looked around, trying to determine the reason for the holdup. A haggard file of civilians was shuffling through a chow line across the square, and yet another column of vehicles was parked next to one of the few undamaged structures. Sim casualties were being carried from the building on stretchers and loaded on the movers, and he decided it must have been some kind of hospital during the siege. The medical vehicles rolled off in short order, and he was thrilled to see the military police directing them to follow.

"They're being evacuated, I bet they're going to the drome." He hugged Trent and Gorman tightly, speaking just loud enough to be heard over the engine. "We just might get lucky enough to ride the whole way there."

They were passing the enemy rocket batteries when the question about staying with the column became moot. The delivery tubes that had changed the hard dirt into mud under the human assault force and then, later, rained death on the scavengers on that same ground were in the very center of the settlement. Unlike the enemy bunkers, they were huge half-spheres of concrete with sliding double-door openings on four sides. They'd been hit by something heavy, probably in the first day's bombardment, as most of them displayed wide cracks and black smudges, but their engineering had obviously been sufficient protection. Mortas was studying them when he saw the doors on one side begin to open, and a moment later he realized what it was. The open mouths of a multi-launch rocket system emerged from behind the doors, dark and hungry.

Someone had called for fire support, and the rocket turrets were about to go into action.

"Get ready! They're about to fire a mission, and I bet these things are loud!"

Trent leaned across him urgently, speaking to both of them. "Cover your ears and open your mouths! Concussion's the real killer!"

They didn't get the chance to do either of those things, as the drivers in the column had noticed the gun activity as well. Instead of stopping and dismounting the exposed troops riding with them, they simply took off at top speed. The three humans barely had enough time to grab handholds on the scout car's carapace before they were barreling along, bouncing in the air with each rut and rise. They weren't past the gun emplacements when the firing started, and it was all Mortas could do to force himself to keep his hands gripping the vehicle. The rockets belched forth with an explosion so loud that he could have sworn someone had just ice-picked him in the eardrums, and the rush of air was a full-body slap that threatened to tear him loose from the car.

The three of them flattened as best they could, trying to bury their ears in one another's torso, and the nightmare ride continued with a bone-rattling succession of jolts from above and below as the firing continued and the vehicles jumped in flight. Mortas managed to press one of his boots against the recon vehicle's headlight grill, finally keeping himself from flying up in the air with each bounce, but the others had no such luck and so they landed on him more often than not. He heard a low, mewling cry very close to his damaged ears and was looking to see who was making that sound when he realized it was coming from his own mouth. The terrifying succession of explosions, wind slaps, and buffets from the armor was reaching a climax that he feared he would not survive when the racing vehicle came to a screeching halt.

Gorman lost his hold and shot forward, skimming across the car's hood and bouncing off the rear end of the towing mover before disappearing between the two stopped vehicles like a rag doll. Trent called out his name in horror before pushing herself off of Mortas and sliding down after him. Taking in huge, panicked breaths, Mortas forced himself to release his grip on the handholds and look around as the rockets fired one more salvo somewhere behind the convoy.

He saw what had caused them to stop, and knew that this was their chance. One of the captured vehicles farther up the line had flipped over in the convoy's headlong flight, yanking its mover to a stop and also crushing one of the Sim troops who'd been riding it. He craned his neck to see better, and made out several limp forms in the dirt around the stricken carrier. Sims from ahead and behind were now running to aid the injured, and he stood up to get his bearings before sliding down to help Trent.

Gorman sported an ugly forehead gash that flowed blood into his eyes, and so Mortas slipped one of the chartist's arms over his shoulder before whispering to Trent, "We're gonna leave them now. Follow me, and no more talking."

Trent was shaking out a dressing from the medical kit, and she nodded rapidly while pressing it up against Gorman's wound. The man's legs gave out as soon as they started to move, so she swung under his other arm and between them she and Mortas were able to hustle him away from the column. Another bunker was nearby, some kind of storage or perhaps ammunition for the rocket turrets, and they managed to get around to its other side without being seen. They halted long enough to tie the dressing tightly around Gorman's head before getting him up and moving on.

He was mumbling about Sere and Cranther and coordinates as they carried him off in the direction of the enemy drome.

CHAPTER 11

"How is he?"

Mortas leaned in, squinting and trying to make out Gorman's features in the darkness. They'd half carried and half walked him to the edge of the spacedrome before discovering the ruined hulks of the Sim craft that had been destroyed in the initial assault. A huge flat area next to the landing strip was simply covered with the crushed, torn, and burnt-out husks of spacecraft and aircraft that had been dragged or pushed out of the way. If the dimensions of the debris field were any indication, it seemed clear that every one of the enemy's flying machines had been caught on the ground.

That's why we didn't see any of their air until now.

The drome itself was a beehive of activity, and they'd gone unnoticed as they slipped into the junkyard as the sun was setting. Mortas had felt genuine relief when the night had finally enfolded them, as if they'd been out of their element moving around in the daylight. They'd found a fuselage that was sufficiently intact to hide them, close enough to the drome to observe the spacecraft that were coming and going, and fitted out in a way that made Gorman as comfortable as possible.

He'd been lucid for most of the journey and swore he was fine, but his stifled cries of pain had suggested internal injuries. After they laid him down he'd started babbling about the sequence for finding and locking in the coordinates for Glory Main, and no amount of arguing that he should rest could make him stop. They hadn't feared detection at that point, because the noise from the drome was an unrelenting roar as aircraft supporting the mopping-up operations took off and landed while every now and then a spaceship lifted off or touched down. Many of the latter were heavy freight carriers, and they hadn't spotted a single Wren yet. Watching, both Trent and Mortas had been flabbergasted when the column of captured human vehicles rolled into the mechanical graveyard and unhitched their prizes right next to where they were hidden. The exhausted Sim infantry force was nowhere to be seen, but the vehicles they had ridden were now parked right next to them.

The salvage efforts obviously continued, as enormous flatbed movers soon began delivering tracked vehicles resurrected from the mud field where they'd been interred. Mortas had waited until the latest movers had departed before sneaking out to inspect these newly arrived wrecks, a diversionary plan already taking shape in his mind. Although the Sims had placed no guards in the junkyard, the blinding lights from the spacedrome flickered and danced amid the wreckage and he'd had to exercise caution. Nothing separated the hulks from the airstrip, and it would have been too easy to get spotted by a Sim worker who'd wandered out there to relieve himself.

He'd located the only tank delivered thus far, and had been pleased to see that its main gun didn't appear damaged. Crawling inside through a blown escape hatch, he'd found the ammunition racks still loaded with their deadly missiles as he'd expected. The memories of a few weeks' training on these massive machines now returned and enabled him to check the power in the batteries without having to turn the engine over. He doubted it would have responded anyway, as the vehicle had probably been left running until it ran out of fuel—and in any event he didn't need to make the thing move.

The batteries were low, but there was enough juice to engage the onboard targeting system and aim the gun. That was all he'd need in order to fire a high explosive round at one of the enemy hangars or, even better, one of the many stacks of barrels and crates that were even then being unloaded. Unfamiliar as he was with Sim heavy ordnance, he still suspected that something in those piles would explode if given the opportunity. Unfortunately, the tank's field of fire on that side was obstructed by the shattered body of a space transport and one of the wheeled scout vehicles that the enemy had parked there. Moving the transport's carcass was out of the question, but the scout car might roll if given a push.

Trent looked up at him when he returned and asked how Gorman was doing. "Lapses in and out of consciousness, but he's breathing well and keeps muttering about how to get to Sere."

Memories of first aid classes and the treatment for trauma passed through his mind, much too fast because the instruction had been so scanty. "Is that good?"

"It's better than no breath at all. I'm pretty sure he's busted up inside."

"Yeah, I thought as much." A huge transport slowly growled by out on the runway, blocking out what little illumination had been filtering in through the wreck's fractured walls. "I haven't spotted a Wren yet, but there's something else we have to do first. They brought one of our tanks in, and I want to use its main gun for a diversion, but there's stuff in the way."

"Stuff we could move?"

"You read my mind."

The circumstances changed radically just as they approached the blocking vehicle. They'd waited in the shadows, letting their eyes adjust to the floodlights and making sure that no Sims had decided to go for a stroll through the graveyard. Then, just as they were reaching the scout car, a chorus of chirps warbled at them from the other side. Trent and Mortas froze instantly, the stealth and silence of the previous nights having slipped into their very psyches. The voices rose and fell but didn't seem to get closer, so Mortas signaled Trent to stay put and slowly crept forward.

He edged up to the car's bow-shaped snout and laid gentle fingertips on the cold metal before stretching up onto his toes to look over. Sound travels far at night, and he breathed out a long, relieved exhalation when he saw that the noisemakers were a good fifty yards away. They looked like some kind of work gang that had been given a chance to rest, and they'd found a patch of open ground between the runway and the junkyard. He studied them closely, and had almost forgotten Trent when she came up next to him. Without saying a word he bent down and lifted her boot up onto the car's front tire. He then looped an arm under her buttocks to raise her up where she could see.

"They're going to sleep right there." She spoke into his ear in a normal voice, masked by the diminished but still-active engine sounds of the drome.

"Nothing we can do about it. But they look pretty dead; half of 'em are already out."

"Wait. What's that?" Her arm extended over the car's nose.

A wall of shadow rose up two hundred yards out, and even though lights moved in the darkness it was impossible to know what they were. Now, sliding out of the murk like some kind of plankton-eating fish, its mouth wide and its fins extended, a Wren shuttle backed toward the open hangar and the piled supplies. Sim ground personnel walked around it, guiding with handheld lights until it stopped and finished lowering its rear ramp to the tarmac. The brightness of its interior seemed to beckon, and Mortas found himself yearning to climb aboard.

Too soon. Not ready. Let this one go.

His heart rate began to accelerate as a chasm of doubt opened wide before him. What if this was the only Wren they'd ever see? What if this was the only one that would come this close?

His mind tripped over itself as he sorted through the myriad tasks they would have to accomplish in near-perfect sequence to catch this particular ride, but a final observation dropped it all into place.

Gorman can't wait. We have to get him out of here.

"Listen. I'm going to release the brakes, and then we're going to push this thing that way." He pointed toward the vehicle's rear, away from the sleeping enemy. "Then you get Gorman—"

"I'm right here." The voice was weak and dry, but the chartist was standing behind and below them. "You thought you were gonna move this all by yourselves?"

Things happened quickly after that. Trent hopped down while Mortas crawled over the roof and slid into the driver's seat. Whoever had parked the thing had left the brakes unlocked, so he climbed up and out again almost immediately. Hugging the car's armor, the three of them slid along its front like a single shadow, their fearful eyes fixed on the sleeping forms yards away. There was no movement and no alarm, and so they slowly turned and began to push. The vehicle gave out a heart-stopping groan as the pressure of their hands and legs mounted, but the ground was in their favor and it gradually shifted backward until Mortas decided that was far enough.

Turning, he saw that the Wren was now changing pilots. Two coming on, two going off, all four holding kit bags and chatting fraternally on the ramp.

No time.

He grabbed Trent's arm and handed her the Scorpion rifle. "Take Gorman and get walking. Nice and slow. Cut around these guys to the left, be ready to hit the deck when I fire the cannon."

Trent looked up at him, blinking hard. "You catch up with us. Got it?"

"I will! Get going!"

And he was running for the tank.

He almost dropped the leg-sized missile when he lifted it from the rack. Under full power the vehicle would have loaded the round itself, but even now Mortas feared there might not be enough juice left to operate the turret. The high explosive was encased inside a hard tube that would disintegrate as it launched, and he wrestled it up onto his shoulder with great difficulty. The open maw of the gun's breach beckoned in the shadows, and he staggered forward.

Shoulda loaded this before going back to the others.

He got lucky and hit dead center, sliding the missile in until it had almost disappeared. He swung the firing mechanism closed, and then jumped into the gunner's seat. A flip of a switch and the cushioned eyepieces in front of him lit up on infrared, a dull green field that had always reminded him of deep sea photography. A targeting array swam into focus before his eyes, and he recognized the silhouette of the scout car that they'd just pushed out of the way.

There was going to be a riotous reaction when he let loose, and Mortas took a quick look to make sure of the escape hatch's location. Returning to the sight, he drew in a long, shaky breath and then placed his hand on the control stick. With a convulsive act of will, he squeezed down on the release and felt power surge into the turret. He twisted too hard, and the gun slewed over to the left with a loud screech that he heard even inside the armor.

Stay calm. Hit the target.

He goosed the gun barrel back to the right in jerky spasms, ignoring the small shapes that had already begun to move at the bottom of the sight's image. The sleeping work crew was waking up, alarmed by the noise the tank was making. He bumped the gun just a tad further, and was rewarded with a blinding white dot. It was the floodlight over the nearest hangar's entrance, and as soon as the infrared adjusted for the heightened illumination he was able to make out the inside of the building. There were stacks of crates there as well, but he now knew they hadn't pushed the scout car far enough to target the other piles.

Would they store explosives inside *a hangar?*

That unmanning thought came to mind just as his vision was momentarily interrupted by a lurching cone, a dark thing moving closer, and he knew it was a Sim coming to investigate. He was out of time, he knew it, and so he made sure the glowing reticle was square on the boxes before jamming his thumb down on the trigger.

The tank jumped, but it was the noise that surprised him. The blast shouted down the sounds of the airfield with an authoritative clap of thunder, and in the instant that he caught sight of the round streaking toward the light he also saw the standing Sim go down clutching his ears. The warhead flew beautifully, almost no arc at such short range, and he was reminded of a glorious moment on the playing fields at school when he had scored the winning goal in the lacrosse championship. The hard spheroid had flown from his racket, curved perfectly to pass over the goaltender's shoulder, and sailed into the net.

The tank round passed from sight, through the open hangar door, and he was anticipating an enormous detonation even as he scrambled from the chair and slid painfully out the hatch. His eyes had become used to the infrared, and he was temporarily blinded as he crouched by the armored beast, his hand on its fossilized tracks and his ears primed, ready, reaching out for the shock wave that he knew he'd created.

One second. Two. Three.

Angry chirps, coming closer, a warbling howl of

pain in front of the tank, the continuous engine grumble from the field, and yet nothing from the hangar.

Four. Five. Six.

Oh no. Nonononononono. I missed. It went straight through. It was a dud.

He looked back into the tank, panicking now, knowing that he needed to do it all again but also sure that he'd never make it.

Gotta try. Can't take off without the diversion.

He'd just grabbed the sides of the hatch when something seized him from behind, talon-like fingers gripping his shoulders, spinning him around. A tall figure, indistinguishable features in the gloom, shouting at him in bird talk. A slap, out of nowhere, stunning him and leaving the side of his face smarting while fireflies danced in front of his eyes. The Sim grabbed him again, this time by both collars, and yanked him forward with a shout that ended in a startled cry.

At first he didn't know he'd done it, but then the hands were pulling him forward and down, the body attached to him vibrating as if hooked to an electrical cable. The grip released and the figure fell away, leaving Mortas staring at Cranther's knife in his hand. Warm blood flowed onto his fingers, and he stumbled away from the dying enemy just as more of them came around the front of the tank.

There was an eruption of chirps, like the aviary at a zoo, and he watched in fascination as one or two of them started to bring up weapons that they obviously intended to shoot at him. Mortas looked down at the knife, thinking of the Scorpion now in Trent's hands, and almost laughed as the moment came when the rounds would rip him to pieces.

The hangar went up just then, sunrise combined with thunder and a tornado, and a belching red cloud of flame raced across the distance. It slammed most of the Sims into the armor while merely flattening the others, and Mortas felt it tousling his hair as he leapt around the protection of the tank and started to run.

The hangar was still standing, but just barely. It was engulfed in flame, swirling spirals greedily licking the edges of the entrance before disappearing into the night sky where the roof had been. Large pieces of wreckage began crashing down around him as he moved, tripping over the Sim work crew's rucksacks. Cinders fell on his exposed head, biting and stinging, but he fought to get the knife back into its scabbard instead of swatting at them.

Got to get to the others. Got to get to the others.

Ahead, in what had been darkness before the explosion lit up the field, he could see the Wren trying to maneuver away from the carnage. Sims were running in all directions, trilling and cawing as they tried to escape the disaster or render aid, and he couldn't make out Trent or Gorman among them.

A section of corrugated metal, ripped and on fire, crashed to the tarmac in front of him. He was just cutting around it when a second explosion went off, lifting him, tossing him—a warm wind from a day at the beach that dropped him onto the pavement like a sack of laundry with bones. Pain shot through his left shoulder as he rolled several more times, and when he came to a stop he could barely move. His cheek was pressed against the flat stone, not minding it now, accepting that the whole silly charade was finally over. He was wondering if that was why Cranther had smiled at the end, but then he saw Trent and Gorman.

They were a few yards away, knocked down, not moving, and the raging fire showed that both of their flight suits were spotted with blood. He tried to come to his feet, but couldn't find his balance and fell over instead. Rolling on his stomach, blinding pain from the shoulder, pushing with his one good arm until he was finally kneeling back on his haunches. Seeing movement, Trent coming to a sitting position, face screwed up in agony, hands grasping something buried in her midsection. Twisting where she sat, teeth gritted, pulling on a spear-shaped piece of broken wood that was clearly stuck in her torso.

Mortas pushed off, still bent over but now standing, and began to totter in their direction. Gorman was motionless, and with a mighty effort Trent yanked the shard from her belly. She flung it aside with a look of distaste before, miraculously, rising to a squatting position and reaching for Gorman. She'd just rolled him over so that he faced the sky when Mortas got there.

The chartist's flight suit was peppered with fragments as if he'd been shot multiple times, and fresh blood spotted the fabric. Mortas dropped to his knees next to him, his eyes reaching for Trent's as the full extent of their wounds became apparent. A Sim rescue vehicle flashed by, trailing flame, and another, smaller explosion went off far behind them.

"I'm sorry. I'm sorry," he shouted, heedless of the enemy running all around them. His hands fluttered in the air, sending another jolt from his injured shoulder racing for his brain. "I thought it would work."

Trent's eyes locked on his, full of fire. "Grab hold of him! It's getting away!"

Mortas looked up to see the Wren moving by, very close, maneuvering to avoid the burning debris that now clogged the runway. Its rear ramp was still down, and he watched as one of the pilots' kit bags lolled onto its side and fell off onto the tarmac.

Trent took hold of Gorman's left arm, pulling him to a sitting position. The chartist's eyes snapped open and he gave out a brief cry of pain before recognizing where they were. Even amid the roar of the fire and the ripple of smaller blasts, his voice could be heard. "Where's the bird? Get me to the bird."

Mortas grabbed his other arm, flinching with the new pain but dragging Gorman to his feet. The Wren wasn't more than fifteen yards away, and they began stumbling toward it like a new form of life, a hybrid of three separate creatures that was just learning how to walk. He stared across at Trent, marveling at the huge red stain on her uniform and knowing that some time, any moment, the dreadful wound would drop her and end this madness.

And then they were somehow at the ramp, tripping

as they clumsily made the big step up and collapsing in a ringing metallic heap even as the craft continued to roll forward. Mortas looked up into the bright lights and the white walls and all the open space, recognizing that the ship had been configured as a cargo carrier. Twenty empty yards ahead both pilots were seated at the controls, concentrating on getting away from the fire, oblivious to their new passengers. Gorman's hands clawed at his arm, his eyes full of pain. "Hurry. Get me to the panel."

Mortas looked up just in time to see one of the pilots moving, somehow warned that they had come aboard, quickly unfastening his seat harness while staring at them from behind the blackout lenses of his helmet. Mortas reached back for the knife, but the drying blood stuck to the sheath and it wouldn't budge. Trent was trying to get on her feet, but the ship swerved around something and she went down again. The pilot, now standing, yanked his helmet off and drew some kind of tiny Sim sidearm.

This is where it's gonna end. He's going to shoot all three of us.

The pilot started toward them, almost losing his footing with the ship's erratic course. He chirped something at them that was lost in the engine racket, and waved the gun as if trying to shoo away a fly. It took a moment for Mortas to see that their subterfuge still worked and that once again they'd been mistaken for Sims.

The pilot came on, snarling now, the chirps run-

ning together into an angry cacophony. He stumbled
again, catching his balance by grabbing a section of
cargo webbing attached to the hull. Mortas pushed
himself up into a squatting position, his good hand in
the air in pantomimed surrender, but the movement
alarmed the Sim enough to remind him he hadn't
chambered a round or done whatever he needed to do
in order to shoot someone. His eyes swung downward
and then he let go of the netting, his free hand darting
for the weapon.

It was all Mortas would ever need. In two quick
steps he was beside the pilot, swatting the gun out
of his hand and seeing for the first time that he was
larger than his opponent. Grabbing him by the back
of the neck, Mortas pivoted and heaved him toward
the ramp like a bouncer throwing a drunk out of a bar.
The Sim lost his balance after one lurching step and
fell forward, tumbling, his momentum carrying him
over the edge. A moment later Mortas saw him on the
runway, still rolling in the light from the flames. He
turned away from the open back ramp, knowing he
was much too far from the remaining Sim to pull the
same stunt.

The second pilot was all frantic movement now,
fighting with one of the buckles that held him in his
seat, but Mortas just stood there, amazed, as Trent covered the last few feet. She'd found the pistol dropped
by the other pilot, but she waited until she was right on
top of the Sim before firing. She jammed the weapon
straight down into the hollow at the base of his neck

so that the round would go the greatest distance through his body and pose the least danger to the ship's hull. The pilot jumped in his harness once and then drooped, and Trent tossed the gun away before looking at Mortas.

"Get Gorman over here!" she shouted even as the Wren ran over something on the runway, bucking and bumping while she climbed into the one empty pilot's seat. The chartist had already started moving, on his hands and knees and barely covering any ground at all. Mortas slipped around him in order to use his one serviceable arm to lift the other man, and the two of them weaved forward as Trent got the controls to respond.

Gorman was making faint gurgling sounds deep in his chest, but Mortas had to leave him standing for the time it took to remove the dead Sim from the other seat. Luckily there was little blood on the dark cushion, and he guided Gorman into place. The chartist's mouth hung open and he was taking rapid, worthless breaths, but his hands found the navigation panel and he began punching buttons. Star charts swirled on the screen, and he shifted a cursor to tell the ship where to go.

Mortas dragged the pilot's body to the ramp and rolled it off, shocked by the carnage receding behind them. More than one hangar was in flames, vehicles and individuals were racing in all directions, and several other spacecraft were following them.

Cover. They're going to give us cover as we lift off. Every ship that can get away from here is bugging out.

He found the one lever on the bulkhead that looked like a means of opening and closing the ramp, and yanked it in one direction and then another until the machinery began to hum and the hatch started moving upward. His last sight was geysers of fire shooting skyward like the birth of a new volcano.

Mortas made his way to the front, hearing Gorman tell Trent to engage the automatic flight controls. Trembling in excitement, the lieutenant squatted down with his good hand on Trent's shoulder, looking through the Wren's windshield and seeing a wide open expanse of runway. Every available light had been switched on by whoever controlled them, and he was reminded of a late night drive only a year before, when he'd passed a blazing sports stadium out in the countryside where some big night game had been in progress.

The Wren's system took over then, setting the course for Sere and wresting control from Trent. She leaned back in the seat, reaching up and taking his hand just as the blast shields slid into place and momentarily blocked their sight. Projections from exterior cameras lit up the blast shields moments later, and the imagery was so precise that it was hard to tell that they were closed. The engines of a slightly larger craft ahead of them flared and then propelled the bird down the track, making them next in line. Mortas forced his numb arm to function, swinging his hand up until it landed on Gorman's shoulder. The chartist's head lolled back, and he looked up with an expression of astonishment and relief.

The engine caught fire, and with a surprisingly light kick the ship raced off down the runway.

"Lay me down on the deck." Gorman's voice was strained and weak. They'd lifted him from the seat just after the Wren had broken free of the planet's atmosphere, gingerly holding his head up and mindful of his grievous internal injuries. Mortas searched around the cockpit area and quickly located a cabinet filled with sealed water bottles. After checking to make sure it was indeed water, he knelt and held the bottle to Gorman's lips.

The chartist managed to keep it down, but his voice remained weak. "Can't believe we actually made it."

"Try not to talk. We'll be getting to Glory Main in no time and they'll patch you right up."

"Thank you for trying, Lieutenant. But I'm going somewhere else."

Trent's words were choked. "No you're not. You're staying with us. We're a team. You can't leave us."

Gorman smiled at that, and he weakly raised both hands until the others each took one. He looked at Mortas.

"Father."

His eyes shifted to Trent.

"Mother."

Trent squeezed his hand in both of hers, moaning in a low voice. "No."

"Sister."

The eyes moved back to Mortas.

"Brother."

Mortas cleared his throat, remembering the words and taking up the litany.

"Son."

Trent managed to join in next. "Daughter."

The three of them started the last line.

"All are one, from the beginning of time until its end."

But only two of them were speaking when it was done.

Mortas collapsed against the bulkhead just after they'd strapped Gorman's body into a fold-out bunk. The prayer had calmed him right up until the moment that they covered the corpse, and then a rush of anguish had taken its place. His knees came up toward his chest, and he wrapped trembling hands around them as he lowered his head and began to cry without making a sound.

Trent was there a moment later, her face streaked with dirt and the torn side of her flight suit flapping open. She tried to take him in her arms, but he wouldn't let go of his legs and so she pressed the side of her head against his own. Sobs wracked them both, and it was many moments before Mortas could speak. He finally blurted out the words that refused to stay inside.

"I promised I'd get him to safety. I promised both of you. I said I'd die before anything happened to either one of you, and look at me now. I'm alive and he's dead.

Shit . . . it was probably that tank round that killed him."

"Hey." Trent ran the back of a hand across her face, wiping away the tears. "Look at me."

He raised his head like a child, his face contorted.

"You didn't say you were going to get us to safety. You said you were going to get us out of there. And you did it. We did it. You, me, and Gorman. We pushed that scout car out of the way together, we crossed the strip together, we took this ship together, and we got out of there together." She glanced at the bunk and then looked back again. "And was he cursing you when he died?"

"He never cursed anybody."

"Exactly. Gorman was his own man the whole way through, and long before he met us. He fought his way onto this ship right alongside us, despite his wounds. He insisted you put him in that seat so we could escape, knowing he wasn't going to make it. And he died content, holding our hands and saying the final words of his people. So if he didn't blame you for what happened, why are you blaming yourself?"

A painful memory. An oblong pile of rocks by a dark stream. Uttering the same words that he'd heard Gorman recite over the dead tanker they'd found in the ravines. Cranther telling him to get the others out, thinking of them even though he was the one who was dying.

Gorman doing the exact same thing. Catastrophically injured, dying and knowing it, and yet urging them through gritted teeth to get him onto the Wren and then to the controls. His final act as a chartist had been to lay in the course to a destination he knew he'd never see.

Mortas reached out his good hand and gently stroked Trent's cheek. "You're one hell of a psychoanalyst, Captain."

"About time I got to ply my trade."

His hand dropped to the tear in the side of her uniform, the ugly rent outlined by a stain of dried rust. He shook his head as he pulled the fabric apart, the bright interior lights showing him that the wooden spear had left a long, shallow gouge in her side but hadn't harmed her otherwise.

"I saw you pull that thing out. Took both hands. I thought it had gone right through you."

"It was hung up on the uniform, that's all." She rose with an expression of satisfaction. "Take more than that to kill me."

CHAPTER 12

Apart from taxiing on the exploding runway, Trent never did get to actually fly the Wren. Without a pinpoint destination on the planet Sere, the tiny ship automatically took up an orbit that allowed them to look down on the mass of dark, barren rock. They'd been discussing the wisdom of putting out a distress call when the ship's console began to beep loudly and then the Wren's nose simply dropped. Moments later the engines kicked in hard, driving them straight toward the surface, and Mortas felt his empty stomach trying to climb out through his throat.

As Sere had no atmosphere there was no friction to slow them down, and the windshield was quickly blotted out by ugly crags of rapidly approaching rock. They both reached out and grabbed the control panel with stiffened arms, a reflex action as pointless as shutting their eyes or turning away, and the Wren began to vibrate with the straining engines. Every light in the cockpit and cargo bay lit up simultaneously, and a voice boomed at them as if a giant were speaking directly through the hull.

"Occupants. Speak in a clear voice and identify yourselves. You have one minute to impact."

They stared at each other from the pilot seats, astounded by the unknown technology and transfixed by the ship's unchecked acceleration. Some sort of loose box whipped past them, crashing into the bulkhead next to Trent, but she showed no sign that she'd noticed. Mortas recovered first, figuring this had to be Glory Main because whatever had taken hold of them could destroy the ship without revealing the presence of the headquarters. No fighters, no rockets, just the wreck of a crashed shuttle on a dead planet. An oddly Cranther-like thought came to mind just then.

Cowardly fucks. Developed this incredible anti-ship device and kept it a secret just so they could stay hidden.

"This is Lieutenant Jander Mortas, Human Defense Force! I carry priority intelligence, given to me by a deceased Spartacan Scout! Do you hear me?"

The ship nosed over further, now pointed directly at the ugly ground miles below. Mortas felt his back straightening, his feet reaching for the deck so that he was practically standing up in the seat's harness. The bones of his right hand suddenly began to compress painfully, but when he looked he was only slightly surprised to see that Trent had grabbed hold of him. Her eyes were wide, staring down, and her cheeks vibrated from the clenching of her teeth.

"I say again, this is Lieutenant Jander Mortas! Carrying vital information concerning a new enemy weapon! Information passed to me by Corporal Tel Cranther, Spartacan Scouts! Do you hear me?"

It was impossible to know how much time they had left, but his eyes swam with vertigo and he finally understood they were simply going to slam into the deck below. A giddy rush passed through him, the awful sensation of falling with nothing to slow him down and the stark reality of his impending death. He twisted in his seat, grabbing Trent's vise-like grip with the hand from his injured shoulder, and she added hers on top of that.

"They don't believe us," she blurted, her eyes on his and her breath coming in short gasps. "They don't believe us. All this way and they're just going to murder us."

The truth of it hit home, and Mortas felt the mad jitter of panic starting to rise in his chest. His heart was thundering with the ground's approach, and he squeezed back at Trent's hands with all his might even though pulses of electricity seemed to be shooting through his shoulder.

This is it. This is really it. No Glory Main for either of us. No hot chow, no safety, no homecoming, nothing. Will they even tell Father what happened?

Father.

"This is Lieutenant Jander Mortas, and you'd *better* listen! My father is Olech Mortas, Chairman of the Emergency Senate! Do you hear me? Olech Mortas! Does that name sound familiar?" His voice broke as he shouted, but their speed didn't change a bit. As if mocking him, the beeping from the console was joined by a warning buzzer barely audible over the roar of the engines and the rattling of the fuselage. Though unable to read the Sim indicators and other signals, there was no need to wonder what this one meant. "Answer me, damn you! Whoever you are, you will *not* survive the *shitstorm* when my father finds out what happened to me! *And he will!*"

He glanced at the nose, terrified to look but too scared not to, the sight of the approaching rock paralyzing him. His mouth hung open, and a low moan drifted up from his very core.

Here it comes. Please don't make it hurt.

"Jander."

He looked at Trent, who was wearing an expression of complete serenity. He tried not to show his terror, but it was too much and he couldn't even answer. When Trent spoke, it was with utter calm.

"Thanks for getting me here, Jan."

His horrified psyche almost didn't register the words, and he never got to ponder them. The Wren's nose lifted with a jolt, throwing them both back into their seats as the engines powered down like a loud sigh. The alarms shut off, but the silence was broken when the compartment filled with commands.

"Lieutenant Jander Mortas! Your shuttle is being diverted to a quarantine bay. Do not attempt to take over the controls at any time. Do not attempt to leave the ship or open any of its hatches until told to do so. Any violations of these instructions will result in immediate destruction of your craft and everyone aboard. Do you understand?"

"We understand." His ears were filled with the sound of his pounding heart, and he tried hard not to stutter. His mouth opened and closed uncontrollably, and he was only able to release Trent's hands with difficulty. "I'm accompanied by Captain Amelia Trent and we have a deceased Forcemember with us, Chartist . . ." Too traumatized for shame, he looked at Trent. She appeared to be in shock, her eyes round and staring at him, but she recovered quickly enough.

"Roan."

"Chartist Roan Gorman."

There was no reply to that, but the ship leveled out and went skimming down a black canyon toward an unknown destination.

"Jander."

"Yes?"

"Your dad really is Senator Mortas?"

"Yes." He wetted his lips. "I didn't want to trade on his name, so I was keeping it a secret. Besides, it didn't seem important until now. Sorry."

Trent's mouth hung slightly open, and she turned her face toward the windshield with a look that was half surprise and half dread.

The Wren followed a tortuous path down a long system of dark ravines, as if imitating the mode of travel that had hidden them the last few days. The voice didn't return, and they left the controls alone as the craft slipped gracefully along. A short time later they passed under an overhang that hid them from view, and just after that a section of the rock moved out of the way to reveal a lighted hangar.

The ship slowed as it passed into the landing bay, and the stark difference between the unmarked rock and the technological vault made Mortas feel as if he'd just traveled through time. In the space of a few yards he'd gone from pre-human desolation to smooth walls of white metal, gauges, lights, ladders, and hatches. He felt his breath catch in his throat as he took in the marvels of modern, civilized living, and he remembered believing at one time that he would never see them again. His mind went back to the moment they'd abandoned the Insert, when they'd crested the first hill on what they believed was an empty planet. He'd looked back on the wrecked piece of equipment with genuine longing, and now felt as if he'd come full circle.

Home.

The ship came to a stop, hovering over a yellow circle painted on the floor and slowly turning in place before touching down. There were no other ships in the bay, but that wasn't surprising because the voice had said they were going into quarantine. Trent touched his sleeve and pointed toward what appeared to be a row of black spacesuits standing against the far wall.

"Banshees."

Even as he watched, the spacesuits began to move

like robot soldiers. He now saw they were actually the armored fighting suits that the Force used on non-Hab planets and in any encounter in space where the atmosphere could be lost. He'd received a brief familiarization in that gear just a few months earlier, and had come away tremendously impressed. Oxygen, water, food, and weapons were all part of the package. A suited soldier could run faster, jump higher, and hit harder than any human who'd ever lived. A soldier in one of those suits could be dropped into an ocean and simply walk out.

The armored outfits contained titanic hydraulics, which had rendered the strength differential between males and females moot. The Hab planets were the most common battlegrounds of the war and, because they didn't require the expensive fighting suits, the units that fought on them were almost all male. The Force did contest for possession of less hospitable environments, however, and so most of the units that specialized in suited combat were made up of females collectively known as Banshees. The helmet on the combat version of the suits completely hid the occupant's face, so Mortas was puzzled by Trent's observation.

"Banshees? How can you tell?"

"See the chest and groin armor? Where the color's lighter?"

The squad of armored suits approached before separating into two columns and smartly marching into position on either side of the ship. Now that Trent had mentioned it, Mortas noticed that the black plating was smudged in an almond color on the upper torso and where the legs came together.

"I see it. What's that got to do with the Banshees?"

"When they go into battle they paint breasts and vaginas on their suits to let the Sims know who they're fighting. Command absolutely hates it, and as punishment they have to wash the paint off by hand after the fighting's done. Takes hours." She grunted in respect. "Doesn't stop them, though."

The voice came back just after that, and Mortas realized he couldn't tell if it was male or female.

"Lieutenant Mortas and Captain Trent. Your port hatch will open in one minute, and you will exit the craft with your hands held high. Carry nothing with you. Do you understand?"

Trent still wore Cranther's skull cap, and Mortas thought of the two knives that had belonged to the scout. Healthy annoyance flowed through him, and he responded in a snarl. "I'm carrying two knives that were the property of the deceased Spartacan Scout I mentioned. I'm not giving them up."

A trace of anger came with the answer. "Lieutenant Mortas, you will obey all commands or you will be executed on the spot! You will carry nothing with you! Do you—"

A female's voice confidently interrupted the transmission. "I think we can handle a fighting knife, Control. Even two."

The voice didn't reply to that, but the port hatch opened as predicted. Mortas gave Trent a big smile and a squeeze on the shoulder as they unbuckled their harnesses, and then he took the lead as they went to the exit. Raising his hands as far as his injured shoulder would allow, he bent over and stuck his head out to find a ramp had been rolled into place. Walking down, he was pleased to see that the Banshees held their weapons ready but not pointed at him or Trent. Knowing how they both looked, him with several days' beard, both of them covered with dirt and worse, and Trent's uniform ripped where the spear had miraculously missed her, he supposed they didn't appear to be much of a threat.

A lone figure stood facing them, and from the condition of her armor she was probably the group's leader. In addition to the discoloration on the chest and groin, her suit sported numerous abrasions and what appeared to be a patch where something heavy had hit her. She wasn't carrying a weapon, and gestured with an armored glove as she turned and started to walk. She didn't look back, and the same voice that had let him keep the knives came from somewhere in her suit as they followed.

"I'm taking you to decontamination now. They'll be burning your uniforms, boots, and any other articles of clothing, so if there's anything you want to keep—like a knife or two—set them aside when we get there." Mortas heard a mechanical whirring behind him, and both he and Trent looked back to see a set of scrubbers descending from the bay's ceiling toward the Wren. The other Banshees had moved away from the ship but kept it under a watchful, helmeted eye.

"One of our people died getting us into orbit, his body's on board. He was a member of the Holy Whisper." Mortas faltered, unsure. "Is there something special we do for them?"

The Banshee kept walking, her heavy metal boots ringing on the floor plates. "Special? How long have you been in the zone, Lieutenant?"

"Long enough."

She reached out with a gauntleted finger to punch a button on the wall next to a large hatch, and it glided open. Inside was a spotless white room, but what caught their eyes was a pair of transparent cylinders that ran from floor to ceiling. Mortas had undergone a practice decontamination once before, but it had been little more than a group shower for new lieutenants and they'd laughed their way through it. He looked over at Trent, who was regarding the tubes in obvious alarm.

"What is it?" He asked in a low voice. "Claustrophobic?"

"You could say that."

They passed the Banshee and approached the tubes. Up close they weren't quite as intimidating; the clear material was hard and immaculate, and there was enough space inside to reach out with both arms almost to full extension.

"See? Not such a tight fit."

"Sure."

The Banshee spoke again, pointing at a long white bench that was bolted to the floor. "Please strip down to your skin. Anything you want to keep, leave on the bench. Once it's been deconned you'll probably get it back. Everything else just drop on the deck."

Mortas sat down heavily, the strain of the ordeal starting to slip away. His stomach growled in anticipation, but he fought the urge to ask about food. He crossed one leg over the other and began unfastening his boots, marveling at how scuffed up and filthy they were. He turned the first boot over once it was off and shook his head when he looked at the wear on the sole. They'd been almost brand new when he'd awakened in his transit tube, believing that he was about to be assigned to his first platoon. That idea reminded him of something he'd said an age ago, when they'd met the crazy major who'd tried to kill him.

This is my platoon.

He looked over at Trent, who was pulling off a bloody sock while keeping a fearful eye on the decontamination cylinders.

My platoon's dead. Only brought one of them out.

He pulled off the other boot absently, not noticing the stains on his socks.

What did Cranther call me, the first time we met? Lieutenant Death.

His torn tunic came off next, still stiff from all the blood, both Sim and human. He poked a finger through one of many circular holes in the back, only now recognizing them as burn holes from the explosion and the fire back at the drome. Dry mud flaked off of his trousers as he slid them down, wincing at his shoulder injury when he reached for the field dressing on his wounded leg.

Seeing his own injury, he looked over at Trent in time to see her slide out of the worn flight suit. If she'd been wearing a bra at the beginning of their experience she'd lost it along the way, and he tried not to stare. Her white skin was streaked with dirt, and just below her left breast there was a long, red scrape that ran around her ribs. A miracle that the spear-shaped shrapnel hadn't impaled her.

"Hey."

She turned unfocused eyes toward him, and he gave her a reassuring grin before reaching out and running a thumb along the scratch on her side. "Thanks for not dying on me."

Trent offered him a weak smile before standing and shucking down her underwear. Though filthy and slightly emaciated, her body was toned and shapely and even in his debilitated state he found it desirable. She pulled off Cranther's skull cap and he was surprised to see how much hair spilled out from underneath it. Stripping off the last of his own clothes, Mortas wondered if they'd be separated after decontamination or if they'd at least be allowed to eat together. He opened his mouth to put the thought into a question just as the tubes, silent and immobile until then, gave off a loud rush of escaping air and began to rise toward the high ceiling. Each one left behind a circular raised pad with a shiny grate made up of small, finger-sized openings presumably designed to let the liquid decontamination spray drain out.

Mortas winced with his first barefoot step, and

looked down to see a pair of feet he hardly recognized. Covered in grime, they still showed the pale yellow flaps of healing blisters and the roughened ridges of cellulitis. Both his big toes bore purple welts that suggested he'd bled under the cuticles, and the nail on his left little toe was actually missing. He felt something brush his palm, and then realized that Trent was taking his hand as they walked. The hand shook until it gripped his, hard.

"It's all right. They're just gonna wash us off, and then we'll get nice clean clothes and some hot food, and then they'll have the docs check us out." She didn't respond, and began to slow down as they got closer to the pads.

"Listen." He leaned in, for the first time becoming aware of how foul they both smelled. "You just look at me while this is going on. All right? Look right in my eyes, until they hit us with the suds of course, but you just look right at me and everything will be fine. Heck, we got this far, what's a little shower?"

That seemed to reach her, and Trent gave him an embarrassed smile. "Thank you, Jan. Get me through this, okay?"

"I promise." A quick hand squeeze, and he stepped up onto the pad. "See? Nothing to it."

The cylinder slid down, locking him in, and he watched as Trent's did the same. He reached out and plunked the transparent wall with his middle finger to see how thick it was, and the stab of pain told him he wouldn't be beating his way out anytime soon. A fan-like orifice opened far over his head, and he watched as a heavy mist descended. It was laden with some kind of liquid, and he shivered just a bit as it washed over his naked body. Unseen particles began chewing deep into his pores, and he passed Trent a thumbs-up that she didn't return.

Motion outside the tube caught his eye, and he turned to see two forms in bulky chemical suits entering the room. They carried large white bags, and quickly collected everything that he and Trent had brought or worn. He beat a flat hand against the side of the tube, trying to get their attention, but they were already leaving. The Banshee followed them out, and the door shut behind the trio without a sign from any of them.

Confused, he found Trent's worried eyes on him and tried calling out her name. She raised a hand to an ear and shook her head to indicate she couldn't hear him, and he gave her a helpless shrug. Mortas looked up, hoping to see the decontamination chemicals on the way, but was surprised to observe an orange circle of light forming around the top of the tube. A similar pattern had appeared far over Trent's head, and it now began moving slowly downward, flickering with an inner energy.

"It's just a scan." He mouthed the words elaborately, hoping Trent would understand. The orange band crept closer, inexorable, sliding, and for no reason at all he was reminded of the fiendish serpents that had lain in wait beneath the water on the planet that had almost killed them.

His eyes then filled with an orange light, and he felt a heat penetrating his skull as the band slid downward. A cavity in one of his teeth jumped in pain as the scan progressed, but then it was warming his throat and he flexed his injured shoulder, hopeful it would relieve the soreness.

Might as well get something *out of this.*

The thought of heat on the injured joint got him longing for the warmth of the shower that he imagined they'd be taking next, and he shut his eyes in anticipation as the scan went on. A long, hot shower, lots of soap, scrubbing off the dirt and the blood and the sweat, sending it all down the drain . . . and then a big meal. Two big meals, both with rich desserts. And coffee and maybe even some alcohol. His system was so completely beaten down that he imagined a good stiff drink would render him insensate, but perhaps a small glass of wine or beer . . .

The alarm startled him, and his eyes snapped open at the noise. It was loud, frightening, a series of grinding woops that came right through the cylinder's walls even as the room's lights dimmed and a revolving red light activated in the ceiling. A mechanical voice began bleating, but at first he couldn't hear it over the horn. His hands reached out for the security of the glass, and he locked eyes with Trent in the other tube.

That is, he locked eyes with whatever Trent actually was.

A heavier mist was cascading down on her, but she wasn't fighting it. Her arms were hanging at her side, and her forehead was pressed against the tube with the blue eyes fastened on his. They drilled into him across the short distance, intense, hate-filled, accompanied by a sneer of such consuming malice that he screamed out loud.

Now he remembered it, the face he'd first seen looking at him in his transit tube, the one that had made him shriek in surprise. This was the face he'd seen then, not the kind, caring Trent but whatever this was. It seemed to read his mind, and the dark sneer changed into a smile of recognition even as the mechanical voice finally reached him.

"Alien presence detected. Alien presence detected. Maximum security protocol in effect. Secure all hatches. All personnel are to remain in place and prepare to defend the station. Alien life form is unidentified—"

The robot's words cut out with no warning, as did the blasting alarm. It was as if Mortas had been suddenly struck deaf. The red light kept turning, throwing insane shadows across the darkened room, but it was the new words, the new thoughts, the new images that now consumed him. Taking over, boring into his mind.

What had Major Shalley said? Just before Cranther killed him? That Trent's words had bored into him. Guess he wasn't so crazy after—

The thought was torn from his brain and blown away like a feather in a tornado, but the spinning winds carried new things. Memories Mortas didn't recognize, images he couldn't have possibly seen, and a voice that wasn't his.

It wasn't Trent's either.

"Trent lied to us."

His head exploded with a series of pictures, a movie made from the chopped-up pieces of someone else's experiences. Amelia Trent—the real Amelia Trent—pinned to a surgical table wearing a torn, soiled uniform, writhing while electricity coursed through her. Screaming, convulsing, tugging at the restraints. Face constricted in true terror, even when the current was turned off. A voice in her head. Pulling, twisting, tearing. Searching.

The same voice that was now in his.

"Trent kept the blisters from me. She was a long-distance runner. She knew about them, but she managed to hide it. You almost caught me with that one."

Mortas felt himself holding a dry, unmarked foot just days earlier. Hers. Its. The feet that hadn't blistered, hadn't sweated, didn't even smell. Then a rush of other feet, covered with ugly bubbles of white and red. He recognized these images. They were his, and Gorman's, and then Trent's because this thing had copied them, transformed itself in imitation. Just as it had transformed itself to become Amelia Trent.

"Took forever to break her, and even then she took a few secrets with her. She was much stronger than we thought, but you wouldn't have expected that any more than we did, would you? That's why we chose her—a psychoanalyst was perfect cover. No skills your group would need, and you had no understanding of her job. You expected nothing from me, believed whatever I said about her time in service."

More familiar memories. Cranther belittling her and Gorman. His own misguided disappointment at being saddled with the two presumably useless bodies from the rear echelon. His anger when they'd found the decapitated soldier in the debris field and he'd believed Trent was studying his reaction. And now knowing she—whatever this *thing* was—had been doing just that.

"Chose you all that way. The perfect team."

Mortas flinched with the new rush of sensory input, his brain vibrating like a motor. His hands slid off the glass, but he didn't see them fall. Instead, a flood of images told him the story of how they'd been selected from all the Forcemembers the Sims had captured asleep in their transit tubes.

Gorman for his navigational skills and knowledge of the stars. Cranther because a Spartacan would be required to head for the closest major headquarters. Mortas to lead them, but so new that he could be manipulated. All lean, all young, all strong.

"That's right. You were all prisoners. Your transports were captured while you slept in your transit tubes."

Trent had been taken much earlier, so that the thing could learn her. Gorman had been captured on a different transport, just a few days before they'd gained the incredible prize of the Spartacan Scout. Mortas now saw teams of Sim technicians circulating among the transit tubes, chattering, examining, making notations in handheld devices while something else, a presence, floated above it all. Slowly descending, circling, approaching the window of one tube, looking in at the sleeping face.

His face.

Mortas sat down hard, still blind, still deaf. Seeing only what the thing wanted him to see, hearing only what it wanted him to hear.

"The attack threw off the whole plan."

An empty Insert, slung under giant flying machines, cut loose so that it fell straight down, cracking open, then dragged forward until it was wedged between two ridges on an orange-colored planet. Sinister movers rolling forward to transfer the transit tubes containing the living prisoners . . . and the dead ones.

"Didn't consider the possibility there'd be an attack. Left the Insert there for three days to let the power run down so you'd wake up naturally. I babysat all of you for three days . . . and somewhere in the middle of that, the humans made a full-on assault on the colony."

A mixed memory now, part his, part hers, part its. Trent's confusion and near-hysteria at not seeing any animal life, any birds. Hiding her true concern, the alarm at not seeing Sim aircraft overhead that would guide them to the colony. The colony that wasn't supposed to be there. The colony that a good Spartacan would have to report to the highest-level headquarters he could reach, if he could steal the ship that had been prepped and set aside for them. The ship that had been wrecked along with all of the others when the humans attacked.

"That ruined the entire plan. But you got me here

anyway, the three of you. Gorman figured out where we were. Cranther and you killed for us. And then, when you completely folded up on me, I got you the rest of the way out of there. I was always ready to do that."

Explosions. He was her now, could feel Gorman's arm over his shoulder, stumbling along toward the Wren, and then both of them thrown across the tarmac, slammed down in a crunching, crushing heap, multiple broken bones, rolling, searing fire in his side and he looked down and there was this spear sticking all the way through him. Pulling it out, marveling at all that pain, already sealing off the wound and mending the bones as a man ran up crying—it was him but how could it be him when he was her, the Mortas figure saying he was sorry, certain that Gorman was dead and that he as she was going to die shortly too.

It ended with a jolt as if he'd been slapped. Mortas's eyes popped open and he was sitting there, emptied, staring at the thing in the tube across from him. The room swam in the red light, but he'd only been given his sight back. The thing pushed off from the glass, coming to Amelia Trent's full height. The malicious glare disappeared, and for just a moment the thing regarded him with compassion.

"You cried when you thought we were both dead. You cried when Gorman went. And I know you cried over Cranther. Maybe you'll cry over me now."

A different mist came down on her in a cloud, and she raised her face to greet it. Her expression was serenely beautiful, right up until the vapor began eating her flesh. She took an awkward step back, bumped into the cylinder, then looked across at him with dissolving hair and skin that was already peeling.

"You were the biggest surprise of all. Brand-new lieutenant, picked at random. There were two others just like you on that transport, but we killed them and kept you. And who did you turn out to be? The son of Olech Mortas—"

The thing convulsed then, jackknifing forward and clutching its stomach as the chemicals burned away more of the skin. It began to spasm, jerking as if trying to escape a straightjacket, and when it looked up for the last time the face was almost gone and parts of a skull were staring at him.

"Just remember that was how I got caught. Simple bad luck. They knew what transport you were on . . . rich kid, senator's kid gone missing . . . and that Trent wasn't on that ship."

It collapsed then, curling into a ball on its side, the mist eating its current form, torturing it, trying to make it reveal its true nature. The spasms took over completely, the rag-doll skeleton shaking all over, and just when it seemed it would simply melt away it burst into a million black specks, tiny fluttering wings crashing around the tube, rising in a cyclone, and then Mortas was able to hear again.

"Alien has transposed! Alien has transposed! Sterilization protocol initiated!"

And the tube filled with a fire so intense that